Return The Goddess, The Lemurians Shall Come

Book II

by

Susan Isabelle

Bloomington, IN 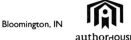 Milton Keynes, UK

authorHOUSE®

AuthorHouse™
1663 Liberty Drive, Suite 200
Bloomington, IN 47403
www.authorhouse.com
Phone: 1-800-839-8640

AuthorHouse™ UK Ltd.
500 Avebury Boulevard
Central Milton Keynes, MK9 2BE
www.authorhouse.co.uk
Phone: 08001974150

First published by AuthorHouse 4/19/2007

ISBN: 978-1-4259-5662-2 (e)
ISBN: 978-1-4259-5661-5 (sc)

Printed in the United States of America
Bloomington, Indiana
Library of Congress Control Number: 2006907593
This book is printed on acid-free paper.

Cover : Mother of Creation   Acrylic by Susan Isabelle

Hello From Susan,

For those of you who have read my first book,
"On Assignment With Adama", hold on!
The Adventure Continues!!!

The Lemurian peoples will come,
Earth shall ascend and
We shall all enter the Gate to find that place of Beauty
in the New World that is forming.
We are creating it!

Spirit has poured out Her graces and we are learning!

The Lemurian culture is based on the Goddess Principles of Love, Mercy
Compassion, Wisdom and Understanding and so much more!

Adama, Goddess, Obed and Melchizedek were
teaching me, how to teach you....

Come along with me as I journeyed a new path to understanding the
Mysteries of the Crystal Skulls and their role on the Earth,
and the Greatest Mystery-
The Goddess In The Kabbala, for
She *is* the Path To Ascension!

Enjoy the adventure!

Susan Isabelle

1

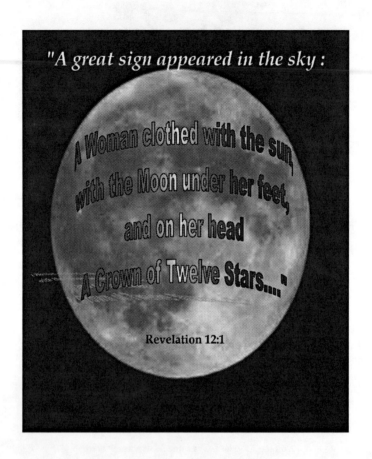

"A great sign appeared in the sky:

A Woman clothed with the sun, with the Moon under her feet, and on her head A Crown of Twelve Stars...."

Revelation 12:1

**On October 13, 2000
We Saw Her!**

Foreword

If I were to tell you this book is true,

You'd say,

"You're out of your mind!"

If I told you it was a work of fiction,

You'd say,

"That book has to be true!"

Let Spirit Guide You

Susan Isabelle

Contents

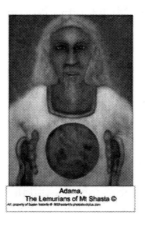

Chapter I

The Flight Home From Belize, Central America

Oh, My God! I thought as I snuggled down into the seat of the aircraft. The small group of adventurers who had accompanied me to Belize was settling in too. We were finally leaving Belize. At least now I can get some rest! I thought. What an incredible journey we had just completed.

Adama, the High Priest of the Ancient peoples known as the Lemurians, had sent me on a mission to reopen an ancient and sacred site in the far jungles of Central America. It was May 2000. It was the time of the opening of the Pleidian Gateway and we had been there!

I remembered back to the day I met Adama six months earlier. I had been meditating in the Kiva, a round house built for meditation, at the base of Mount Shasta in a small town called Mc Cloud in Northern California.

Suddenly, I was no longer in the Kiva, but had been literally pulled out of my body! I stood in the presence of a gigantic being of pure light! I was inside the mountain known as Mount Shasta and I was with the Lemurians. They are an ancient ascended race of the lineage of Melchizedek and dwell at Mount Shasta and in the inner earth. At the time, I had never heard of them before. That was about to change!

When I first saw him, he smiled and introduced himself as Adama, High Priest of the Lemurian peoples, and stated, 'We have been waiting for Al'lat Le Andro Melchizedek. Come, we will show you what you are to do."

"Wait a minute! Who are you? I rebelled. I don't know you!" He held up his hands. I watched the Earth spinning between his hands. It began to fade in and out. Then I knew we were in trouble! The earth was about to disappear from the present dimensional reality. He stared deeply into my eyes. I understood everything with his glance.

"We will come at that moment to hold the integrity of the Earth through the transition but it must be with the assistance of humanity. Will you go?" He had asked me. I understood that at some future moment Earth could come close to losing its right to exist in an elevated dimensional space. A Universal transition was to occur at a future date and I was needed to assist the Earth forward in time if Earth were to survive! The Lemurian peoples had called me to assist them and they would help, if we as a people agreed to work cooperatively with them.

"Yes." The words just fell from my lips. My life then took on new purpose and I had agreed to open thirty six areas to Light and bring balance on the Earth. Through working an elevated Light frequency energy through the earth's own meridian system, I would do it! Meridians are electrical grids, a system that flows over and through the earth. The grid may be altered, enhanced and directed for beneficial purposes by "working" that flow with Divine Light Energies.

I had now just completed the second of the thirty six sites Adama wanted me to reopen. I understood 'reopening sites' to mean taking the latches off a container, the Earth. Bound countless years ago, the Earth had been kept isolated, contained within a certain space. This was necessary for Earth was in a battle zone of Light and dark. That darkness had held a firm grip on this planet. Now it was time for ascension, not just for Earth, but for all Universes!

Humanity, Earth, and the outer Universe are in a phase of evolution called the "In Breath of God." We are all about to ascend, or transform into a higher state of being and the latches and bindings must be removed from the minds, souls and that of the entire planet. All that is not of Light will cease to exist in this reality, for it cannot be drawn back into the Divine to ascend to the next cycle of evolution. Remember: Like attracts like. It is a fact, a part of the Divine Order and Law of the Universe. Soon, light and dark will not co exist, as in your current world.

To help, the elevation of consciousness on Earth would be required. Because of the shortness of the time, intercession from other cultures and ascended peoples would be necessary. Also, the planetary grid systems would have to change to a higher Light containment so as to pass through the Gate. I had been sent here from my home far away in the outer universe to help in the process. My 'home', as I call it, is not on Earth. I had learned that I had been "seeded" here from another Universe, that of Andromeda. That universe is one of the oldest in all of creation. Our peoples have previously experienced this process and survived and now desire to assist others in their evolution. We are seeking the elevation of all. It was necessary that I come here.

Why? To do this work. My true Spirit , that of Al'Lat Le Andro Melchizedek , took on physical form on planet Earth knowing I would one day remember why I had come to Earth, and become active in the service of the Divine Plan. Adama had helped me to understand that when I spoke to him on that day in 1999. What plan, you ask? In the ascension of a planet there are many factors that push and pull on its conscious development. There are many within this universe and other universes that sincerely desire to have planet earth ascend. First of all, for the freedom of the peoples of Earth and secondly they desire Earth's progress for their own ascension. Yes, the ascension of other planetary systems and multitudes of races and beings are also dependant upon Earth's rising out of the third dimension.

But, there are forces that would just as soon not ever have the planet Earth ascend. Power and control, the "I -want" mentality and desires, pull us all downward and that feeds the will of lower beings of lacking higher consciousness. That lower consciousness does not easily release its victims, but sets up a perpetual contest of will and draws in anyone who is not prepared or unaware. As Buddha's teachings explain, lack of attachment and enlightenment is required to find release. As Christ explained, we are then to seek the Highest and live in the Light!

"Adama," I said aloud while pulling the blanket up around me, "if you have thirty four more sites like this one in Belize, I don't know if I can do it!" Oh, yes, Adama had been waiting for me in Belize, but I didn't realize that others were also waiting, both light and dark beings. Belize had held both. Here again is a universal truth; where the highest concentration of light is; so also the contrast presents the highest concentration of darkness. Forces would oppose the work I had come to do. I had descended into the realm of the lower worlds while in Belize to learn command and authority. I had met the darkness, met the challenge, and with the words, "I am of the Light, I do not belong here!" I overcame and was given a great honor and an incredible gift. Faced with a challenge we all shall one day encounter one way or another, I was freed from the icy grip of fear that night and the site in Belize had been opened! Fear, hatred, revenge and all lower thought energies must be overcome by the ascending soul.

Our small group of Lightworkers had been met by a specter in the night who told us of a force that had been wrecking havoc across the country. It had been freed because of the 'ignorant ones' who had reopened his tomb! Not only had Adama waited for us, so too had the people of Belize, the Maya knew I was coming and knew something about me I didn't know at the time. I would re-entomb the vile creature of darkness, an Atlantian of the old culture. It had kept the people in fear and in its grip of lower consciousness. I would help rid Belize of this with the assistance of the small group who had accompanied me. None of us had known the dangers we would face from the seen and the unseen.

Now finally, we were on our way home. The whining of the plane's engines sent me into sleep. All too soon the stewardess bumped me into wakefulness and I accepted a cup of coffee. There really is nothing like Guatemalan coffee and I couldn't resist one more cup before reentering

11

the States. I reached down into my back pack and touched the little glass head the Maya man had thrust into my hand. "Here! Take it! You will know how to use it!" He said tearfully. My family said I am to give it to you. We thank you for the gift you have given me in my hands, and I will never have to dig ditches again!"

Yes, what a fond memory. As a Master Teacher, I had given him an attunement to Shambhala Reiki Energy, an initiation that gave him the empowerment of Light to heal others. After I gave the attunement to him, he had gone back into the jungle to heal his people. Before I left Belize he appeared at my hotel from Guatemala to make sure that I had the glass head as a gift from his people. He had returned from the jungle in tears to tell me the story. Apparently, when he went to his small village, many people there had been healed of ailments through his Shambhala Reiki Energy! He was now their village Shaman Healer!

Now, in the airplane flying 35,000 feet or so above the ground, I held the mysterious head in my hands and turned it over gently. Amazing! It had a complete brain inside and seemed to glow with a mysterious shine that came from within the stone. It peered up at me with hollow, alien looking eyes. I considered the small head once again. What exactly was this? Was I just a tourist getting a sell? No, I knew that was not true. I had experienced something very real. It was a gift from the Maya people to me. Now, responsibility for the head was mine. I knew the head was special, magical somehow.

Because of that little glass skull or head, I had been brought face to face with the Lords of Light of the Ancient Mayan Priests. I had met the Lords of Darkness just the night before. All in one night this happened. It was a

12

night of shear madness-yes, madness, or so it seemed to me at the time.

I knew this little head was responsible. I knew it was a gift but I wasn't sure I wanted to have such a gift! It scared me but I had to follow through with the responsibility. It connected me to a realm of the Angels and the Maya Lords of Light and I knew we had a work to do together. My fears were simply because I knew so little about it, I reasoned.

I picked up the little book I had bought in the airport just before boarding the plane. The book was titled *Sastun, by Rosita Arvigo.*

No longer sleepy I read....then all became clear. As I read what the author Rosita had written, I received an explanation of all my wondering and questions. Her book told me all about the spirit that roamed the county side causing illness. I knew that it was the Atlantian we had entombed! Her book explained that the spirit had been freed by the archeologists who ignorantly released it. When they did so, many of the men present died on the spot and many others became ill. This had been documented and was a historical fact.

It was the same spirit we had been called to re-entomb in the deep jungle. The rogue spirit had now been returned to the tomb. We had done it! This was my confirmation!

It also explained to me that what the Maya had given to me in the form of a small crystal skull was called a "Sastun". A Sastun was a gift from the spirit world's Lords of Light, in the form a crystal or stone. The owner, or rather "keeper", would have to demonstrate mastery over the lords of darkness and enter into the realms of Light *prior to its use.*

"Mastery over three worlds was required before use." I sighed. Read the label next time, Susan! I said to myself. Only thing was, there was no label. One strike and you're out! Had I fallen in consciousness of fear and allowed their control of my mind through fear, I would not have overcome. I kept on reading. I began to understand even more. I learned that by surviving the test to prove one's mastery over the upper, middle and lower worlds, it allowed the keeper to heal and receive great knowledge.

Just as our Maya guide had explained to us while in Belize, the Maya believe that the Ceiba tree is sacred. It represents to them great mysteries;

> The upper branches form the 'heavens" and there dwell the Maya Lords of Light. These are beings of great consciousness, the Angels and realm of God

> The middle of the tree, bark and lower tree represents the middle world where we as humanity dwell, caught between the realms of light and dark, a place of decision.

> The roots go deep into the Lower underworld world where dwell the lords of darkness, beings lacking light and captors and tormentors of mankind.

I had met all three challenges on that night and had been taken into the realm of the Maya Lords of Light for instructions. Now, they would be with me to help me on the rest of my assignments. I had a very powerful tool from the ascended Maya of a culture of long ago!

Thank God, I had passed the test that night! I shuddered to think what may have happened had I not. Suddenly,

I realized what this meant. Oh, My God! A *real* Sastun was inside my backpack! It was flying back with me to the US! *

* On Assignment With Adama

Chapter II
Did You Say Rum?

My husband, Will was waiting for me at the airport when I arrived back home in Manchester, NH.USA. I had just come back from an incredible adventure in Belize. My second assignment from Adama had been quite a trip! I would have so much to tell him! I was so excited! As soon as I saw him I began to blurt out parts of the story.

"Will, you're not going to believe what I brought back with me! I thought it was just a piece of glass! Boy! Was I wrong! I have a *real* crystal skull from the Maya priest. He gave it to me! Wait until you see it and what this skull can do! I can't believe I have this! I need some rum."

"What?" Startled, he answered me, "Susan! You don't drink!"

"Will, please, we need to stop at the liquor store and buy some rum."

"Susan, tell me what you want the rum for. You haven't taken up drinking since you've been gone have you?"

16

"No, I haven't. Just stop over there at that store and get me some rum." I grumpily sulked. This was not going well. He slid into a parking space, parked the car and looked deeply at me.

"Susan. I am not going into the store until you tell me what you want the rum for. Why do you want rum?"

I looked at him deeply and seriously answered, "I need it for the crystal skull."

He burst out laughing! Great roaring laughter. He could hardly contain himself in the car.

"Will, it's not funny! The skull needs it!"

"Why? What are you going to do? Get it drunk?" He laughed even harder.

Surely, my first hour home was not going well. I always used to joke with him that he kept me for entertainment purposes with all the unusual things that seemed to be constantly happening around me, but now I was getting ticked off. I was not being entertaining.

With a stern voice, I said, "Will, I need the rum. Pure rum. I need it now!"

"You're serious?" He asked incredulously, studying me this time. He'd heard my voice.

"Yes, I am. I'll tell you why later. I'm tired."

"Ok," he said slipping out of the car. A few minutes later, he was getting back into the car.

"OK!.....this I've got to see."

Back at the house, he carried the bags in and set them down. We sat on the couch together. I took out the small skull and placed it in my hand so he could look at it with me.

"See, Will? Look how it glows. As I held it for him to see, something amazing started to happen. "Oh, my God! Will! Look!"

As we watched, the small skull began to glow a beautiful blue color. Then something else started to happen.

"LOOK!" Across the top of the skull a glowing pulsing energy began to emit from it and the skull began to grow in size. The top of the skull lifted before our eyes. It went from sitting flat in my hand to a rounded skull.

"Woaaa, I'm not sure about this, Sue," he said looking up at me with stricken eyes. "I've never seen anything like this."

"Neither have I, Will. What a great gift. A gift for the world! The Maya made sure I received this little skull. It's supposed to be here." I looked at him pleading. He had to understand.

"What is it? What is it used for?"

"Well, as I have been reading," I said holding up the book I had found in the airport, "this is a Sastun, or a gift from the Maya Lords of Light. It speaks to the Keeper, now me, in dreams and messages to bring knowledge and gifts of healing, I believe."

"What kind of knowledge? He asked me in quiet tones. And what do you need the rum for? Does it drink?" He asked, much more seriously now.

"No, I answered smiling. Rum's used to clean the skull and remove all negativity and energy it collects. I need to take it and clean it now. There's no telling how long it's been since its been cared for."

I went into the bedroom and placed a clean towel on the floor. I found the passage that spoke of Rosita's experience with the Don, the Maya Healer she had been studying with. I knew how to prepare the skull.

Holding the tiny skull in my hands I began reading the prayer directly from the book.

I quote,

"Sastun, Sastun, Sastun, by your great power,"

I continued the prayer as it was explained and just as the book told me I ended with,

"I believe Sastun is able to do all these things

By the power of the Father,

The Son and the Holy Spirit. Amen."

Nine times I said the prayer and made the sign of the cross over the tiny skull. It gleamed in the light brighter each time the prayer was said. It cleared and became more translucent.

Each time I said the prayer, great swirls of energy spun inside the skull, warming my hand. I could feel it wait and pause each time I came to the prayer sentence,

"And help me to understand...."

It seemed to be speaking to me and responding with its energy. The tiny skull looked pleased and relaxed in my hand somehow.

**Susan Isabelle
with El Aleator,
the Sastun
Skull gift from
the Maya**

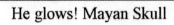

He glows! Mayan Skull

Chapter III
The Vision Of Empowerment

An exhausted, but fulfilled woman went to bed that night. Sometime during the night, I had the first dream- vision. Actually, I was out of my body. My physical form lay inside the warm bed. I was somewhere else.

"Susan," the Voice spoke, "Look!" As I looked about, I was outside my house in Manchester, NH. How did I get out here? Who were these people in white standing with me? I wondered. What did they want me to look at?

Suddenly, a huge jaguar sauntered slowly walking across the back lawn and toward the front of the house where I stood with three men robed in white. The jaguar was majestic and I was mesmerized by the beauty of the beast.

We did not run, but stood perfectly still as he passed by and walked down to the lake at the end of our road and then disappeared.

The White Being by my side then pointed toward the bay window. I could see plainly into my home. Inside the house paced a cougar back and forth in front of the window.

The huge creature paused, glared out at us, staring at right me with its vibrant yellow eyes. They were filled with massive power and might. The cougar then resumed its paces.

Suddenly, I realized the beast was *inside* my house. I panicked!

"My Kitten!" I shouted. "Where is my kitten?"

I ran past the White Beings and bolted into the house. My kitten was inside somewhere. I began to rummage all though the house. I was frantic.

"Where's my kitten? What have you done with my kitten?" I shouted as I looked everywhere.

"Why do you need a kitten, when you have such powerful beasts at your command?" I heard the Voice speak.

"It is my kitten and I love it," I answered. "All this power means nothing to me" I cried.

The Being spoke, "Look over there."

As I did, I saw my kitten, small and starving over in the corner under a blanket. I ran to it, picked it up and cuddled its small body next to mine.

"This is what shall be." The Voice spoke softly to me.

"NO! I shall never let this happen to my kitten!" I shouted.

"This is what shall be. To what you must for the All, you must take command of the powers that surround you." I looked around the room at the symbols of power being given.

"Look Susan." There before me with the sweep of his hand, I saw the Earth. "Remember, this is what you have come for, to the All. For now, there are those you must leave behind."

"How can you be so cruel? It's just a little kitten. I would never let anything happen to those I love!" I cried into its furry little body.

"NO!" I screamed and awoke.

Crying I held my pillow tightly and wept into it. Over and over again I saw the image of the Being manifesting the Earth and his voice saying tenderly,

"Look, Susan. Remember, this is what you have come for, to the All. There are those you must leave behind."

And my response to him was, "I will never let anything happen to those I love!"

But the realization of the great responsibilities to come, sunk in. I cried myself back to sleep.

In the morning, I understood what the prayer of Sastun would bring to me. I would have vivid experiences so real, so profound, that my life would never be the same.

I also knew the day would come when I would be leaving those I loved on order to do what I must. I, Al'Lat le Andro Melchizedek, did not come for enjoyment of the comforts of Earth, but to do a job.

Adama had been one of the Beings there that night. It was his voice I heard in sympathy. Just as before, he had shown me the Earth and now the sacrifices I would be called to make.

"Yes, Adama,
I am still with you and the Lords of Light protect me
and help me!
I will continue to do the work."

I remembered what had happened to me when I was just twenty three years old. Now it was time to go and help the people.

Remembering GO! 1972

I was in my kitchen washing the dishes. My two sons were outside playing. My little boys were now five and six years old. We lived in our own home on Lake Attitash in New Hampshire. My hands were in the soapy water scrubbing away when I heard a loud voice command me from out of nowhere! I heard the Voice say:
"Susan, go see Martha Payne!"

It startled me so that I dropped the dish and backed up against the wall. Still dripping wet, I shook as I picked up the phone and called the only person I knew who would know where Martha now lived. I hadn't seen her for two years. She had moved away.

"Sylvia, I would like to see your mother. Where is she living?"

"Why, Susan, she is here with me. She is dying and has come home to be with me. She doesn't have much time left and she won't be able to speak to you."

"May I see her?"

"Yes, you can come over now if you like."

The next call was to my neighbor. "Florence, can you watch the boys for about an hour or so? I need to run an errand….."

Before I knew it, I was at the door of Sylvia's home. Right behind me was another friend, Jane Harland.

"Jane! Susan! Welcome! She's in the bedroom in the back." Apparently, Jane also had been summoned.

As the three of us entered the room, we could see Martha lying on the bed. Her abdomen was swollen and seemed to engulf her small frame. She was unable to speak, but we could see that see that she recognized us and was happy that we had come.

We had all been members of a local Baptist church and Martha had a bad habit of spreading malicious rumors. She had wrecked havoc in the church until she had to leave, but not before causing much pain for people I had loved dearly. Now I saw a woman in terrible pain and near death. I had good reason to dislike, if not hate this woman. I felt a wave of compassion for her come over me. I felt pity.

All three of us sat around the bed feeling inadequate somehow, not knowing what to do. Then I got it! Yes! That could be the only reason we had been called here, I thought to myself. After a few minutes of silence, I spoke.

"Martha, do you want us to pray for you?"

She nodded, "Yes". That is what she wanted. I bowed my head and began to pray.

"Father of All Mercy, have mercy upon Martha and ease her pain. We are thankful for the time that we've had together and all the lessons we have learned......"

I don't know what else I said. Something happened to me and I don't remember what I said.

Something happened though. All I remember was that the whole room was filled with light.

When I became aware once again, Sylvia and Jane were sobbing and looking at me strangely. When I tried to make eye contact, they began sobbing even more. I got up, kissed Martha on her forehead, and walked out. In the air outside I gasped a deep breath. What had happened? Jane and Sylvia wouldn't speak to me anymore afterwards. In our church, things like that weren't supposed to happen. We could get in trouble with the church authorities. We were not charismatic, and this would be considered something like that. Later Jane would die in a car crash and I never did know what happened that day.

I went home to wonder and was filled with a beautiful peace. Three weeks later, I was once again in my kitchen when I heard the commanding voice,
"Go to Martha!"

 Once again I called Sylvia.

 "Susan, she's not here. She's close to death now and is at the hospital in a coma." I jumped into my car and flew to the hospital. This was urgent! I ran into the hospital.

"Where is Martha Payne?" I asked the desk. I went straight over to the room and opened the door. When I went over to the body on the bed, I thought sure this couldn't be Martha! I went back out to the desk.

"You made mistake!" I accused the desk person. "I wanted Martha Payne's room!" I was horrified to discover I had been give the correct room. Yes, I had the right room! But that couldn't be Martha! I went back in and approached the bed. The figure on the bed was really Martha. I recognized the ring on her finger. Her eyes were rolled back and her tongue was swollen out of her mouth. She had no hair. Tears welled up in my eyes and I said,

"Martha, do you want me to pray for you?" I timidly asked, remembering what had happened last time.

Unbelievably, she nodded! I began to pray. Once again the Light filled the room. I could see that Martha's spirit body was being held by some force that appeared to be claiming her! I called on the Love of the Christ. Jesus appeared in the room! I watched and prayed as He spoke to the being claiming her. I prayed for Martha with all that I am. I was aware of the door opening in the room and closing, but continued the prayers. This was a fight for Martha!

As quickly as the first time I prayed for her, it began and then it was over, but this time I had seen what I think the other two women had seen the first time. I saw Christ! I filled with tears and started to run out of the room. As I opened the door, a little girl, a candy striper volunteer about sixteen years old, was standing facing me in the open doorway. Tears were streaming down her face. She had seen Him too! This child had opened the door and seen the Christ. I nodded at her and smiled. She smiled back through her tears at me and then I ran. I ran to my car and cried for hours, until I could contain myself enough to go home to my family.

That night I lay in bed close to my husband. My two children were sleeping peacefully in their room. My young husband was very ill. His asthma rocked the bed as he tried to breathe. His labored breathing had gone on all night long. I looked at the bedroom clock; it was now 3:00 AM in the morning. Finally, I heard his breathing soften. He'd make it through the night and now I could go to sleep.

I had prayed upon each of his breaths that God would spare him. I was twenty three years old, had a gravely ill husband, and two little boys to care for. I prayed a lot even as my thoughts were comforted by the vision of Christ in Martha's room. I rolled over and went to sleep.

My eyes opened in a panic to see the early rays of first light. Something was wrong!

"What's happening to me? I can't breathe!" My mind screamed.

Something is wrong! I can't breathe! I realized a great pressure all over me. I was being squeezed from head to toe! With super human effort, I rolled to try to wake my husband, but it was too late! My arm never made it to touch him but fell limp on the bed. I died.

I floated above my body, looking down at the death it held. Without a thought, without regret or even wonder, I turned and headed toward the tunnel of Light above me.

Speeding through the tunnel I could see the bright Light ahead. I "saw" my body, a speck of Light without form; pass by multitudes of others even as I am.

"I am dead" I thought, then simply popped through the Light, into the fullness of the Light. Pillars of moving rainbows greeted me.

All was absolutely silent as I floated through the maze of Rainbows. It was as if I knew somehow, exactly where I was going. I entered an area that was a big as the entire Universe. Great streaming rays of multicolored light emanated in rows of great rays from a great inner circle of Light. It was a Throne of pure light with a white fire that surrounded the Throne as a moving, living river. From beneath the river, the rays spread outward forever. Above the Throne light were concentric circles of rainbows of color, layer upon layer of colors that rose up as far as I could see!

I made my way down toward the center toward the Light, into a ray of pure sapphire! I seemed to know were I belonged and was entering into the sapphire ray.

As I did so, I recognized that I was sapphire too and was joining my sapphire light to the Light of trillions upon trillions of others of the sapphire ray. That ray was people; people and beings just like me! Our Light formed the sapphire ray! That ray spread out upon a sea of crystal. I made my way down toward the Throne and into the ray.

Just as I was about to enter into the row, or sapphire column of Light that is my home in Heaven before the great Throne of God, I heard the Voice,

"Go Back! Go back and help the people!"

Oh, no! I thought and sadness filled
me. But again I heard,

"Go Back! Go back and help the people!"

29

My Light was being pulled back! Back down through the tunnel I sped.

I slipped back into the body and awoke! It was 6:00 AM. The children were already stirring and my husband needed to sleep. I rose out of bed and just wondered. I cried softly as I hugged my children. They were so little, they needed me. I had returned.

We dressed for church and I decided not to wake my husband, but to let him sleep. He was so sick! At church I sang with new heart. I had seen God in the Great Throne Room! I now know where my home is, and I have seen the Christ. When I arrived back at the house, my husband met me at the door saying,

"Susan, Sylvia called. Martha passed away at 4:30 this morning. She wanted you to know."

I went to my room. I knew he thought I was crying, but I feel to my knees and praised God. In my heart I know that Martha and I had traveled into heaven together. She was to stay and I to return, but they wanted me to know she was there. I know she is. The prayers on her behalf and the calling of Christ at the last moments of her life saved her. She's home.

I tell you this because there are so many today that will tell you that God is US, humanity. That we *are* the I AM. By my experience I say, "Not so!" In all of scripture there is a thread of truth interwoven that is so needed to be understood right now. Beware!

You may take this literally, or symbolically, I will not argue the text as it is not necessary. The message is the same; I encourage you to consider this;

1. The original falling of the Angel known as Lucifer, or son of the morning, was that he wanted to put his throne above God's. *He declared he was as God.* That <u>cast him out</u> of heaven. Angels were also cast out that followed this teaching.

2. Eve's 'fall' was in temptation that she could be as God and ate of the fruit. By her and Adams actions, *they declared they could be as God.* They were <u>cast out</u> of the garden.

Are you seeing a trend?

3. The Anti Christ; Scripture teaches that the anti Christ will one day stand in the temple and say "I AM God! Then there will be destruction. The spirit of anti-Christ <u>will be cast out</u> and into the lower realms.

4. Today, mankind is on that slippery slope. The teachings today say that we are God! Millions are declaring they are Gods by quoting a few scriptures out of context. The issue is "God verses god". The small 'g'- god. Perhaps the "temple" the scriptures speak of is really the temple within mankind, *each one of us*; perhaps the temple doesn't have to be built in Jerusalem, but the temple *is in* us?

Perhaps the false anti Christ spirit is a lie within each one who is declaring their godhood? When the spirit of anti-Christ declares itself to be <u>G</u>od, millions shout right along, agree and say, "So AM I!"

Mankind will have made the same mistake as those before, and declare themselves as God.

Those of Mankind doing so; what of them? A 'casting out' will occur just as it has always happened in the past. This time, its 'cast out' of ascension.

What? How can I say that? Think about it, please.
It is robbery to take that which is not yours.
It is theft to steal the owner ship of the land, the Universes and declare they are yours. Will a man rob God? We were told to take care of those things. We haven't.
Instead, humanity is declaring ownership and destroying it.
Theft. The *original sin*, the- *I will take* the throne of God and declare it to be mine!
That friends, is a low energy. It is not one that will make it through the ascension.
It is power, control, manipulation of the Highest.

We are not God. God is in Heaven. The Kingdom of God is within us. In that lies a potential of what shall be; a fact of great Mercy toward humanity. One day GOD will choose to grant us the full status as Sons and Daughters and GIVE us all, but not yet; its' not our right to take it now. It's been promised to us but we're not to take it. That's like waiting for your parents to die so you can take the inheritance, not nice, agree?

God/Goddess has a throne that is magnificent. Christ shares that throne with Him as the only Begotten Son and all things are put into His hand through the time of ascension and until all things are fulfilled. Then you shall receive the gifts.

Then there shall be a new heaven and a new earth. That day is coming soon. The Maya have given us a time frame and its 2012. The River of White Fire is the Holy Spirit Shekhina, and we come out from Her in manifest form *and lesser* light than the Father's. We are the children. I am a created being. I am a part of the ray of sapphire that makes up the glory around Him. One day I will bask in that Light forever and be at perfect peace and enjoy Mother-Father forever. I am not God.

Native American
White Shell
The Changing Woman

But I am blessed!

Chapter IV

June 2000
A Shambhala Class

I was back teaching at the Shambhala Center in New Hampshire. The Center had grown so much! Students filled the Center night and day.

I had started a new system of shared space based on a model of a cooperative Center for Energy Workers. It was hugely successful even in its infancy. Energy workers often struggled for money as their life styles and beliefs held by them did not allow for the usual rat race mentality of the world and they suffered financially because of it.

Financial prosperity was often denied to them simply because their beliefs prevented them from obtaining money by compliance to systems that were endangering the earth's environmental systems. I had been given a plan for shared energy and space.

The night visions from Obed and Melchizedek had shown me how to establish a Light Center that would welcome those from all walks of life and belief systems. All would benefit. Soon, my classes were filled to overflowing. Obed is my Angelic Guide. His name means, 'Serving.' Melchizedek is the High Priest of El Elyon or God most High. The Office of Melchizedek is a Christ power held to bring the sacraments of God to the people. They were always with me.

After returning from Mount Shasta the growth had become phenomenal. Now, I had returned with a crystal skull from the Maya.

In my classes, I began to teach about the skull.

"Susan, what do you mean by saying you have a crystal skull from the Maya?" one of my students asked.

"Well, when I returned from the trip to Belize I was educated on the plane about the skull by reading a book called *Sastun,* by Rosita Arvigo. She was a woman who lived and apprenticed under a man called Don, a Maya healer who was 104 years old. He used a special crystal he called Sastun to assist him in his healing work. He taught her that it was a gift from the Mayan Spirit world to help him." The class considered the words spoken by me with interest.

"The Spirits, or Lords of Light, choose the one they would contact and gift with a crystal Sastun. He taught her about the Sastun although she did not initially want to use the crystal gift she had been given."

Why not? Alison asked.

"Well, she had quite a first night with her new Sastun!"

I have to admit, my first night with the Sastun was a bit unnerving! The first night I had the crystal skull in Belize I met the Maya Lords of Light and also the dark lords presented themselves!"

"The Lords of Dark?" she asked, timidly.

"Yes, the Maya believe one must master all the realms of creation in order to be a true master, not unlike many of our systems of belief throughout the entire world."

"What did you do?"

"I remember when faced with my challenge that night I stated to the dark, "I am of the Light, I do not belong here!" Then I was immediately transported into the brightest Light with angelic beings of the Maya. It was beautiful, but I didn't understand very much at the time. Since I've been back, the skull has been teaching me during the night."

"What? How can that be?" James asked, now interested.

"The skulls seem to have a way of transmitting information to me while I am asleep. I awake in the morning with knowledge."

"What kind of knowledge, is it dark?" He asked.

"No, not at all. The knowledge I receive is to help me to assist humanity in its ascension and understanding of Light. I receive visions and see future events that may happen. I am shown this so I may know where to go to do my work. I sing and pray at these places and release lower energies to that of the Light of God. One amazing fact I have learned is that the skull calls itself, El Aleator and I am calling it that too."

"What does that mean?" Another student asked.

"El means "Lord or Master. The word Aleator means language, tone or speech. So the skull is telling me that it is a Master of speech and of tones or Light Vibration. During the night I've been taught how to pass on this vibration to others."

"Why do you want to do that?" James asked.

"Here's the exciting part. What I have been shown is that El Aleator has come to us at this time to begin the process of activation of the people to knowledge and understanding of many of the ancient truths."

"Why? Don't we have enough truth to deal with as it is? The world's really messed up with all that we have in technology. What do they want us to know?"

"Good question, the truths taught by the Maya does not deal with human technology. Their teaching is about the truth of Spirit, about living in harmony with the earth and all of the variables of nature." I paused.

"The Mayan calendar teaches us that the ending of this system of time is at hand. We will soon enter into a time of change and possibly the end of this earth system if we do not grasp the truths they are attempting to convey to us."

"Susan, that sounds very serious. Isn't this just a bit negative?" Linda asked me.

She has a positive outlook that burdens her, I thought. Some people are so involved in the movement to think positively, that they have ceased to understand a great truth:

All things work together for our good,
even when we don't understand,
And even if we consider them to be undesirable at the time.
To hide ourselves from those actions,
And all of our human experiences that surround us,
is to hide our heads in the sand.
We fail to learn our lessons.

People have come to believe that if they don't see something, it doesn't exist. So, if you don't think about it, it will go away. Or, if you only think wonderful thoughts, all will be wonderful. What a deception to the mind!

If I had chosen to ignore the Atlantian and what he was doing to the people every night and if I only wanted to think good thoughts, I would have run. He'd still be terrorizing the people of Belize and keeping them trapped.

The real challenge is to
Overcome our attachment to the emotion; the fear,
Identify, observe only, what truly is, have discernment,
Do so without prejudice, in mercy and compassion
and then
Perform a compassionate action;
Do what is right and good,
For the Highest Good of All, in purity of Spirit
With grace and ease...

We cease to learn and grow by denial of perceived negatives. To grow, we must become the observer, to transcend the emotions and accept all with understanding and experience peace within our souls, not by denial. I sought a way to help her overcome her fears, for they are fears. So I looked directly at her eyes and stated ....

"Negative? Not at all. It is our greatest hope for the future." She looked stunned

"How could crystal skulls possibly help us with that?" James asked.

I looked at all of them and wondered if I should continue. Not all could or wanted to understand. Skulls were simply too far out for most.

"Think about it for a moment, I know this sounds really wild and about as far out as one could possibly get, but listen. If you were an ancient civilization that knew that for the next 13,000 years humanity was going to go through

38

a time of darkness and the darkest ignorance would overcome the minds of the people." They listened.

"All you knew in your culture was about to be destroyed for whatever reason. You had a single opportunity to preserve knowledge for the generation that would one day reappear that could translate your wisdom to them and benefit, perhaps even save the whole of humanity."

"WOW!" Someone exclaimed. At least someone understood. I continued.

"Now suppose that in your day, crystal technology was such that people were so advanced they had learned how to project their thought patterns into a crystal formation. They would decide to leave behind their library for that generation to come." I paused as they absorbed the idea of a universal library. Continuing,

"They met and decided to choose something that the future people could recognize as a place of knowledge. They could project their thought patterns into a crystal formation. They would decide to leave behind their library for that generation to come. They met and decided to choose something that the future people could recognize as a place of knowledge."

"Where would that be?" James asked.

"I ask you. Where do you store your knowledge, in books, on stone tablets on paper? None of those would last the many thousands of years to come." Several students looked up blankly at me. Others seemed to be understanding, so I continued.

"The form would be of the human brain, the human skull. The brain is where you store knowledge, isn't it? They put it in a crystal skull!"

"I get it! They expected us to understand. But today the skull is a symbol of death or of outlaws" James exclaimed shaking his head.

El Aleator, below. As you can see, he is amplifying the colors around him.

> **Skulls come in all types....**
> **They represent the place to keep Wisdom and**
> **Knowledge, even as your own skull does.**
> **Hand tooled Skull from Tibet on left,**
> **Center, El Aleator from Belize**
> **Right, Brazilian Jade Skull**

Chapter V
On Assignment: The Cape

"Lucy, would you and Raael like to go with me to Cape Cod for a weekend?" I asked my two friends. They had both previously accompanied me to Belize.

"Oh, sure! A vacation!" Lucy replied.

"No, no, not that. I have a class scheduled and I could use some help driving down there. It's about four hours, but it would be fun. We could go to the beach too, after class of you'd like!" I offered.

"Ok!" They both looked excited about the trip and a few moments of rest. We'd all been pretty busy.

A few days later we were off toward Cape Cod on the east coast. The Cape was known for dangerous storms in winter and wonderful summers of fun for boaters and sun worshippers. I'd met my second husband on Nantucket

Island on a ferry ride from the Cape ten years prior, but hadn't been there for quite some time.

"I have all the instructions and its pretty straight forward to her house. We just have to find our motel and two miles from the motel there's a donuts shop. That's where we take a left and she's about three minutes from that point. Our class starts tomorrow morning, so we can have a few for rest and relaxation!" I said as we began our trip.

As we entered the Cape, it was slow going, a lot of traffic, a highway parking lot! It took us several more hours just to get to our motel. We were tired and exhausted as we checked into the motel. We looked around as we waited for the attendant to finish our paperwork. Lucy quipped,

"Oh good, they have coffee at seven AM!"

"Could we have a 7 AM wake up call?" I asked at the desk.

"Sure thing! All set!" The attendant said as I signed the charge slip. "We'll have the coffee ready!" He smiled.

We decided to have dinner just down the street so as not to get caught in any more traffic.

"Oh good, that'll give us a chance to see her turn off at the donut shop," I said getting into the car.

We drove the two miles to the donut shop. It wasn't there.

"She said it was two miles from our hotel. Well, we'll go up another mile."

We clocked the mileage again, but still could not find the store. For those of you who have never seen this store, it has a big, bright orange and pink sign that glows for miles and the best coffee!

We ate dinner and decided to drive back slowly. In the near darkness we searched for the usual and familiar, brightly lit sign. The next thing we knew we were back at the hotel and still had not found the shop.

"Well, Lucy and I will get up early and get the coffee and try one more time. Otherwise I'll have to call her again in the morning." I said to Lucy.

It was three weary souls that feel asleep that night. Bright and early, Lucy and I awoke about the same time. I turned on the television to check the weather. The TV said 7:15 AM.

"Hey, Lucy! The attendant didn't call us like he said he would." I complained.

She said, "Well, its only 6:30. Didn't you tell him 7 AM?"

"Lucy, its 7:15." I replied.

"No, it's 6:30. That's what my watch says." She retorted.

"Have you ever known the cable TV to be wrong?" I asked. We both just stood staring at the TV. It now said 7:17 AM

"Ok let's so to the front desk to get our coffees anyway and ask him."

We walked across the empty parking lot to the desk. "Funny, there are no cars," I thought to myself at the time. "This place was packed last night." Then we saw that the front office was closed.

"They're not open! Look! It says 7 AM opening! I told you its 6:30." Lucy exclaimed.

"Well, I'm up and I want some coffee. Let's go find that donut shop!" We jumped in the car and started the engine. The car clock came into view when I started the car. It said 7:25.

"Look at that Lucy!" I said while pointing to the car's clock. She too saw the difference in time.

"Oh, My God! This is getting weird Susan!" Lucy pulled back her hair in her nervous little way as she wiggled around in her seat.

"Uh- Huh" I replied driving out of the parking lot and onto the road. I'm going to clock the mileage again. We went the two miles and did not see the shop. We drove past where we had eaten the night before, still no donut shop.

We decided to stop in at a small corner 24 hour convenience store to get our coffee. Lucy and I asked the attendant who was behind the counter, "Where's the coffee?"

He motioned across the empty store to the counter. Lucy and I walked over, took out three cups and began filling them.

Almost immediately the attendant was by my side. He opened the trash bin beside me and began to pull out the garbage bag by the green plastic handles. He pulled, but it was so overstuffed he couldn't get it out, then, in anger, slammed shut the bin.

I began to fill my second cup when again, to my surprise, the attendant was by my side again.

This time he opened the bin, and with no effort at all, he pulled out a half empty bag. It was easy. Lucy and I looked at one another, then took our three cups of coffee and turned around. We were shocked.

The store was completely filled with customers waiting in line. The attendant who had stood beside me was behind the counter. There were so many people we had to walk to the back of a line. Mind you, we had entered an empty store just minutes before. There were no customers. We were the only customers and we had seen no one else come into the store. There was no one other than the attendant in the store, and now we had to walk to the back of a long line of customers.

We were both too shocked to say anything at first, then Lucy whispered to me while we stood in line, "Susan I don't like this…."

"I know Lucy, let's just get out of here and do the class and go home!"

We returned to the hotel quite somber. I tried to call my clients home but the phone was busy. The hotel clerk still was not in the office. I took out an old map and found her street and decided that we would follow the map and forget all about the donut shop. We told Raael what had happened.

Soon, the three of us were turning up the road where the donut shop was supposed to be. It still wasn't there. We wondered what we were getting ourselves into by entering this house. We did not speak as we got out of the car and went up to ring the doorbell.

"Hello!" A jolly woman greeted us at the door, I am so happy to see you! Did you have any problems following my directions?"

We just looked at one another as we entered the house.

"Well, to be honest with you we never found the donut shop; I just followed an old street map." I replied to her question.

"Why how could you have missed that!" She exclaimed.

"I know that we are just meeting, but do you find this place a bit strange at times?" I asked.

I could see her questioning expression. "I mean like people changing their minds or acting out of character, or sometimes it seems like you're just forgetting things a lot?"

"OH!" YES!" She exclaimed again. "Sometimes I think I am losing my mind. I'll start out somewhere and end up somewhere else!" She laughed. Then, examining me more seriously said, "I'm not senile, you know."

"I know that, Monica, but this is a very unusual place that you live in. I'll explain more as the day goes on, but we do have a lot of material to cover, so let's get started!"

At noontime, the class decided to have lunch at a café next door to the donut shop. Lucy, Rachel and I just looked at one another.

"This will be interesting" Raael said as we opened the car door.

"Ok! Right there!" Monica giggled as we drove up. "Here it is!" She got out happy as a lark oblivious to the strange happenings around her or the comments we had made to her.

The three of us stared in amazement at the donut shop on the same corner we had turned only a few hours prior. At that time, there was no donut shop or the big pink and orange glowing sign. It was here now!

Shaking our heads, we went in and had lunch with the group.

After lunch, we returned to the class. I spoke to them all about the happenings, especially the time flux and the disappearance of material items suggesting extreme changes in reality and dimensional shifting.

"Monica, if I were you, I'd leave this place." I stated boldly to her and her friends assembled for the class.

"You know, that's what my ex husband said before he left. He said the place was making people drink like fishes," she giggled, then more seriously, "yes, there are a lot of alcoholics around here."

"I would imagine if I lived here, I'd take up drinking too, that is, if I didn't have a better explanation of why this is happening...."

Then, I saw it....a vision. Ever so fleeting, it came to me as if I was watching a film, a video. In the vision I saw the beach with waves. There were people; thousands of people were in the waves. They were being tossed upon the waters. They were helpless to reach shore. It was horrible to see them struggle and drown. At that moment, I told no one of the vision. As quickly as it had begun, it was over. I felt a chill and a knowledge come over me. I was being called.

"Monica, where is the closest beach?" I asked.

"Oh, it's right down the road, about five miles...." I cut in, "Tonight, we'll go there to place a support pillar of Light to help secure the area."

The two women who had come with me just rolled their eyes..…. "Oh, boy! Here we go again!" Yelled Lucy.

After the class, we decided to go to dinner and discuss a plan before attempting to find the beach. We entered a restaurant that had all the ambiance of the 1950's. A waitress, small and uncommunicative, directed us to a table clear across the dining room. Several tables were empty and we walked right past them. A few tables were set with antique looking dinnerware. Patrons spoke quietly and we could not hear what they were saying.

Seated, we looked around the room. It seemed to have a fog, mist floating in the air. It was like looking through a glass that had a film over it. The people in the room seemed lower that we were, or that somehow we were suspended in a dimension above them.

Lucy spoke, "Susan is it safe to eat here?"

"Well, Lucy, I don't really know. Let's see what happens."

"Yeah! We've got the floating table!" Quipped Raael.

We ordered our food and very shortly afterwards, it was served. We looked down at what had been placed before us. The food was bland and colorless, just as everything else around us. No one picked up a fork. We sure didn't have an appetite but were mesmerized by the events that were unfolding.

Finally, I spoke, "I'm not really hungry. I think we should leave."

A "Me too!" Shot from Lucy.

And a nod from Raael was all it took. We stood up and walked out the door. To this day, I do not remember paying the bill. It was as though we walked out of a dream. We walked out into the night.

We began driving out toward the beach as Monica had directed us. For a place that was built on tourist business, it seemed so strange we could not see any signs for the beach.

We kept driving back and forth looking for a sign.

Lucy spoke, "She said it was just five miles from her house! We've gone back and forth at least three times."

Raael added, "Let's just forget it! Maybe we're not supposed to do this!"

Just then a car pulled in front of us going very slowly. I had to slow down to about fifteen miles per hour. Lucy became impatient.

What's the matter with you?" She began yelling at the car in front of us. We couldn't pass on the double yellow line.

 "Why don't you go faster? What is the matter with you anyway?" She yelled! Something was happening to Lucy.

"Lucy it doesn't matter." I tried to calm her.

"It's so dark we need to go slow in order to find the signs." I touched her arm. At that very moment the car in front of us turned to the right.

"Look! Shouted Raael, there's the sign. There's the sign for the beach!"

A small white sign about ten inches long was nailed to a post. The sign had been posted on the telephone pole and was now directing us to the beach area. If it hadn't been for the car turning off at that moment, we never would have seen the sign.

"Guess what guys! That car was sent to help us find this place. See? We've got angels on our side, we can do this! Angels just don't know how to drive a car!"

They laughed. "Hey! I really believe the angels are really driving that car!"

As we followed down the road shown to us by the mysterious, slow car, we soon drove into a parking lot. In the quiet of the night, the street lights cast an eerie glow over the car and into the parking area.

No one moved to get out of the car. We sat in silence as the shore winds gently rocked the car. We watched the waves crashing on the sands just ahead of us.

"Well, here we are." I said at last with a sigh.

"What are we going to do?" Asked Lucy.

"I really don't know just yet. We'll have to do a pillar to stabilize this area." I answered.

The depth of the darkness I was feeling pressing into my being left me cold inside. This would not be pleasant, I knew that already.

"Obviously, something has happened here that is causing the dimensions to shift and we have been experiencing realities that shift every few minutes." I said thoughtfully.

I wondered as they sat silently with me just what my statement would mean and what affect it would have upon us once we got out of the car.

"I think that's pretty serious. All that I can think of to do to help is to set a pillar. "

"What do you mean?" Lucy broke her silence.

"About the Dimensions?" I asked. She nodded. "OK. If you can imagine a pile of 100 blocks, each one rests upon another. If you pull one out, they all tumble or shift their place downward. To add another block somewhere in between, you lift all those that are above it."

She nodded again to show she understood the concept.

"When we do experiments that disrupt the levels, the blocks, we are actually shaking loose foundations that are set for all our protection."

"That does sound serious!"

Yes, every dimension is shaken by fooling around with the energies that separate them and hold them within their time lines."

"How?"

"It all has to do with the flow of light, time, space and our so- called, 'assigned places' within that flow. It seems obvious; someone or something has been moving the energies that secure this area. Most likely, some Tesla experimentation has occurred here."

"Who or what is that?" She asked.

"Tesla was a brilliant scientist who discovered many of the secrets of time and space. I thought though he had destroyed his findings because even he knew it was too dangerous to use the technology he had discovered. I guess not." I paused to consider the thought.

"He's dead, but someone must have continued his work. This place is all out of whack! It's the only thing I can think of that would toss time and realities around like this."

We sat looking ahead at the beach and the pounding waves in absolute silence for several minutes. We were all thinking. My thoughts were if we'd ever get off the beach and back home again.

"OK! I'm ready!" Raael exclaimed! She jumped out of the car and ran to the beach.

Lucy and I looked at each other, shrugged, opened the car doors and followed after her, out onto the sandy beach.

Raael was tucking up her long skirt into her underpants when we arrived. We watched her, waiting to see what she was going to do. All of a sudden, she raised her hands above her head and ran screeching into the ocean!

"We are HERRRRRE!" she screamed to the black sky above us! She raised her fists and then swung her arms as if she was holding a sword up at the veiled moon.

At that instant, a gust of wind came out of nowhere. It tossed Lucy and me completely off our feet, and threw us face down on the beach! We lay across from each other on the sand.

Lifting our faces up out of the sand and spitting it out of our mouths, Lucy and I just looked across at one another in shock.

I turned over looked over toward Raael who had a horrified, shocked look on her face. She had seen what had happened to us just moments after at her announcement to the unseen world.

"Raael, don't you EVER do that again!" I scolded. "Now you've got their attention!"

The wind had risen to such a gale, we could no longer stand. Rachel came and crouched down beside us on the sand. Apparently, someone or something had heard her challenge and we were not welcome!

"Sorry".

I nodded. "OK, let's do this." I said.

Three times I tried to set the pillar, grasping the Light of Heaven, but the Earth connection could not be made. It had no "bottom". Usually, when setting a pillar, you could attach it to something. There was nothing beneath us. There was nothing beneath the sand we were lying upon. We were in a dimension that didn't exist, on earth anyway, and had no solid base. This was frightening.

Then it started. A groaning and wailing from deep within the earth began to rise up between the three of us. I could hear it faintly above the wind at first, but then it got louder and louder. The cries of agony touched my soul and I wept. Tears began streaming down my cheeks.

"We've got to close this!" I cried out and in tears, I looked at my companions.

They were hearing it too. Lucy's eyes were terrified as she looked across at mine.

"We're in hell!" She whimpered. "Oh, my God, we are in hell!"

"Lucy, hang on! We can do this!" I prayed. I prayed for the release of the torment of the souls and I prayed for the earth's protection.

"Dear God, I don't know what they've done here, but please, help me to close this!" I said.

I reached up into Heaven to receive the Light from God to close the portal that had been ripped open somehow.

My companions held the energy with me as I brought it down to the earth in one more attempt to set the pillar. The groaning and cries of pain grew louder; the wind whipped us with sandy venom and shook us threateningly.

The Light held strong in my hands.

As it went down and my hands touched the earth, I saw that instead of connecting to the earth's core, the energy of the pillar spread outward. It spread to the North and to the South. The Light was connecting to other places! Then, I heard the words,

"Susan, you must go to Rhode Island and to the Gaspe Bay to secure the ties or this will not hold. It must be supported elsewhere with pillars that are set on solid earth."
The wind stopped and we fell onto the sand exhausted.

"It's done, I whispered, but only for a little while. I've got to get to two places to secure it or the coast will rip wide open and all hell will break loose upon the people."

Lucy and Raael just looked at me. Neither one offered to go on the next trip.

"Just how am I supposed to get to the Gaspe Bay in Canada *and* to Rhode Island in the next two weeks?" I asked God aloud as I fell into the car.

My two friends were silent as we drove back to the motel. In the morning we were all too happy to be leaving. We decided to get off the Cape before even considering breakfast. The car was packed and we began the journey back home. Pulling out from the parking lot of the motel, we had to wait for another car to turn into our motel lot before pulling out. As I looked into the driver's seat of the car coming toward us, I gasped!

Do you see what I see? I screamed!

"Do you mean the man with no face?" asked Raael. A ghost was driving the car. He, or IT, had no face.

"Let's get the hell out of here shouted Lucy!" We drove straight home.

"Hi, Sue!" Will gave me a big hug as I walked in. "Boy, you look beat for someone who's been playing on the beach at the Cape!" He teased.

"I'm not even going to discuss it, Will. It was a real hard class this weekend." I softly answered him. He could see I was troubled.

"OK," he said. "Take a rest and when you get up, I've got something to talk about."

Too tired to even speak I went for a nap. Arising a couple hours later, I sat at the table in my comfortable home as Will brought me a cup of coffee. I could see he was excited about something. I nodded to him.

"Sue, you know I want to buy a boat," he began.

"Uh- huh," I nodded sipping my coffee. I hated deep water. I had nearly drowned in Florida as a child. I really didn't like boats.

"Well, I think I found the one I want. It's in Newport, Rhode Island in a slip there. I'd like to go see it."

I nearly dropped my coffee mug! I visibly shook. Seeing my reaction he quickly cut into the moment.

"And then we can drive up to the Gaspe Bay in Nova Scotia, all along the coast! Wouldn't that be a wonderful trip?" He looked pleadingly at me.

He thought I'd disagree and was making an offer I couldn't refuse. I realized he didn't know that those were the two exact places the Angels the night before had told me to go to. It was there I would set the two pillars to stabilize the Eastern Coast from the rip in the dimensions.

"When do you want to go?" I asked, hardly breathing.

"The owners told me they could see me Wednesday. This week, Sue."

"Ok, Will, I'll go with you. There's something I need to do there anyway." He looked at me with questions, but decided not to ask. He was getting excited now.

"And I've already made our reservations! Tuesday night we'll be in Newport so I can look at the boat before the meeting on Wednesday!" He looked so happy!

I forced a smile. "I'd better start packing. It's already Monday morning." I was stunned at the organization of the universe.

I was "On Assignment". Once again.

Newport Rhode Island

Tuesday afternoon found me dockside in Newport Harbor looking at yachts. I used to go to air shows with him and I know I looked at least ten thousand airplanes. Now, I would be looking at boats. "OK" I thought.

It was always a strange feeling within to have had some of the Spirit-filled experiences I'd been having for the last several years, and then suddenly find myself thrust into the world of planes, cars and now, boats.

I live in two worlds. I realized that now more than ever as he was excited about boats and I was desperately searching for clues as to where I was to place a Pillar from God. I tried to pay attention, really.

I know he was disappointed in me as I just couldn't find the enthusiasm he wanted from me. I was distracted by every person we met, seeking a clue or a message from one of them. Nothing happened however, and finally we went to find our motel.

Outside the confines of the city, we drove up a hill toward our room for the night. As we went higher on a windy roadway, the sign of the motel came into view. Peeling paint revealed the name, "Gateway Motel". What better place than a Gateway! We were here! HERE was the place for the Pillar!!! I laughed until I saw the motel. Will had sought to find a motel that was really cheap. This one was very cheap.

I refused to stay in the first room we looked at. It was awful and dirty, smelled of old cigarette smoke and stale air.

"Will, I can't stay here. Please, can we see if there's another room, please?" He nodded and walked toward the motel office. I followed him.

The attendant was kind, and we were given another room. Higher up on the hilltop was a small cottage. This would be our room for the night. We opened the cottage door and walked in.

I was immediately struck by the décor. The bed was covered by a deep green velvet bedspread. There were emerald green curtains hung on the windows. It was so dark inside you couldn't see a thing coming from outside.

I pulled back curtains to bring in some light. Looking out the window, I could see a giant tree further up the hill. I opened the window and a soft breeze filled the room. This would be good.

"I like this one, Will." Now all I had to do was wait for the sign and location to place a pillar.

Nothing happened all that evening. We had dinner down the hill and came back to sleep. We were tired from all the sun on the docks. The soft emerald green velvet cradled me to sleep, its colors healing and soothing my soul.

I awoke early with a start. "NOW!" I heard the Voice speak urgently to me.

I jumped up and threw a wrap over my nightgown. Will was still sleeping soundly as I slipped out the door in barefoot in the first rays of dawn.

I walked around the back of the cottage in the soft dewy grass of early morning to see a spectacular sight.

An ancient tree towered up into the glowing dawn. On one side of the tree was the massive amber and golden glow of a rising sun. The pulsing, rising sun was suspended in the east over the ocean.

On the other side of the tree, hung a globe of pure silver beaming its light over the receding nighttime sky. A near full moon contrasted the sky.

The hilltop formed a crest between them with the Ancient One standing between them.

I ran and sat between the sun and the moon facing the tree and went into trance.

"Al'Lat" the Voice spoke gently, we have come to show you what must be done.

I saw Adama and several others who were with him, in the trance mist with me.

"Why? Why did this happen?" I asked, pleading for humanity. The memory of the cries of the trapped in time overwhelmed me for a moment.

"Al'Lat, the people are unknowing of the damage they do." Adama spoke.

He paused and communicated the energy of his thoughts to me. I could see his distress.

"The powers they unleash are magnificent, but without understanding of the wave of retribution that is unleashed by the powers, they endanger us all." He paused again as I considered his words. "The "rip" as you call it, is expanding and multiples of realities in this area intermix causing great confusion and disorganization throughout the universes."

I was given a vision of bulges of dark energy rippling across an ocean of light. Planets bounced as fishing bobbins bounce upon a lake in the wake of a boat as it passed.

"Know that what is does affects the Whole." A solemn Adama looked into my eyes.

I could see the ripple effect upon many concentric circles of times and universes as he projected the image into my mind.

"You have placed a patch on the damage, as we have. One day they will understand the powers, but now are as children playing with matches in a basement." I could hear his concern as a parent and for his own peoples.

I was then shown what to do.

I could see the two pillars on solid ground, one North and one South. The stabilizing energy of the two outer pillars would "hold in place" a center pillar.

Just as if I were building a fence by placing fence posts, one would support the other in a line. The unstable pillar on Cape Cod would be supported by the Light of God from the two other pillars to be built. Now I must set this pillar.

I could see this, even as the tree stood between the sun and the moon. Its branches stretched out to touch the sun and the moon, holding their energies and strengthening it.

"Yes" that is what you must do, Al'Lat." The trance was over. I stood. Now I understood the concept and what I must do.

I began to sing a song to the moon. As I sang, the essence of the moon began to flow out from the moon.

Using my voice, a moon's milky essence began to flow out from the moon and down toward the earth. Using my hands in a sacred dance, the essence was directed into the great tree!

A great force was being created at this moment! The tree would receive the essence and be strengthened by the moon's own energy! This would hold the power of the southern pillar!

I turned toward the sun. Dancing between the sun and the moon before and ancient tree, I was filled with ecstatic joy!

I danced the Dance of Times. Upon other planes I had visited in ages past I had learned the moves and the songs. I remembered and I danced a wild sun dance!

She too began to release her golden sun's essence in great beaming rays of magenta gold!

I directed the sun's elixir down though the sky into the ancient tree! Its' golden rays of sun essence was flowing into the tree even as the moon's.

Standing back, I could see what was happening. The Male force and the Female force were now flowing into the tree.

It was to be the standing Southern Pillar of God.

Taking both arms, I stretched out one hand to the sun and the other to the moon.

I breathed in deeply. As I did, I drew a great force of energy from both the sun and the moon at the same time.

I breathed it into the tree and secured the energy to the core of the Earth. Mother GAIA received the energy and the Pillar was created, set and sealed.

I fell to my knees and offered prayers to God most High for all that He has done.

In prayers of thankfulness I honored the Spirit of Truth and Knowledge.

Humbled by my experience, I thanked God I had been used to bring a compassionate action to the Earth and many universes.

"Thank you Father, Mother, Christ
and Adama for your love."

Yet, there would be one more pillar to set. Crying softly, I slipped back into my healing bed and let its waves of emerald green caress me back to sleep.

Below, The NH Telos Site Meditation

The Third Pillar Nova Scotia, Canada

When I awoke, I looked out at the great tree one more time. It stood tall and magnificent, towering into the sky. I thanked the Ancient Sentinel and promised that no one but me would ever know its purpose or true location.

Soon, Will and I were well on our way up the Northern coast of Maine, heading toward the Gaspe Bay Peninsula, Nova Scotia, in Canada.

Will was driving straight through. I slept much of the time as he drove. Vivid images began to fill my sleep.

In vision, I could see the Pillar of God now stood strong and souls were already ascending in the established Light on Earth all along the coast from Rhode Island to the Cape.

So many were trapped in a time wrap. Now they would be freed. The Light of the three Pillars had been drawn down from Heaven, with the blessing of God. Light so powerful shone along the entire coast as a great beacon. Its rays of freedom shone deep into the dark recesses of time and offered a way home to those welcoming its brightness and immersing themselves in its freedom call.

A rip had been closed, but now a penetrating Light had created a path toward Heaven. The Angels were now able to descend upon that Light and reach the deepest depths of their human despair and break through the barriers of time and the energy signature that trapped them. A gateway and highway had been established to escort the lost home.

There was joy in Heaven as families and soul groups were reunited. The souls took on their true form of Light and were now free. The Light of Christ had freed them. He set the captives free. He always has.

We drove all the way up into St Andrew and decided to stay there for the night. We began looking for a room to stay. "I'm sorry" was all we heard. We couldn't find a room anywhere! Finally, at one of the hotels, the attendant was kind enough to call a central tourist bureau to locate a room for us.

"Well," he said. "They have one room in St John available, but it is an hour and a half backwards from where you are going."

"You mean to tell me," asked Will incredulous, "that there is only ONE room in all of the Canadian Gaspe Bay for us?"

"Yes, Sir," the attendant apologized. Will looked at me.

"I guess that's where we're supposed to be, Will. Let's go back."

He shrugged his shoulders and said, "Tell them we are coming. Here's my card number. Hold the room."

I walked outside as the transactions were being completed. I could see the Hand of God in this. We had to go to St John. Interesting it would be there. St John. He was a great Pillar of the Church and of Christ's ministry. Yes, we would go there.

After the long drive backwards, we found the old seaport town of St. John. The building were quaint and old and still reflected the air of times past when this had been a busy port on the coast. Harboring ships from distant lands, many people disembarked from those ships for they had come here from Europe to seek a new life and home.

Our bed and breakfast house and room was snuggled in between two other buildings facing the harbor of St. John. We parked along side the curb of a narrow street and walked to our location.

"Hello!" The motel attendant greeted us. The quaint seaside village was closing up for the night. We had arrived just in time.

After checking in, we were about to start up the narrow stairway to the third floor of an old captain's house. Before we did however, the attendant spoke and pointed to a little room.

"Tomorrow morning your breakfast will be served in this room," he stated. "By the way he said turning back to look at us beneath him on the stairs. "Did they tell you about the room?"

"No," answered Will.

"Oh, I am so sorry they did not tell you."

"What?! What about the room?" Interjected Will, becoming impatient. We were tired.

"Sir, it is haunted." he spoke apologetically. Will's expression was of total confusion. He just couldn't respond.

I looked at him and touched his shoulder saying, "Will, it's OK. I'll take care of it."

The attendant quietly let us into the room. The frosty air of the specter was all around us. This room was really haunted. It would be difficult resting in this place. We stood very still in the room for a few moments. The attendant put down the bags and stepped quietly out of the room, not even asking for a tip.

"Susan, what are you going to do?" Will asked, his eyes pleading with mine. He didn't like things like this. I always tried to prevent my world from entering his.

"Leave for a few minutes, OK?" I asked.

"No problem there!" he said, stepping out of the room shaking his head.

I walked over to the side of the bed. Allowing my mind to open to the unseen world around me, I saw the image of an old woman. She was dressed in an ivory muslin nightgown, her hair white long and flowing about her shoulders. She stood by the window looking out over the harbor. She rocked with tears and seemed not to notice me.

I attempted to communicate to her with my mind. Suddenly, her full body shook and she looked up from her crying. With amazement, she turned toward me. I nodded to her and sent waves of love to her. She seemed to sigh. I could now see that she understood I could see her and she was now waiting for me to speak.

"Why have you called me here?" I asked.

"I desire the Light of which you carry. My name is Martha Johnson and I have been waiting for someone to come."

"Martha, do you now desire to leave this place?

"Yes, she answered. I have been here waiting.

"What year is it, Martha?" I asked.

"1680, she answered. He is not returning. I want to go now."

"Martha, I am very tired and am not able to do as you wish right now. I promise in the morning I will call for your release. But you must not touch us or disturb us. Do you understand?"

"Yes!" She lit up with acknowledgement of the fact she could go home.

I hated to be touched by ghosts. They can do most anything, but not touch me. I had a terrifying experience on St. John Island in the Virgin Islands. I was awakened there one night by the touch of many, stroking my face and arms. They were trying to awaken me. Many, once slaves, were trapped there and they wanted to be freed. I understood, but it was pretty bad. No touching! That is my limit! Strange, it would be once again at a place called St John!

The room warmed as she drew back.

I called Will into the room. "We're OK". He nodded. "I need to go outside to the dock for a while, Will. I'll be right back."

He didn't question me as I left him standing warily looking around the now warm room.

Outside in the yard of the house the full moon shone brightly. I said the prayers and set the Pillar, connecting the three to hold the coastline. I was finished, it was done. Prayers of thankfulness were said as I rose to go back inside.

I snuggled in next to Will, grateful to be warm and comfortable beside him. How much easier his life would be if I were not in it in this way. From an old school, he much would have preferred me to be the woman he had married. Now he had all kinds of experiences with me and some he'd rather not have. Sleeping in a haunted room was one of them.

As I lay thinking about all that had happened, he fell into a sleep. Just as I was about to close my eyes, I saw Martha materialize next to me.

With an icy finger she reached forward, touching my shoulder. When she did, she said, "OUCH!" and then instantly disappeared.

I sat straight up and sent out an angry but amused message, "Martha! I TOLD you Not to touch me. If you do that again- I will leave!"

She was a spunky little thing, I thought while concealing my smile. The Lady of the house, she'd not often taken commands from strangers. She was playfully teasing me. Her little "OUCH!" was saying she'd not harm me and was likely a bit insulted by my inferring that about her earlier. She had played a little trick and I could feel it was not with any ill intent. She was so like a little child! She had been a little child, trapped and waiting for centuries to finally go home.

In the morning, I kept my promise to her. Christ and the Angels came and escorted her home at last.

Author's note:

At the time this was occurring in 2000, I had no idea that the site we were at on Cape Cod was the same area that the local Indian tribes had been massacred in the 1800's.

At the time of this writing 2006, I have just learned that there had been a raid by Colonials assisted by opposing tribes from the Great Lakes area. They wiped out all the coastal Indigenous Indians, driving them onto the beaches and into the ocean. This area also had been the scene of many shipwrecks along the stormy coast. Many had lost their lives.

People have asked me how souls can become trapped in this way. I have asked Spirit and this is what I am told. Sometimes, the soul may be unprepared for horrific death and its trauma. The ensuing denial, grasping for life and emotional trauma marks the current timeline with an emotional energy 'stamp'. That event causes an energy signature, a memory, which remains locked in time. The scene becomes as a video that replays itself, over and over and the soul refuses to let go of the drama.

Somehow the rip had opened into that timeline, deep in the recorded history of this nation, allowing it to surface as a bubble breaks through the waters of time.

Chapter VI

July 13th, 2000 The Challenge

"Hurry! Let's get going!" I shouted to the group assembled at the Shambhala Center early one morning. We were going on a trip. We were on our way to the White Mountains of New Hampshire to the Eastern Telos site for the day. This was the first site Adama had directed me to open, November 1999, six months before the May 2000 Belize trip, the second opening. When the site opened the earth shook as the powerful energies of the opening went from the east coast to the west coast to Mount Shasta. Three loud booming noises were heard and a measurable earthquake had occurred. I looked up into the sky. It was going to rain. I hoped that further north the weather would be better.

My students had wanted to go to the site and perhaps see some Lemurians or the White Spirits of the White Mountains that I had been speaking about so often. Curious, they had heard the stories of the students who had returned with me from Belize and secretly, I knew some on this trip were very skeptical.

70

Also, some were pretty haughty in their attitude toward me and the others that had been in Belize with me. This would be a test; I felt it all around me. It made me a little nervous, but I am not one to prove myself or do miracles 'on command'. Spirit does not work that way.

Just recently, a man had badgered me constantly with phone calls and emails. He had seen many people at the Center receive healing. He had seen Lilly's straightened arms and others who had received miraculous healing. He had brought his friend to me for healing of a pancreas that caused his friend constant pain and illness, as well as a progressive kidney failure. Soon, his friend would be on dialysis.

I had given all that Spirit had given to me in his session. The man, his friend, had not been healed. Day after day I would receive angry and hurt calls and admonishments.

"WHY?" Why don't you heal him?" He cried! "Why don't you do this for MY friend? You do it for others? What's wrong with me?" He would ask pleading for his friend.

"It's not you." I'd explain, "Healing is a gift of Spirit. Individual karma and life contracts must also be understood," I'd try to explain over and over again.

All my attempts to explain to him that it is not my decision as to who gets what or when went unheeded. I tried to explain that it is Spirit and God that heals, not me. I am the vessel of the energy, but not the Maker. He couldn't understand or accept the fact that God was not, at this time anyway, going to heal his friend. He blamed me.

Today, he was on this trip with me. He had signed up before I knew he had done so. When I initially rebelled, Spirit had told me he must come. There were others too.

"OK", I thought. It doesn't really matter what people think about me. I am on a mission. I had adopted an old saying of my mother's, "Come hell or high water I'm going through!" Ever since I had come back calling myself Al'Lat Le Andro Melchizedek, many had thought I'd lost my mind in Mount Shasta. I knew that.

To say one has been assigned to help save the world, does sound a bit delusional, doesn't it? I laughed to myself. Yes, quite delusional according to the standard of the world.

Having come from a social work background, I'd seen many people have had breakdowns and appear delusional, or psychotic. They would see and hear the unseen. But, I am not delusional. What had happened to me in the last few years flew in the face of all I had been taught. I hear voices, and speak to that which is unseen. But this work, this mission, is not under the standard the world has set. Many visionaries and even great scientists had received messages and assistance in dreams and visions.

Another world existed and I had been gifted with an ability to tap into it. I placed a new bumper sticker on my car which said, "I'm not weird, I'm gifted!" I could not change. The world would have to become educated as to the alternatives all around it and find release from the bindings set upon the minds of the masses. I would try humor and every other way to break down the barriers.

I always sought confirmations too. A confirmation was most often a series of events that led up to a desired result and an outcome that could be reasonably perceived. 'Spirit proof!'

Confirmations, of my sometimes unpredictable actions to others, most often held undeniable direction. That direction, guidance from above, most likely came from

Angels, Obed, Melchizedek or Adama. It came in rapid order, such as the Pillar at the Cape. I moved as quickly as I received the information. I also found that after having experienced many such occurrences, that my Faith and ability to perceive the Spirit's direction was becoming highly tuned in. I am deliberate.

It was becoming easier and easier to follow my inner voice and the clues Spirit placed in front of me to provide my stepping stones on my path. Not many would have the spiritual maturity to understand this life I was now leading. Sometimes my actions appeared to be scattered and not as 'scheduled' as the world would have it.

For some, it was confusing, others were as excited as I was at the occurrences, and others saw this as weakness. But in fact, I was becoming stronger. Challenges were coming from those who saw an opportunity to seize power, enhance their own standing, and an opportunity to discredit the Center in Manchester. Where there is great Light there is also a contrast of great darkness. It is a fact.

This undercurrent was perceived and known by me. "Spirit will instruct" was what I had been told in the night. I would wait and be patient. Some at this event today, were the skeptics and challengers. I was about to be tested by them in front of many of my students.

We had a mix of energies on this day. I would have preferred to cancel, but Spirit continued to give the "go ahead" for the event.

"Ok. Let's hit the road!" I consigned myself to the waiting day and unknown outcome. The drive was over three hours long to the mountain. As we entered the mountain range on Route 16 it was pouring rain. We stopped at the southern base of Mount Washington. It towered over six thousand feet above us. On the northern side, around the mountain, was the site.

I prayed. We had come so far! Could rain like this stop our efforts? I got out of the car and sat on the grass in the rain and prayed. They were all watching me. The rain stopped. The group and I watched as four columns of white swirling mist formed in the shape of twisting, dancing funnels. Each of the funnels must have been five hundred feet high. Everyone got out of the cars to get a closer look and to watch.

"WOW!" Someone shouted. "Look at that!"

Spirit opened my mouth and I spoke saying,

> "These are the Spirit keepers of the sacred area.
> They have arisen and are going into the site.
> We can go now."

We all watched as the columns of white passed in front of the mountain, then slid behind the crest. They disappeared into the area where we were going. Excited now, the group jumped into the cars to follow. An hour later, we entered the Town Brook Trail just above the Dolly Kopp Campground on Pinkham B Road.

"Listen!" I shouted to the noisy group. In the background, the sound of drumming could be heard and soft singing in the breezes. People were getting very excited now and started to run up the trail.

"Stop!" I yelled, "Wait!" They didn't listen.

Then they hit the wall. Not one that could be seen, but one that certainly could be felt. They all stopped short where they stood on the trail. They could go no further.

At the same instance, I heard something and the word "OMNI-PAW!" was spoken.

They all heard it from the ethers, the unseen realm, around us. A few looked frightened.

"OMNI PAW– what does that mean?" I asked the group, as I was confused too. I didn't know what that meant.

"Well, I speak French and that means; 'One Step' a student spoke.

"So, don't take another step! That would be a good translation, don't you think?" I asked the faces looking down at me. "Well, I guess we cannot enter without asking for permission from the spirits here!" I said to the confused looks on many faces.

They were beginning to realize that this was not a game and it was real. I began to pray,

"Spirits of the Ancient Ones who guide
and protect this sacred space,
We come to you to seek entrance onto this sacred ground.

We honor you and your presence.

We have heard your drums and they
are beautiful and your songs.

We thank you for allowing us passage and
we will hold sacred this place."

I prayed aloud to all assembled there, seen and unseen. Some in this group were unenlightened and disrespectful. They had not yet learned that spirit is all around us. There are those, unseen by human eyes, which protect sacred ground. They are the keepers that hold ancient rights to the land by eons of time. Sometimes, we simply 'run them over' with our arrogance and we show no respect. There are often consequences for our actions; but because we are so unaware, that we can't even relate the events to our actions. Today, that was not to happen. It was 'in their face', so to speak and literally! They would not be allowed in without intercession on their behalf and some training on the spot!

This training would come, not by me, but by Spirit. Now I understood what Spirit had told me about being patient and letting Spirit handle this. As soon as the energy felt calmer, I began to walk up the trail as the somber, humble, and aware students now followed.

Magic At the Falls

There was dead silence as we began the ascent to the triple falls and the recently titled, Lemurian Eastern Gate Site. Clinging to their drums and precious items the solemn group walked in the gentle rain that had once again begun to fall. As we entered the sacred area, a dignified gentleman who had come on this trip, approached me with a very worried look.

"Susan, I must be losing my mind. Do you see that it is raining?"

"Yes" I answered, while glancing all around.

"I just set my drum down over there beneath that tree and looked up." He looked at me with a strange look, pleading. "Susan. It is raining, but the rain stops just above my head."

Indeed, it was. The rain fell, but did not touch us. His pleading looks made me feel compassion for him. He clearly could not comprehend what was happening. That which is spiritual often cannot be comprehended with the rational mind.

"We're not getting wet. It's raining, but we're not getting wet!" He looked as though he was going to break down.

"It's alright," I said touching his arm reassuring him. "We are here now and there is much to do."

Still stunned, he walked over to the rest of the group. I could see him looking up. I did too. I could see the rain coming down just above my head. It stopped and simply disappeared about two feet above me. I looked over at the other students. They too knew about the rain and were giggly with excitement.

"Look over there I said pointing out the rock with a large face peering out at us. That's the site entrance. You may go in and sit and meditate at the entranceway into the mountain and the tunnels of the Lemurians, but remember to respect. All." I continued as wide eyes looked up at me. By now, they were beginning to realize that we were in a sacred area and there was magic all around us. They had learned to respect that which is seen, and unseen, the All.

"Up above the first waterfall are two other sets of falls and they are beautiful.' I said pointing upward. "Just above the second set there are some rocks I want you to see. Kneel down when you find them and touch them lightly. There are messages and empowerments there for you to experience. These too are gifts for you."

They looked up at the towering rocks above them.

"Over there, I said pointing to a large rock formation. You can see the stone guardian of this site. It is about two hundred feet tall. If you climb up there you can see all three falls and pools of water. You'll be standing on the top knot of his head. Trying singing up there too!"

I smiled at them, "Now GO!"

They just about flew off into different directions like excited children on a picnic. I couldn't blame them. I did the same thing when I first saw this place. All over the rocks faces peered out at you made of moss that was alive with Spirit!

"Susan, Look!" someone shouted. "On that rock there's an Indian riding a horse and over there an Indian maiden with long hair."

"Take pictures, all around you, everyone." I shouted, "They are speaking to us in their way, in clouds, in trees and on the rocks!"

Cameras were flashing all over that mountain!

I went quietly into the sacred site of the Lemurian portal and sat down. I held the little skull, the Sastun, in my hands. I had so many questions. I could only hope that here, in this place, I would find some answers.

I remembered the legend of the Native Indians. I learned of it when I took a photo to a respected Mohawk Elder. The photo was of spirit form of Adama, a Native American and an Aborigine. He explained to me that the Indians had been waiting for this. They too were waiting for the White Spirits of the White Mountains to come and save the Earth. They knew all about the white spirits.

Soon, warm washes of energy were flowing over me. I was going into what I call a 'trance'. For me, the experience is like being a speck of light in a room full of light beings and colors. The colors swirl and move. From those colors an entranceway is formed between the worlds and I can communicate to the unseen. My physical body is often unable to move and I am often unable to communicate to the physical world around me. Sometimes, I have even appeared to be dead as my pulse is not found and my breathing slows.

I understood, but those around me would not. This is America. We don't do things like that here. I knew some here would be horrified to see me in trance. For them, it would be 'embarrassing' and really not very 'professional'. The swamis of India did this. This is called Samadhi and it could last for a long time.

"Let no one see me, please," I silently asked. Lifted up in the energies, Adama came forth from the tunnel before me, actually a dimensional doorway.

"Adama! It is so good to see you!" My mind spoke to him.

"And you", came the answer in return.

"Adama, I have returned from the second site and ask now where I am to go next."

"I am sorry; I cannot tell you at this time." Inwardly I gasped, "Are there to be any more?" I asked.

"That shall depend upon the events of the next several months." He replied. "Remember I said to you that it must be all with the cooperation of humanity?"

"Yes", I answered.

"Over the next few months, events that have long been awaited will begin to manifest. Not only you, but others who have been called into this time, must respond to their call." I felt his uncertainty. "Something so wonderful that I can hardly speak shall manifest on the earth at this time IF all shall hear and see that which is unseen and unspoken."

"Adama, how can this be? Adama if we cannot hear it or see that which is, what we are to do?"

"Al'Lat, it is heard and seen within the heart, Dear Child. You will know, we are confident, but the others, that remains to be seen."

He paused to make sure I understood. I could feel love flowing out to me.

"Be aware, be awake and follow your heart and be strong. It must be so. We are with you and support you in prayer and in All Light of Love and strength. I must go now." I watched as he returned into the Light that he had come from. My body shook as my Light returned to the physical.

I opened my eyes to the earth once again. Breathing myself back into the body, I was once again physical. I hurt. My body was such a burden. I realized I had been sitting in one place for over an hour. Stretching and forcing the flow of Prana back down my legs I struggled to stand. Only one person sat staring, gaping at me.

"Hello" he said quietly. Are you all right?" He asked with concern.

"I will be!" I said smiling and trying to cover what had just happened. I struggled to stand up on shaky legs .When I stood up I could hear the others excited voices in the distance.

"Back to work"! I quipped.

"What just happened?" He asked. His gaze and wonder were speaking his curiosity.

"I'd rather not talk about that right now." I answered with a smile. What had happened was not to be spoken of at that time. About a half hour later, two women came running down the side of the trail.

"Susan, you should have seen it! Oh, My God! You should have seen it! We both saw it and it spoke to us, it gave us directions!" Lily shouted.

"What did?" I asked.

"We were by the rocks you told us to kneel down at. We knelt down together and all of a sudden the leaves by the rock started to lift up and swirl around." Lily stated, ignoring my question.

"There was no wind," Joan said, assuring me this was not an action of the wind.

"Yes! The leaves swirled around and, Susan, they formed a little man-they formed a LITTLE MAN!" She was nearly shouting hysterically.

"A leprechaun," Joan interjected. "He spoke to us! He really spoke to us!" She shouted as she was pulling my arm, "Up there, he spoke to us!"

"OK!" Calm down," I said. "Let's sit over here. My senses are telling me that this was meant for you both. Let's find out what he said."

"He told us we were to do earth healing," Lily began

Joan interrupted, "And that we would receive a special gift today."

Lily was wiping away tears as she stated, "We must use it for the earth. The two of us together." They smiled at one another.

"I think that this is for you, not for me. I will leave you two to write down everything. Do it right now, so you don't forget– write down every single word he said." I walked away from them as Lily ran to get her note book. I left them taking to one another in excited and joyful glee! The others were coming down the mountain with stories of their own.

Spirit had promised to teach them, and Spirit had. Each person on this trip had faced the unknown realms and had overcome doubt. They knew. They knew this was real. Some had learned respect, some had learned humbleness.

Some had learned fear. Yes, fear. In today's world many think that they know everything and they cannot be taught. To try to fill something up that is already full, is an impossibility. To try to teach someone who is already certain they know everything, is extremely difficult. Some times, Spirit and a good teacher, must shake the student out of the comfort zone in order to teach. Today, Spirit had allowed some to 'hit the wall' to experience something they had no knowledge of previously. They became confused and disorientated. They emptied enough to be filled with something new.

For many, the security of whom and what they have formed themselves to be is knit tightly. To perceive the world differently, causes fear. Why? Fear of the unknown. If you know everything, you are comfortable in that. To not know moves us into uncertain waters. That's frightening. That means you must incorporate and integrate new knowledge, change, and adapt.

What is even more frightening is that sometimes those who cannot adjust, or be flexible to change, can become violent in their attempts to secure their own perception of the world. They force others, manipulate others, into the rigidity of their perceived world and will not allow growth of other individuals. Why? To maintain the borders of their own little world. They do that so as to not experience fear, to keep themselves "comfortable. " Hence: religious wars etc:

We finished that day after doing the Earth Healer Attunements and learning how to use the gifts for the Earth and for all of humanity. The Earth Healer attunements are a combination of five symbols given to us by the Acturians through a channel in England, Kathleen Murray, and a toning method to help us restore the waters, the air and earth.

Used with another system, they were powerful! St Germaine had given me the new attuning symbols and the empowerment for the five Acturian symbols some time previously. In this place, I found the attunement was extraordinary and powerful beyond anything I had experienced with this attunement process. Many were blessed this day.

I had given many, many Earth Healer attunements before, but now, I would bring people here as often as I could to tap into the Lemurian gifts of ascension energies in this place. It was blessed!

It was a tired but enlightened group that made their way home from the mountain. They had truly met the Lemurian energies that day and would never forget the miracles they experienced, or so I thought.

They had seen with their own eyes the miracle of the rain stopping with prayers. They had seen the Spirit People five hundred feet tall glide over the mountain as mist.

They even heard the guardian tell them not to go one step further without permission and they had hit a solid wall of energy that denied them entrance.

They had seen the faces and pictures in the rocks and seen a leprechaun speak to them. They had seen it raining on each other and themselves, but not get wet.

Spirit had spoken in miracles to them. Some were filled with Spirit and a love that would forever change their lives, but some still could not accept that and denied Spirit's working. Some hearts grew even colder that day. Some, just a few, became very jealous.

Even though it was very late when I arrived back home, I decided to pop the camera photo stick into the computer to see if anything came up on the screen.

As I looked at one picture, I was puzzled by the blurry globes leading up to the top of the screen. I was just about to discard the photo as a blurry mistake when it hit me.

I was looking at the picture of the waterfalls and the guardian BEHIND something that was in front, causing the blurriness. Stepping back from the computer, I could see more clearly and the image over the waterfall as the image appeared in fullness.

The spirit of an Indian stood in front of me. His form covered the entire photo. This was a Spirit showing up for his photograph! Was this the image of the one that was the Spirit Guardian who had shouted at the irreverent new comers to the site, "OMNI-PAW!" meaning, *Not one step*? Likely.

He was proud, tall and wore a fur animal on top of his head as his hat. The face of the animal peered out at me. The Indian had feathers streaming down the side of his head and he held a shield with a face painted upon it. In front of him flew a mallard duck, all in spirit! That was another confirmation to me as that was the chosen new location of the new Shambhala Center on Mallard Pond in Manchester, NH.

To the right of the picture, a bear looked up at me and another face of an Indian was clearly seen. To the left, a bird man flew with wings outstretched. The face of a gnome stared out from the photo. Most amazingly, a FAIRY was in front, holding a stick as her hair streamed behind her!

The next morning I made copies of the picture and sent it out over email. We had met the Keeper of this sacred site, heard his voice and received the blessing!

I was especially delighted to see the Mallard duck in the photo. I remembered that only about seven months previously, I had been searching for a new center location and was drawn to a small abandoned mall area. It had been closed down for years. When I first looked at it I was deterred by the old buildings, broken glass and boarded up windows in the mall. I didn't think I wanted to completely redo the location.

I knew, however, that I had been drawn there for some reason. After walking through the empty parking lot, I left and drove back to lunch at Wendy's, a local stop down town and ate my salad. While there, two Mallard ducks waddled up to the car! I couldn't believe my eyes!

I rolled down my window and threw out some salad, but they just looked at me. Then they flew off in the direction of the mall I had just visited. How strange! How strange to have Mallard ducks come to your window in the middle of a city!

I drove back to the old mall. There at the top of the marquis was a sign that said, Mallard Pond Plaza. I walked around the back of the buildings to find a swampy area filled with hundreds of Mallard ducks. I called the realtor.

Now, six months later, I was in a beautiful new Center and the whole mall was being transformed by new tenants! Mallards are a sacred bird! I had been invited!

It was also in that new Center, that I had first met Lily. She and Joan were the ones who had experienced the leaves forming into the leprechaun earlier in the day.

Lily had come one night to one of our free healing clinics in the newly relocated center. She had a condition in which both her arms had a rare bone disorder that caused her forearms to grow in a twisting, curling and painful way. She wore braces on both arms to try to stop the curvature of the forearms.

Spirit led me to tell her to remove her braces. At first she was hesitant, but removed them. Her arms fling upward across her chest, all twisted and torn. As I began to send the Loving Energy into her broken arms, she fell into a deep sleep. Time after time I pulled the energies down her arms. Each time, the arm would straighten. I watched as the miracle occurred for her that night, the twisting smoothed, the arms lengthened and the fingers became straightened.

That night, she left with both arms straightened. When she awoke, she saw a miracle. She never had to wear the braces again. Her hospital and therapists began referring their incurable patients to me.

Lily was so grateful, that she became a volunteer at the Center. Soon, she realized she had great psychic gifts and became a popular reader at the Center and really helped many people on their path. People loved her! I did too, but I couldn't shake the feelings I was having. Her personal growth was astounding, but she hadn't time to grow in the wisdoms of Spirit that only time could give. I watched warily, but supported her growth in all love, and taught in patience many truths.

One day I noticed that students were looking at me with very strange looks. At first I thought it was about the skulls and then soon realized something was amiss! I spoke to a close friend and asked why the looks.

"Katrina, do you know why people are staring at me?" I asked.

 She shook her head 'no', but I pressed. "I think you do. Please tell me."

Finally she gave in. "Lily and her friend are saying you are possessed."

"WHAT?" I was shocked! "Why in God's Name would they say that?"

"Well," she said hesitantly, "sometimes you look different."

I nodded. Indeed I did, and I knew it. I didn't think others would notice it though.

She more confident began again, "Your eyes are different. They even change colors, Susan; they think that's a sign of possession."

"You mean to tell me everyone is looking at the color of my eyes? To see if I'm possessed?"

I laughed.

"Yes," she answered shyly.

"OK. I'll take care of this, I said. Don't worry, I am not possessed."

She smiled. "I know." I knew exactly what I was going to do.

The next day I would handle the problem. In the morning I went to my 'real job' as a social worker for an n organization that works with children of special needs. I was the crisis worker there. Even though my Center was growing, my heart was with the children and their families, I couldn't leave them..

They really needed someone who cared and would help them. I was afraid that if I left my position, the next person would not be so compassionate to their special needs.

It was a reality I could not face. Also, I had discovered that I had special gifts myself. I could use the energy to help the children and calm the parents.

On this particular morning, I was scheduled to visit the home of a young sixteen month old child who had an inoperable brain tumor. I had also found that I could "Take On" the ailments of children into my energy body to assist their healing. In my heart, I had offered to do this for this child days earlier.

As I held the fragile little girl on my lap, her mother spoke. My healing energy just flowed, there's no stopping it sometimes, especially if someone is ill. Spirit turns it on.

Only, on this morning, things didn't go as planned. The child felt the energy, stiffened and turned around and slugged me in the face with her little balled up fist! I was stunned! I heard her say, "Don't do that!"

"Why?" I asked.

"I don't want to be healed. That's not what I came here for." She looked me square in the eye as she communicated her thoughts. Instantly, I knew she had come on mission. She had come to assist her family in the teachings of Spirit through her illness and her death. What an incredible child!

"Well, can I at least hold some of your pain just for today?" Understanding, I offered.

"OK" She replied. I felt the energy of her tumor enter my body. She relaxed. It was done.

I drove back to the Center for my lunch hour. The two responsible for spreading the rumors of my possession were both there together.

"Come on, I said, I'm taking you to lunch!"

What about the store?" Lily had asked.

"Don't worry, let's go, I've only got an hour!"I demanded.

We got into the car and drove the short distance to a small restaurant. After our orders were in, I spoke to the two women.

"I want t you to look at me. I want you to really look at me." They both gulped. A bit of sweat broke out on Lily. They both knew I knew what they had done, and they were in trouble.

"NOW LOOK!" I demanded.

"Oh, MY GOD!" She exclaimed! You've got a brain tumor!!!"

"No, I -I do not have a brain tumor, I have the ENERGY of a brain tumor. It is NOT the same."

"HOW?-HOW can you have a brain tumor and not have one?" She looked confused. I explained to both of them what had happened with the child.

"You see, when you see me looking different, it is because I am using the gift Spirit has given to me; when it is chosen by Spirit to assist or the time to help someone who is sick or in need of the special gifts I have." I paused to allow them time to think a moment.

"I take on the *aspect* of their illness for a specific time. It is transmuted while in my body back into light and dispelled. That is how I can do some of the things I do. It is a part of the gift I received in my coming here, and it is a part of the way I can heal people, just like you, Lily. I have always done this; however, I was not always aware that I was doing it."

"Now that I am doing so much work at the Center and people see me almost every day, you can all notice the differences in my appearance. I can't hide anymore." They both realized I knew they had started the rumors. Ashamed, they hung their heads and Lily began to cry.

"We didn't understand." They apologized.

"You have so much to learn! How after everything you could do this?" I shook my head.

"Well, take it as a learning experience and undo what you have done"

Susan Isabelle, Shambhala Master Teacher at the Shambhala Temple she founded in Manchester, New Hampshire USA.

The Temple was the largest training center on the Northeast USA for alternative teachings and energy initiations.

Weekly Light worker gathering, and free clinics were held for students and those needing hospice care/ and or training.

The Center served as an example of the principles taught by the Lemurian peoples to Susan of an Energy Co-operative.

In a cooperative, all share the work and the joys of service to humanity.

In 2003 Susan was directed to start a new work in California at sacred Mount Shasta, home of the ascended Lemurian peoples.
A new Center has begun!

They both nodded. By the time we got back to the Center, we had a new understanding. There'd be no more possession talk.

Chapter VII
The Mystery of the Skulls Unfolds
August 2000

The July trip had helped to dispel the rumors and the misconceptions of most of the group. I became very busy with the new Center and more and more people were finding us. It was humorous to have a medical center call us and say, "We have a client for you and we believe this person will need six treatments!" Humorous because it is Spirit that heals, not us. Miracles are not scheduled appointments, but Spirit continued to heal, even the referrals. Soon though, Reiki became so valuable a money saving resource for insurance companies that they began to pay for sessions.

My fascination with the tiny crystal skull grew as I began to understand the wonderful gift that had been bestowed upon me. I had received the skull in May and by August I had learned I could transmit the energies of the little skull to other crystals. Those holding a crystal that had been activated in this way could then experience the same vivid dreams about the Maya and Angels of Light. The energy of Sastun, at least in part, could be transmitted to others! We all began to learn of the gifts we had received.

Each weekend of classes became an exciting journey. I found in meditation, I was able to take students into the Chamber of The Crystal Skull at Altum Ha, Belize. This friendly crystal skull had become activated while we were in Belize. When we visited her on the astral, she welcomed our arrival. She gave messages to the students. Her pulsing message, "It is time, Awaken!" was clearly heard and felt by all.

One afternoon, after doing a class meditation in July, 2000, a student from another state reported she had been told by the Altum Ha Skull that another skull would be coming to Vermont. She had been told she needed to be there. None of us had any knowledge of another crystal skull coming into the Northeast, but I told her if she were to hear anything, to please contact me. In late August 2000, I received a phone call.

"*It's coming*! She explained! *It's coming*!"

"What *is*?" I asked.

"*The skull is coming to Vermont next month. I just got a flyer telling all about it! It is from Guatemala!*" She was very excited and so was I.

Soon, I was to understand that the skull was an artifact that had been in the care of a woman from Texas. She was coming to the Northeast to another center in Vermont. She provided viewing times with the skull!

The message the woman had received in class that day was very true! We would go!

We quickly called to Vermont to set up our viewing times and made arrangements to bring our own crystals for further activation.

I sent off an email to our Shambhala group.

> *Hello everyone! This is a notice about something that has come up! I have just found out that in September, that another crystal skull, a very large skull, from Guatemala is going to be in Vermont.*
>
> *I feel this is very important, but I don't really know why right now. As many of you know, I have been giving activations from El Aleator, the crystal skull from Belize and they've been pretty powerful!*
>
> *I'd like a number of you to come with me and those of you who have skulls, if you want, to let us take them to Vermont and expose them to the energy of both skulls at the same time! I'm curious to find out what's going to happen!*
>
> *And, as a reminder of what happened last May, here's a review....*
>
> *On May 20th, 2000 at the site of Cahal Pech just outside of San Ignacio in Belize, Central America, the crystal skull now know as El Aleator was activated in sacred ceremony under the rays of the Cosmos. That date was the same date set within the very structure of the Temple Chitzen ITZA in nearby Mexico, the time clock of the Maya. In its watchful waiting for centuries of our time, the Temple was designed as a signal to the world that the GATEWAY of the Pleiades was to open on this very day; it was a timepiece.*
>
> *The Maya also looked forward to the return of Quetzalcoatl, a Christ-Like being, who was to appear at that time. This moment started the countdown to 2012. There were to be 12 years to the end of this world as we know it, and now is the time to make preparations for the next world to come. I didn't know that at the time,*

but was later to read a book on Maya Cosmo-genesis, describing the day and the date.

I know what really happened that day......

The Gateway did open, the tiny Sastun skull, El Aleator and I received the activation and we have a lot of work to do!

The Pleiades, or 7 Sisters of the Heavens were flooding the Earth with knowledge; the Sophia of higher consciousness!

With new understanding from the Pleiades, the Earth will transform.

El Aleator is an activator of the thirteen skulls, a time keeper and now is the time for the activation of at least one!

Sign up soon or get your skulls to me if you want this!

Love All Ways, Susan Isabelle

Now I would wait to see who would join me in Vermont. Spirit always leads. I wait.

What's This All About?

That night, I had the first dream.

I found myself in a large room that was all white, glowing light. Looking around there was nothing in the room, any way out or windows. There was nothing in the interior room, other than a table. It sat in the center of the room. As I looked closer, I saw it was set with ten bottles placed on top of the table in a certain arrangement.

Then I saw above the table hung a large globe of radiant lights. There were twenty lights, all differing colors, glowing in beauty and intensity. I heard an instruction;

"Fill the bottles with ALL the Colors, but only one color in each bottle."

I thought about it until I awoke the next morning. I couldn't do it. How can you put twenty colors into ten bottles and not use each bottle twice? That dream bothered me all day.

I had put it out of my mind until my eyes closed in sleep that night. Again, I found myself in the same room, with the same situation, and again heard to fill the bottles.

This time I tried. I went over to the table and filled one of the bottles with the glowing light. It seemed to slide right out of the big globe with my thought. Well, at least I know I can get the light out of the globe, I considered as I awoke the next morning. I felt satisfied and decided to put it out of my mind.

Falling into bed from a long day's work, again I was in the room. The bottle with the light stood on the table as it had the night before and glowed with color. So I filled another bottle. This went on for ten nights. On the eleventh night I stood in the room with ten filled, glowing bottles.

"You must use ALL the colors", a voice from no where spoke.

"How can I?" I asked frustrated now. If I try to put the other colors in, I'll be using two colors for each bottle. You said not to do that!" Then I awoke.

The next night I tried emptying a bottle, then tried putting another color in. I couldn't. The glowing filled bottles would not empty. I was stuck. I was confused and getting angry at a lack of sleep! I was getting very tired of this. Then I remembered the message from Adama.

"It must be with the assistance of All," he had said.

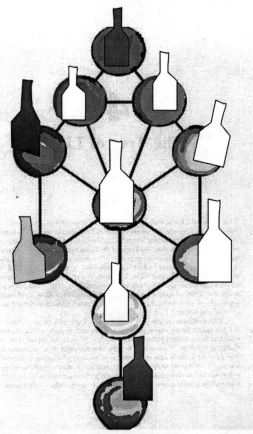

In the vision, I saw ten bottles placed on a table in a very certain way.
I was told to fill the bottles. Each bottle was to be filled with only one color and to use ALL the colors, but there were twenty colors.   A Mystery!

I wrote an email out to the Shambhala group once again. This time I explained what I had been going through, but did not mention the arrangement of the bottles or the colors.

Within a few days, several students had either come into the Center to speak to me, or wrote back. All had suggestions, but unfortunately, I had tried them all.

I announced to the Shambhala group that I would be purchasing crystal skulls to take with me and activate to the larger skull from Guatemala. Several persons called and we made the arrangements. As I spoke to each person I reminded them of the vision I had seen and asked their interpretation;

> I saw a vessel (ball) that had 20 colors within it and a white table with ten bottles, or receptors on it. They were clear. It was also made known to me that I was to put the 20 colors into the 10 bottles. I tried all sorts of ways to put 20 colors into 10 bottles without duplicating the color in the bottle, or putting more than one color in a bottle. It was a mystery.

Only I knew how the bottles were arranged on the table and did not share that. The bottles were arranged on the ten sefirot, spheres of the Kabbalah.

I tried several times to get the group to validate my vision, to confirm it to me, but that did not happen. The closest was someone who spoke of a tree formation. I saw the Tree of Life-the Mystical Jewish Kabalistic formation made by the bottles on the table. I had no other information regarding the vision. It was profound. Something was being communicated to me, but I couldn't understand.

I knew I wanted to activate my own crystal skulls in Vermont with the larger skull. I offered the opportunity as directed to those requesting activation. I bought 7 skulls to activate for those who requested them in time.

I was to go with three others to view the skull on Friday, 22nd of September 2000. As I was making my way out my front door, I was halted abruptly by Obed's voice (my Guide)

The BOOKSHELF!" He shouted at me. What did I need with another book? I'll be too busy to read, I thought.

I went to the shelf and was guided to an old book I had bought in 1988-or something. I had never read it, but kept, as at that time I did not do energy work!

The book was old and fell apart as I opened it. Out fell a page onto the floor. When I picked it up, it was the Kabbalah, the Tree of Life! Only this time it was different. There were COLORS associated with the round circles that made up the tree. 10 of them! Ten colored circles!
**Instantly I knew that these were the colors of the bottles to be filled-all ten of them!
At least ten bottles would be filled with a color.**

I now had ten skulls, 7 from my students and 3 from my own collection. 10 Kabbalah colored circles and 10 skulls! Was the larger skull from Texas the colored ball that would fill them?

"*Yes*!" was Obed's reply. At the very last moment, I was being given the instructions! The ten skulls were to be the containers! I had found the colored ball of Light! Now ten little skulls would be filled from the larger skull. This was fantastic!

I was running late. I was going to pick up the other three persons riding up to Vermont with me. I stopped at "Copy Max", a copy and office supply store on the way. I would make a poster size enlargement of the colored Kabbalah. I thought that I could place a crystal skull on each of the 10 colored circles. I bought colored markers to fill in the circles with the corresponding color.

When I was with the two powerful Central American Skulls, I would activate the Pillar of Light and "FILL" each of the skulls (bottles) with the energy they produced. I had ten skulls! Ten Sefirot of the Tree! I was excited!

The attendant making the poster made a duplicate poster as a trial run and gave the extra poster to me at check out. He didn't even charge me. In my haste to pick up the girls, I didn't even stop to consider that now I had two, full- sized posters. But, now my vision was complete, or so I thought!

We made it to the Vermont Center just in time to hear the keeper of the large skull speak. We each had an incredible first meeting with the skull on that Friday night. The Light and vibration that came from it was amazing. The skull was so large! The keeper spoke to us and told her story. It has been an adventure of a lifetime for her. A very beautiful soul exists in her little form.

When we arrived back at our hotel, we pulled out the poster of the Kabbalah and colored each of the round circles, using the colors as directed in the book. Then we decided to find the spot we each wanted to place one of our skulls, choosing our own colored spot in preparation for the next day. We took out our skulls. I had ten. The students brought even more. We took a count.

To our amazement, we now had 18 skulls and my Sastun. My El Aleator Sastun from Belize had an amazing quality- it liked to change color. I had never been able to figure out how or why it chooses certain colors, but it did. (It acts like a mood ring and changes color for different days or people.)

Now we would have to color in the other poster too! We colored in the other poster's ten circles. As we placed the skulls we discovered between us we had 20 skulls when I counted my Sastun, El Aleator and the Guatemalan skull. If we laid the two posters on the floor the larger skull could be on one poster and the El Aleator on the other, but that wasn't quite right. The larger Guatemalan skull wouldn't be able to fill the other poster from that position.

As we played around with the positioning of the skulls and posters on the floor, it finally came to us to overlap the two posters. If we put the Guatemalan skull in the KINGDOM-PURPLE space on both of the posters where they met, they would overlap. That would take up two spaces. I could put El Aleator on top of the large skull in that space. We would then have 18 crystal skulls to place on the 18 open and seen, spaces. If we placed my mood color Sastun on top, on the two overlapping Kingdom spaces, it would all work out! 20 Colors, twenty skulls, 10 spaces made into 20. This would fulfill my vision exactly! 20 into 10! Twenty colors into ten bottles or containers unduplicated! We then marked each space with each person's name. We prepared slips of paper to secure the skulls and the owner's names and location on the Kabbalah- we were ready!

After the flurry of activity was over, I sat back with the others and just looked at what we had created together.

We now had 20 colors, laid out in the 2 posters-10 Kabbalah circle configuration, making 20! The vision was now complete. Now all we had to do was activate the Pillar!

The next morning, we set out to meet again. We would all be together for an hour and a half with the Guatemalan skull and its keeper, as well as the owner of the center. They joined us at the beginning of our ceremony.

We were now 6. Six, is the number of feminine energy. Together we brought down the Pillar of Light and secured the energy. We toned the long tones to bring in the connection to the Divine, then the Knowledge tone and Peace tones. By then we were pulsing!

Now I understood why I was called to be the Keeper of the Multicolored Sastun. It actually had been directed to me for that very day. Spirit had arranged it all.

The Pillar of Divine energy was pulsing upon on the Guatemalan skull, through the Colored El Aleator's many colors. I know that twenty difference frequencies were pulsing into the crystal skulls. There it was expanding and activating the frequencies of the colors. My little Sastun, El Aleator sat atop the larger skull. El was beaming happily away, shifting, changing colors and sending the energy frequencies into the larger magnifying skull.

By the radiating of its powerful energy, it multiplied the force of the energy and color frequencies. Each skull, placed upon its corresponding color, was now being filled with a specific RAY of energy! I felt in my being that this had not happened since the last time the two skulls had been together! Who knows, that may have been over twelve thousand years!

I took my Master Crystal, that's a crystal I use that has a special ability so I call it a Master, and directed the pulsing energy and color, into the corresponding skull. The little skulls sat upon different colored circles of the Kabala. We sent the colors to little skulls on the posters according to the color given to us by the two skulls. We each did this several times. When we were done: each of the little skulls was pulsing a DIFFERENT frequency that could easily be discerned with our hand. Some of the little skulls actually changed color!

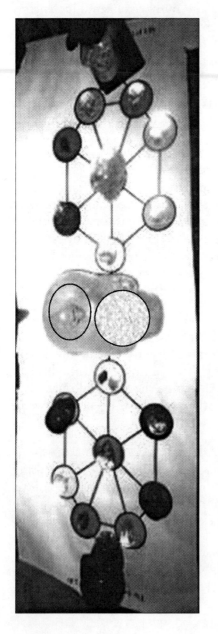

El Aleator activator from Belize, atop Skull from Guatemala

The activation of all the skulls.

Center : El Aleator on top of the skull from Guatemala, Kingdom position

*Large, center skull from Guatemala is part of a private collection and face is not shown

I had the Skull's Keeper come over to experience this-it was amazing! I didn't have the opportunity to explain to her what had happened in detail as she had many customers waiting for her, but she commented as she walked into the room, "He *(the skull) is VERY happy!*" She was beaming.

As I held the larger skull between my hands,   I kept hearing a chant,
" Kith-saroc(d)-ma-sha".

Over and over again I heard the chant. "Lucy, can you hear it?" I asked

"I hear something but I can't understand it," Lucy replied.

I keep hearing it say, **"Kith-saroc(d) -ma-sha"**. I'm going to write it down, just as I hear it," I said. "I haven't a clue as to what it means, but I am going to find out!"

 As soon as I returned home I began to search out the meaning of the mantra. Looking in several books, I found the meaning,

KITH means "Friend" that's how it is pronounced

SAROD means a musical instrument, one that has many strings

MA-meaning 'mother'

SHA-is the prefix for peace, as the Hebrew "shalom."

So, the meaning is

"Friend *—toning the Mother of Peace*".

I exclaimed,

"The skulls are feminine! The skulls are used to tone, or bring in, the Mother of Peace!"

105

I was so excited and called the three students that had gone to Vermont with me. Lucy was the first. Her Catholic background gave her a special appreciation of the knowledge.

"Oh, Susan, it's such a beautiful mantra and call to the Mother! I knew this was so special!"

"Yes, Lucy, you are a friend who is calling/toning the Mother of Peace with your crystal! The skulls will now tone Her Energy out to all the Earth!"

All those who accompanied me to Vermont were so blessed!

"Adama, they did it! I silently sent out to him. You said we'd all have to do our part. They came with me and we did it!!!" I could feel his smile all around me. What an amazing discovery! Now I would have to study the Kabbalah and get more understanding. Now I knew,

The Crystal Skulls are a part of the return of the Goddess energies!

" Kith-saroc(d)-ma-sha".

How the Earth so desperately need the Feminine energies! So many wars, so much destruction!

Now my new search began. I was disappointed at first to discover the Kabbalah books seemed to have a completely different meaning, and many different spellings! The books spoke of paths and seemed to be very difficult to understand.

I hope not to offend anyone, but something was not right and much too complicated. I understood the ten circles on the Kabbalah to represent, Strength, Wisdom,

Understanding, Severity, Mercy, Beauty, Splendor, Victory, Foundation and Shekhina or God Presence.

Weren't those all feminine qualities except for severity? Looking deeper, I found that severity actually meant dominion, control, discernment.

Spirit had used the skulls to bring in a feminine energy and it had been on the Kabbalah. It MUST be feminine, I resolved. So from that viewpoint, I began to formulate an understanding.

Malkuth was called the place of Shekhina. Shekhina was a feminine energy as I understood it.

The She, Ki Na? 'She', is feminine even in English, Ki means energy….hummmm….I thought.

Just above the globes representing Splendor and Victory was a globe called Tiferet, or Beauty. In some books it was called the place of the Universal Womb. If Tipareth was the center of the Kabala and was called the womb, wouldn't that be the logical place for Shekhina and not Malkuth? Jewish followers used to light a candle on Friday nights to honor the Bride of God, the Shekhina. Wouldn't that indicate a Mother? A Wife? Many books stated Malkuth was the place of starting on the Kabbalah, but that didn't seem to fit.

There would be much to learn, I decided. In my own understanding, Kuan Yin represented mercy and compassion. That place for mercy on the Kabala was just below the circles of wisdom and understanding. To follow the paths from Malkuth upwards would put mercy then wisdom. Then the final place was at Kether, or strength.

Athena was a warrior Goddess representing feminine Strength, who sprung from the mind of God, called

Zeus. I understood Sophia to be all Wisdom and Understanding.

In Christianity, Mother Mary birthed Splendor and Victory into the world through her Son, Jesus. He was called the Foundation and the Gate. The place of foundation was just before Malkuth, the Presence of God. Foundation was a gateway, a narrow gate to enter, ONE Way as the Christians believe.

So if Tiferet was really the Womb and Jesus the Gate, maybe the Kabbalah was being viewed upside down? Maybe Malkuth was really the end? Maybe it was God Presence? Maybe the Shekhina was the Mother Goddess?

Well, who am I to say something like that! I thought. Jewish mystics have been studying this a lot longer than I could even imagine! It seemed as each book gave a different pathway. The skulls remained a mystery and in all my attempts to understand, only a few things were understood.

I just knew; the Kabala was feminine! Each of those skulls was infused with a new energy that had been activated by the two Maya skulls. If each one was placed on the Kabbalah globe representing a feminine aspect, then each held a new energy for the earth! The skulls held a special energy that could, and would, tone in the MOTHER!! A new day was upon us!

My next email to the group read,

> *We have brought into the earth plane 20 RAYS into 20 vessels. Each of these skulls now holds a frequency of feminine energy, a new RAY for the earth that is a new frequency. They are metallic and opalescent colors. Each of the skulls was placed upon a circle of the Kabbalah, which held a color*

but also a LAW. The New Law, which is to renew the earth. I will explain to each of you as to your color and law that is contained within the skulls.

You who are owners of these skulls are now Keepers of the Frequencies. I honor you and your willingness to serve humanity.

What a gift! From you, the new Rays will spread across the globe. You will be given instructions as to how to activate crystals belonging to others with your skulls. There is a formula and a way to determine who is to get what. I will share that with you! I am convinced the skulls are feminine, or designed to hold this energy! I know there are many of you who will disagree with this, but that is my understanding and I'll hold to it.

They are directly connected to the Kabbalah feminine nine energies, even if they 'present' with a masculine demeanor. That's "OK" and it will work just fine. Even as humans, we all carry both masculine and feminine energies!

Namaste'

"Adama? Adama? Where are you?" I'd call each night before sleep. He'd been very silent. I felt something was up! I hadn't heard from Obed either. My dreams were also silent. I wanted confirmations of the discoveries that were being made, but the usual flurry of activity was only apparent at the Shambhala Center.

Each time I'd go into the Center, there'd be a line of people waiting to speak to me. I value my privacy and am really a shy person, so this took some getting used to. Days went by. I was busy activating skulls and holding skull classes. It seemed everyone wanted a skull! I felt this was a good thing as the more skulls out there in the world that could hold the energy of the new frequency, was just a day closer to a reality I wanted for the Earth!

I remembered the vision Adama had shown me of the New Earth to come while I was in Belize. I had seen that a new energy source would power the Earth's needs, as people lived in small communities in total harmony with all of nature. People were happy and lived in a light form that also allowed a physical reality, and travel was almost instantaneous!

Yes, I could imagine a world filled with mercy and compassion, inner strength, wisdom and understanding, beauty and Splendor! Yes! If the skulls were assisting this, then bring them on!

John Lennon's song and vision as he wrote *Imagine*, filled my being. I found myself singing a lot! Imagine all the people living life in perfect peace.....

Chapter VIII
He's Torching the Earth!

I received a call on October 7th, 2000. A student and friend invited me to go to her home to join in a ceremony. She described it as an earth healing ceremony, to be performed by an Indian at her country home that evening. I decided at the last moment to go and arranged to pick up two other students.

As we entered her spacious barn, we found what we thought was going to be a Native American Indian ceremony, was in fact Indian, but from India. An Indian priest was present with his attendants. My friend introduced me to her friend, the priest, who was garbed in his flowing robes.

About thirty people were in the semi darkened room. Piles of fragrant sweet, roses were placed on an altar and heaps of grapes lay beside them. In the center of the barn was a cement foundation which held a fire pit, yet unlit, that rose up from the cement floor. It was made of bricks piled up one atop another to make a pit.

I immediately felt this was somewhat unusual. Piled next to it was a bundle of wood and kindling. Around that were four placemats for seating. As I usually sit in the east, I again choose a place directly behind the east position and set my mat down there.

After a while, people began to find places to seat themselves. My friend had been invited to sit at the position in the west on the raised platform with the priest.

The priest came and sat down on the platform pillows just in front of me in the eastern position. He too liked to sit in the east.

He turned and asked, "Would you like to move so that you can see better?"

I told him, "No, I am fine, thank you."

He turned his back to me and began to speak. He stated, *"I have been called here to do a healing ceremony for the earth. My peoples have been doing this ceremony, the Hindu peoples; this has been done for centuries."*

He paused and looked around the room filled with Northerners from a culture that had little knowledge of his culture.

He seemed to hesitate, but then went on,
"In the ceremony, I am going to call on the fire deity; the fire deity to bring up a cleansing, consuming fire to purify the earth."

He stooped to pick up a small pot beside his cushion, and then continued.

"I am going to put the fire deity into this little pot, then make the fire in the fire pit with the energy from the fire deity."

He stood up and stated with resolve and motioning his hands over the fire pit,

"I am going to take the Earth and plunge it into the fire provided by the fire deity to purify all the Earth and the elements of the Earth!

Then, nearly at a shout he announced,

"I will immerse the earth in the flames to purify it."

My heart began to pound…the pit of my stomach told me it was time to run out of there!….

Another priest began walking around the room, passing out roses and grapes to each person seated on the ground around the four priests in the center. When I was handed a rose, I took it and the grapes. My hands were shaking. He went on,

> *"You will take the rose you are being given and the grapes and put them onto the platter at the proper time to be thrown into the fire to represent the purification of the elements of the earth."*

Beside him he had his little fire pot containing a fire to which he intended to call in the fire deity, and then use it to prepare his fire in the pit. My mind was racing……

Think, Susan! Think! What's happening? I scolded myself. Time was at the crucible, right now! I considered what was actually happening at this moment:

1. He had before him a fire pit in which he was going to call a demon and then descend the earth and all its elements into a furious fire.

2. He was then going to offer up to the spirit the four elements of the earth and throw them also into the fire.

He said this was for the healing of the earth, but every fiber of my being was horrified. How could anyone call this purification when this was total destruction? This was to burn it all to ashes!

I began to understand.…..*The pit clearly represented the PIT and the fire is the prophesied fire of Armageddon that will destroy the fourth world.* All of heaven is offering us the freedom from this curse, and here before me was a man who was about to invite the fires.

I was sitting directly behind the priest. His fire pot was next to him in front of me on his left.

On his right side was a platter of the elements of the earth, ready to be thrown into the fire.

Not a good situation.!!!! It couldn't get much worse!

Every fiber of my being wanted to jump up and run right out of there. I held my rose and began to cry. The rose, such a symbol of love!

Was LOVE to Die this night? God forbid!!!!

As he began the ceremony, he called in the god, the spirit of the fire. He called in the demons.

All around me darkness descended. A deep, deep blackness filled the room. I had a difficult time remaining in my clear state and had to fight to stay off its energies. I could hardly focus my mind in its attempt to control me.

I looked around the room at the people who were there. They had glassy eyes and stared straight ahead.

I thought, *My friends! Oh, My God! What had I brought them into?* I felt the pulling on my spirit and the attempt to control me increase. I fought the darkness invading my mind. I began to chant a chant to call in the Armies of Heaven to help me,

"Kodosh, Kodosh Adoni Tsebayoth-
>	*Holy, Holy, Holy is the Lord God of Hosts,"*
>		*"Kodosh, Kodosh Adoni Tsebayoth-*
>	*Holy, Holy, Holy is the Lord God of Hosts,"*
>		*"Kodosh, Kodosh Adoni Tsebayoth-*
>			*meaning*
>	*Holy, Holy, Holy is the Lord God of Hosts,"*

Over and over again I chanted until the entity's power was removed from me and a protection was given by Archangel Michael. My prayer had been heard!

When the Angel appeared, there was immediately established a wall around me and my two friends. They sat beside me, one on either side. I could see the dark lift from their being. They were freed from the dark veil that covered everyone else's mind. I breathed a sigh of relief, but not for long.

Now the priest was at a fevered pitch! Wildly he called in forces to manifest the Earth. It began to appear over the fire pit in a physical form. I couldn't move from my protected space. As the earth was being manifested, I could see the horror rise in my friend to my left. He now understood what was happening. We looked at one another. I nodded, *yes, do what you must,* I sent out to him on my thoughts. He began to hold the earth in a protective shield within his hands.

He was praying over the Earth. His guides were all around him too, assisting and holding his energy in the onslaught of this powerful entity. Suddenly, I could see him convulse. He was being kicked in his back by something! He was in pain and I could not help him, I had to fight this powerful entity! He held on. He held the Earth and would not let go of it.

I continued rocking in place all the while chanting,

"Kodosh, Kodosh Adoni Tsebayoth-"

"Susan, call on the Mother!" I heard a voice in the darkness call to me. I was directed by that voice to call in the feminine energies to protect; to call in the feminine aspect of God.

"You cannot lend your energy to this, or all is lost! You are the Melchizedek!"

The Voice pleaded with me. Now, more than in all of my life, I knew we needed all the compassion, mercy and love of God for the children and the planet! Only the Mother could protect her children now. The fierceness of Mother would fight for her child. I had clearly understood from my recent studies of the Kabala that God is both male and female in aspect and composition. All Aspects dwells within the One.

We needed all the compassionate action of the Christ Light who is action, force and energy to come forward *now*!

Tears flowing down my face, *I called HER!*

"OH, Mother save your children!
The Children will die, the Earth will perish,
Mother, COME NOW!"

As soon as I cried out I was amazed to see before me the etheric forms of Kuan Yin, Mother Mary, Athena, Sofia, Ix Chel and The Shekhina come around the perimeter of the room! Not one, but All Her forms appeared in the darkness. They hung as glowing lamps.

GAIA was under assault in the center in the form of Mother Earth, ready to be consumed by the fires! I felt someone behind me. I knew it was Christ. Christ was beside me on my left, shielding me. They positioned themselves in this order: Mother Mary stood about three feet above the floor in her Blue gown, Her head was down and her hands were held in prayer. She was about twenty feet away from me in the far right corner.

Kuan Yin, a beautiful tiny figure gowned in a flowing iridescent white robe, was in about the midpoint of the room at my right directly behind the North positioned priest.

IxChel, the Rainbow and herbal Goddess of the Central America's stood behind the west priest, behind my friend who was mesmerized in the ceremony.

Sophia, Wisdom, gowned in the deepest shimmering violet, stood to the far left behind the people on the South.

Shekhina, a glowing essence in the form of a Dove, hovered above the room and watched from above. I saw them all clearly and knew exactly who they were.

Christ was now on the left behind me, I felt His Presence as He watched and supported my strength.

Athena was present and in her form of a spider, right next to my male friend. She began to make a web right beside him. He too saw and watched in amazement as the spider rapidly spun a web that extended in diameter of two feet or more.

Something began to happen.

First, Kuan Yin glided from her spot on the right wall area to the left of the priest, still floating above the ground; she went right over the fire pit.

She now stood in front of the priest who was ranting his prayers. She was unmoved by his ranting and seemed not to even notice him. Her focus was on the fire pot. The priest was now at the point of his ceremony where he had already called upon the fire deity to embody the flames of the fire pot.

It definitely had entered the fire pot, and it was blazing furiously.

She moved once again, gliding past the priest. I watched as Kuan Yin

Gracefully poured her nectar out of the bottle that she held in her left hand. She poured it into the demon fire pot. She looked up at me and smiled a shy smile, then glided back into her position across the room.

The nectar glided like sweet honey, down on the fire pot. I watched it all as if in slow motion. As it did so, the nectar covered the pot.

The flame simply went out. Poof! It was gone. No more fire! No smoke arose-it simply dropped and went out. No emotion, I just observed .The fire deity was vanquished, but the priest had not seen what we had seen.

Moments past that seemed as years. My attention was drawn once again to the spider. Athena was spinning her web furiously as she worked in the corner. The web was forming before our eyes!

He reached over in the midst of his chanting prayers to the deity to take up what he thought would be a flaming fire pot.

"What?" he exclaimed," The fire has gone out!"
The fire has gone out!"

He jumped up from his seat. Now very disturbed, he began with the others to attempt to make another fire in the little pot. It wouldn't do it. Finally someone went into the house to obtain another fire from the fireplace inside, to restart the pot.

After a while, they got another fire in the pot, but clearly the deity was not in this fire!

Its power was vanquished by Kuan Yin.

The priest's assistants relit the fire with coals from the fireplace in the main house, then took the false fire and put it into the center of the big fire pit.

The flames ignited the bon fire. The flames went straight up. The priest and his assistants were relieved. They started another round of prayers.

All the while this was going on, the people still looked like zombies and moved robotically, without expression. Their eyes stared dumbfounded into the fire and their bodies swayed with the force of the breath of the priest as he ranted.

I during this time, I sat, rocking, crying and praying while holding the rose that had been given to me. A beautiful rose, it represented *Love*, love of the Earth and humanity. It is the symbol of Mary and Kuan Yin.

A Voice spoke to me, saying,
"Susan, pray into the rose!
Pray for the healing of children, the
Earth, the creatures of the Earth,
mothers, fathers and humanity."

Many, many prayers went into this rose with pleas from Mary, Kuan Yin, Sophia, and Athena going into the rose. All the love of God in the aspect of feminine energies was being chanted into the rose.

"Oh, Dear God," I cried,
Please forgive them!
Please intervene for us all!
Father, I pray for humanity;
Please, save the Earth and
Let not love die this night."
"Oh, Mother, Father,
I pray for my children, for all children.
They do not know you as this, but I pray for them.
You said if there be but five righteous to Father Abraham,

You would not allow destruction.
Father, There are many more now upon the Earth that
honor you.
Mother, you who bore, nurtured and fed your children
Upon the earth,
Come now on behalf
of your children
To plead for them and
to save them this night...."

I rocked and cried into the rose, so many prayers.
Do not let these people, who are bewitched and delusional
by the darkness, do this...."
I prayed
A wonderful sweet scent began to rise from the rose.

As I chanted, my tears flowed, Mother's Tears. I am a
mother, my children would die.

I cried as the Mother of All would cry for her children.

Now the ceremony was at a fierce pitch; the fire in the pit
was flaming high.

I prayed, chanting all the more as now the priest began to
call forth the elements to be thrown into the fire.

I had hanging around my neck, the Sastun from Belize.
It was hidden beneath my cloak which I had wrapped
around me. I heard from behind me, soft, gentle, male
words speaking.

"Susan, take the Sastun and direct it at the back of the
priest, toward the fire pit"
"Just hold the Sastun, do nothing."

•

I know that voice! Jesus was with me! I took my free hand and slipped it under my cloak and held it up toward the back of the priest.

Something was happening, but my eyes were closed as I rocked and prayed into the rose cradled in my other hand. Jesus would do this, I knew. He too loved the Earth and gave His life for it!

With that, the Goddesses began to move. I felt them.

I opened my eyes. What are they doing? All the forms as a soft mist, floated over toward my male friend who was still mesmerized by the rapid spinning of the spider. Thankfully, the kicking of my friend's back had finally stopped. He gave me a nod that he was OK when he felt my focus on him.

I wondered as I saw them taking the web from the spider, the Athena, who represented strength and warrior energy.

The small web, about two feet across, began to expand in their hands. They spread the web, stretching it and elevating it above the fire, now raging in the center pit.

Each participant that was seated around the fire glared into the fire like stoned zombies. They were now throwing articles, bundles of dried pieces of wood into the flames to make the flames go even go higher. They had no idea what they were doing. They were under the influence of demonic forces. The flames shot up about six feet into the air.

Athena's web was now securely placed above the flames, and then I watched as the Aspects of the Goddesses stood back. The scene before me was unbelievable! The Earth was held suspended above a net that spread clear across the room. Six glowing forms were positioned about the room, and a crazy man was dancing around a wild, demonic fire!

Then, there was silence in the room for a few moments.

"Susan, the Earth will have to go through the net..."

I heard someone speak to me from across the room. My heart leapt in me. The thought that the Earth would have to go even near that fire was horrible. I shook and sweat began to pour out from my face, mixing with my tears.

Then, I heard Shekhina, the Beautiful Dove watching above it all, as She spoke,

> *"Do not fear,*
> *Although it must go through the net,*
> *it shall not be to destruction.*
>
> *The Earth will have to go through the net,*
> *But the fires of destruction will be extinguished.*
>
> *Do not fear: The earth will pass through unharmed."*

The priest motioned to his attendants. They began to pass a plate in front of each person in the room. The glassy eyed people began to place their roes and grapes on the plate as it was passed around.

He asked that each one place their rose and grape upon the platter, as they represented the elements of the earth.

They were to be thrown into the fire along with the earth. He called it 'purification', but no, this was intended to destroy. The darkness bore down harder upon the room.

The sweet grape! The grapes, the Fruit of the Vine that represented the Spirit of God! The Fruit of the Spirit! Love, Joy, Peace, Gentleness, Truth, Patience, Wisdom! Were the Fruits of Spirit intended to also die this night?

"My God, How can they be doing this?" I cried!

The death of Beauty, the death of Spirit, the death of all upon the Earth! How could anyone do this?

He then asked each participant to place their hands over the plate and to 'bless the elements' on the plate, then add an element of their own.

"No wonder they wanted me here tonight, I thought. *If I had blessed this ceremony, this torching of the Earth as the Feminine Melchizedek, the forces of darkness would have controlled this.*

"Please Dear Spirit, Help Me!"

When the plate neared me, I heard Kuan Yin say,

"Susan, you will take one petal for each of the Goddesses
and place it on top of the platter.
Keep the rose and the grapes,
I will take care of the rest.
Do not, as you already know,
bless the plate as the others have done."

I did as instructed and placed the petals on the plate. As soon as I did, I was filled with joy! I knew!

I could hardly contain myself, now completely freed from the influence of the forces, I was ecstatic!

I was also told at this point, that this ceremony, even though celebrated throughout the earth by this culture, would never hold the destructive element again.

The net had been formed. The plate was given to my friend on my right, the last person in the room. He did not put anything on the platter.

My, and Mother's, rose petals lay on top of all the roses , grapes and elements the others had put on the platter.

The priest held the plate high and chanted his prayers over the plate.

As he tipped the platter upside down and dropped the elements into the fire, I watched my six little petals float down before the whole platter.
As soon as those petals touched the fire, it died, the fire was completely extinguished!

Completely- dead- stopped- cold.

A dead smoke filled the whole room. Its grey, dirty mist began to float over the dead looking participants. For all intents and purposes, this ceremony was over. I heard Kuan Yin say to me,

"Leave now!" and I did.

I ran out leaving all my possessions behind and ran up the hill in toward the car in joyous laughter and saying,

"Did you see that? It just went out.
They put it out!
Incredible!
Mother put out the fire!!!

My friends and I were ecstatic in joy! We fell to the ground away from the others in the woods. Gashing for breath,

125

laughing with uncontainable joy, we shared our stories! We had all seen Goddesses! Mother Mary had put out the flames of destruction! My friends were amazed as we spoke of the work of the Goddess and of the guides. James had seen Athena spinning the web beside him and was telling us about how he'd never seen a spider like that or one that could spin so fast!

"And Susan," he asked, *"What were you doing under your cloak?*
I saw blue flames coming out of your chest and at the priest.

What was that?"

"Wow!" You saw that?" I was astonished. "I really don't know. I was told to do that, I held up the crystal skull beneath my cloak and directed the skull at the priest. Jesus told me to do that. I heard Him speak to me, but I was so busy with the prayers I never saw what happened."

"Well, I saw blue flames coming out from you at the priest! I'll never forget it!" He said.

I was left wondering what had happened! I am not afraid of very much in my life, but I want to honestly tell you, that this was the most frightening event of my life!

Today, 2006, I still have the rose. It is a fresh and beautiful as the day it left its stem. It will never die, it is in my heart.

Author's note....

I was later to learn that this young priest had never performed the ceremony before.

The element of purification had been turned somehow into the actual performance of destruction of the Earth and all of its Beauty and Spirit.

I hold no ill towards him or those of his religious beliefs. He simply was trying to perform something he hadn't been prepared for properly, and the dark forces took advantage of him as well as everyone else in that room.

The occasion was such that it was necessary to have been played out just as exactly as it had. That very night we were on the verge of war in the mid east.

The next morning Barak of Israel changed his mind and extended the deadline to the Palestinians indefinitely.

War, and a fiery destruction had been averted by the hand of Mother Mary and her aspects of the Divine Compassion!

I found this in my unread emails after the event of the 7th of October 2000.

I sent it to the Shambhalatemple group. Quoted,

"The Vatican has recently release the contents of the famous third secret of FATIMA:

A VISION THAT SHOWED THE VIRGIN MARY HALTING AN ANGEL FROM TORCHING THE WORLD"

A statue of the FATIMA Virgin has just arrived in Rome for an important ceremony in which :
THE WORLD AND THE MILLENNIUM WILL BE ENTRUSTED TO JESUS
[Note: Many believe the true start of the millennium is 1st January 2001]

A word to my students from Susan Isabelle:
It is my hope that in all love, you will offer up a
"Thank You! to Kuan Yin,
(embodiment of Compassion),
Ix Chel, (The Feminine Healer),
Mother Mary (Mother of All Love to mankind),
Sophia (embodiment of Feminine wisdom)
Athena, (of feminine strength),
the Christ and the
Shekhina Glory for their work on Monday night.

Together, the embodiments of the feminine aspects of the
Godhead have
HALTED THE TORCHING OF THE WORLD-
I saw it happen.

Susan Isabelle

Authors note: Fatima is the name of a place in Europe where three children were visited by Mother Mary prior to the world wars. Mother Mary came to them several times and at the last visit caused the sun to move and the Earth to be dried up from rain. 70,0000 people saw this happen.

One of the children, Lucia, was given three prophesies to hold for the Earth. The first two gave warnings to the people of Earth to avoid the coming war and to pray. The child had been instructed to hold that final one secret. According to this email, the third and final message had been released.

Chapter IX

The Miracle of October 13th 2000

On this day we went to the Lemurian Telos site in NH behind Mt. Washington once again. It had been previously scheduled but now we were going to celebrate the wonderful occurrences that happened on Monday at the fire ceremony.

Kuan Yin, Mary, Athena, Sophia, Ix Chel and The Shekhina worked a miracle to save the Earth from the fire. That fact was confirmed to us by the email from Michael in London. The Vatican had released the 3rd secret of Fatima.

The secret was that Mother Mary had been seen in a vision halting an angel from torching the World! The 13th of October was also the anniversary of that date back in

1917 in France at Fatima, when the 70,000 or so people saw the sun dance in the sky!

Now I understood; I wanted to celebrate, and we also had the energy of the full moon. I was excited! We too had seen the near destruction of the earth and the Goddess in Her aspects had come forward to halt the destruction!
I was told that the earth would have to go through "the net". I understood this to mean that the earth would come really close to the consuming fires, but a "net" or filter, would be established to temper the effects of that fire. We would not be destroyed!

We also had gone up the mountain to do the Earth Healer's attunements. Eleven of us had gathered together to go to the site, traveling from Manchester, New Hampshire on that Friday for the Attunements.

Kathy and Nancy from South Boston had come. They had previously experienced their own miracles of working the energy and power of time as part of their gifts of Shambhala.

Polish speaking Yola was with us, as well as the woman from the Cape who we had visited there and trained a few month earlier.

Mala was there too. She is a Korean woman who works with the angels for her homeland.

Jan, a long time friend and crystal skull keeper joined us along with young Tim and Lorraine from Connecticut. He had been at the October 7th night of the fires.

Jai, a Vietnamese woman rode in the front seat with me. Soon, we were approaching the Mount Washington area.

"What is that smell? Someone asked.

"Roses! Its roses! Did someone put on cologne?"

The car was filled with the lovely scent of roses that grew stronger as we approached the site. As we neared the site's location, we could smell the roses completely permeating the car! It was beautiful!

As we parked the cars, people were jumping out. Everyone was excited-the roses! We soon discovered that it was not just our car that was filled with roses, but that everyone had the scent of roses in their separate cars! All around us the air was thick with the beautiful scent of roses.

"What could this mean?" We all wondered aloud to one another. How beautiful to be greeted this way. After all, it was a rose petal that fell to extinguish the flames of destruction!

Once we had entered the path, we stopped by the large rock that guards the entrance to the falls. It was at this spot that we heard the "OMNI PAU" warning before. This time, we did not need a warning. We stopped to ask permission from the Ancients Ones who guarded this sacred ground. Then we went forward, up the path.

As we neared the site by the waterfalls, several faces on the rocks could be seen, and the faint sound of Indian drumming was heard.

We spent some time to look at the rocks and the images upon them, honoring those who were revealing themselves to us. Many were taking pictures of the mossy rock images.

Excitement was all around. One picture we took was a moss image of an Indian woman. Another image on the rocks ahead of us glared out; it was an image of a man standing by what appeared to be a spaceship. Another image was of an Indian on the back of a buffalo.

Everyone was awed by the size of the stone guardian, who is about a couple hundred feet tall, who they named the real "Old Man of the Mountains," the gorge flowing with water and the water spirit, who was clearly seen.

As we climbed the trail we soon came to the Lemurian site by the falls. This place is called the lower falls. It is where the Lemurians had directed us. Lemurians seemed to be guiding our way today along with the Maya and the precious skull I now had in my pocket.

As soon as we sat down, the group began to exclaim," *The drums*!"

All around us now the beat of Indian drums was heard. We all heard it resounding, coming from the ethereal realms; it beat a soft, but definite beat.

The ancients were joining us! They were waiting for us. This was going to be a real celebration! Even the heavens were joining us! They had come to provide our group with the sacred music of ceremony.

We had temperatures in the 70's, a beautiful blue October sky, and the colorful foliage was red, yellow and vibrant orange! The combination of the sights, the beautiful scent, which permeated the air and beautiful scenery around us, and now the music, was amazing. It seemed we had it all!

We spent time to clear a space for our belongings in the overgrown brush of the past summer months. It had been several months since I had been here. Now I was returning home to familiar ground with much to tell Adama at the Lemurian portal just in front of me now.

I lay flowers at the entranceway. Others had done the same. They brought crystals and small gifts for the Lemurian peoples who we knew were once again enjoying their old lands. Once everyone had had time to complete their ceremonies, we gathered together. We sat down by the stream. It was so beautiful.

The waters gently flowing, the earth safe once again and our joy was lighting up the whole area.

I began to tell the little assembly of highly dedicated and Masters in their own right, of the night of the halting of the fires by the Goddess and her representations, or aspects of the Goddess, in personages. I told the group the entire story about the Monday night fire ceremony and the incredible intervention of the Goddess. In doing so, I mentioned the name of 'Athena'.

At that moment we all heard,
"EEEE-AAAA-YAH!"

The 'Xena Call' came resounding through the gorge- from her!

She, in this aspect, is a bit wild! We heard it one time only; but it was enough to let us all know she was present.

"That was Athena!" Someone shouted! Everyone laughed. She was with us and she had made herself known!!

After the laughter and amazement calmed down, I began to continue my story. My heart was so filled with the awesome events of the past week. All their faces were turned upwards toward me as I spoke to them.

I felt such love for each one. These were good, strong Masters of the energies and they were rejoicing with me. We were gathered together to rejoice in the love of God and Goddess for the earth.

The efforts of prayer warriors and activists such as these seated on the ground in front of me had made a difference. Earth had turned a corner so to speak, in its evolution. Now we were ready to face the challenges ahead, knowing full well we would not be facing destruction.

I looked up toward the giant stony faced guardian watching over the ancient, sacred ground. The water was falling gently down the babbling brook and dancing on the rocky stairway to the ocean far away.

Something flashed behind them and my eyes were drawn upwards to the sky to see the most spectacular sight I have ever witnessed!

The sun was just cresting the top of the Stone Guardian. My attention was drawn to look at it.
I couldn't believe my eyes.
The sun was pulsing rainbows! It was pulsing rainbow colors down in great circles of energy. It looked like a funnel with color whirling toward me in wider and wider circles.

I stared and could not speak. I was looking into the sun through rainbows! I saw the sun move sideways, not up, but sideways to the right across the gorge as I faced it.

It then changed to a large golden disk, a flat gold, which was easy to look at. It began to move toward us!

The SUN was coming toward me!

Moments passed. I was stunned. I couldn't speak. I was fascinated by the beautiful sight all happening behind my students. Finally, I found my voice and shouted to everyone,

"Look UP! Look up at the Sun!"
I pointed behind them and they, seeing the incredible sight, jumped to their feet!

Everyone gasped as they saw the same miracle I was seeing. The golden sun was vibrating a million rainbow circles that began to radiate colors down upon us.

As the rays were coming toward us, the woman from the Cape fell to the ground and pulled her coat up over her head and sobbed.

The others stood with outstretched arms and absorbed the energy. One poor woman prayed and sobbed uncontrollably. All the while, we were being attuned to the radiant energies.

"I've never looked into the sun before!" someone shouted, *"but I can see into it-there are symbols!"*

"Oh! The colors! They are so beautiful!!!" Someone shouted.

"I see it spiraling and moving!" someone else shouted.

"It looks like the Yin Yang symbols moving in the sun!" said another,

"Look, Susan! When we speak! Look! There's incense coming out of our mouths!" Janice hugged me as she was wiping tears from her eyes and laughing at the same time.

Yes, as we spoke to one another, puffs of white came from our mouths, scented with the fragrance of roses. Incredibly, with each word we spoke, a cloud of incense

135

floated out from us, bathing each other in a beautiful aura of roses.

"Susan, Susan! Look!" Malama was pointing to the waterfall next to her. She had been seated on a large flat rock by the falls, but now was jumping up and down on the rock with excitement. The falls were flowing backwards, back up toward the sun! Laughing and crying we played as children in the glory of it all!

"Oh, How Beautiful! I exclaimed! Then, I heard a voice speak to me, *"Tell them to close their eyes, Susan."*

"Everyone, I was just told to tell you, please close your eyes for a few moments, they want it so." I said apologetically. The group quieted down and silently closed their eyes. I then saw something that will be with me forever. There are no words to express the glory of that moment.

I saw the form of a golden, veiled woman,
I believe in my heart,
To be Mother Mary, Divine Mother.
She was standing on top of the sun,
And in the sun.

Her form was as the sun in golden glory!
I saw that around her head, suspended up high, in gold
rays of glory
That there were many, many multicolored globes.
Balls of fire energy were making up Her crown.

I watched in amazement as they were moving
and now descending down upon us, one at a time!
Each globe would descend until it was over us then burst.

136

As soon as that was done, another came and did the same.
Each fiery globe transformed into a radiant ray of color to
bathe us!
I was given the gift of seeing this with my own eyes and I
Also felt the colors enter my body through my eyes.

When She had completed the process
She disappeared back into the Golden globe of the sun.
Then, it was over.
"OK!" You can now open your eyes!

Just as they were opening their eyes, another miracle was occurring. In the air were millions of confetti-like sparkles of energy! Just floating in the air they sparkled and shone like a million little butterflies of pure silver and gold!

The water in the stream beside us was still flowing backwards. The water was drawn upwards toward the sight before us. The Korean woman was standing on a large flat boulder beside the waterfall as she watched the sparkles descend around her. She was closest to the water watching in amazement as the water ran upstream toward the sun!

Time stood still for who knows how long. All of a sudden, the air was transformed . Suddenly, the air flashed silver, then gold! As I looked up again into the gorge, the sun had once again resumed its normal position.

We would never be the same from that day onward. We all knew it, and were solemn in the holiness and realization to each awakening soul. After quite some time, we came out of the attuning energies and back to the physical. We relaxed and shared together what we had seen.

We wrote down the symbols we had seen in the dirt at our feet but we'd never forget them. By now it was late afternoon. I asked Spirit if I should continue with the plans of the day and do the Earth Healer attunements.

After what had happened, I was content to just rest in that wonderful glow of the miracle. Spirit said to do the attunement, so I did. I understood they still needed the symbols in their hands and the specific frequencies of those symbols. I asked the students and they too agreed.

The scent of roses permeated the air and the drums of the ancients drummed the entire time I did the attunement. Lady GAIA was present and powerful as she attuned each one and they received the symbols.

Our day was so incredible; but it did not end there-it was the beginning. After giving the attunements, I fell to the ground, passed out and entered the Tunnel. I died. I lifted up, and was taken out of my body. My physical body lay in a heap on the ground. My spirit soared toward heaven.

No one noticed because they were in their own glorious space in the energies too! I was taken up into the Light. There was no thought of return; I was in the Presence of God.

I stayed there for a long time as the students rocked in the Light of their own experiences. I was not aware of anything on the Earth, for I was no longer on Earth.

"Susan, Susan! Are you OK?" I heard my young friend say from somewhere far, far away. " My guides commanded I touch your feet. Are you OK?" He asked in concern, while pulling on my legs.

I felt myself being pulled back into my body, once again I was returned to earth. Groggy from my return, I said to him, "You have just done your first resurrection."

I know I had passed to the other side. I didn't have a conscious memory, but I knew I had passed over. He brought me back.

There is no death, just LOVE. Beautiful!
There are no words! Just Love for all of us.
I was in LOVE....

It was dark and very late when the group decided it was time to go back home. Everyone had changed. We had so much to share with one another and we knew that each had been gifted beyond anything Earth could offer that day.

A Korean, Polish, and a Vietnamese woman were on this trip and one of them now sat beside me in the front seat of the car. I have a little Buddha that I have pasted on the dash of the car that had always faced me as I was driving. It was for good luck and safety as I drove, often times like today-half out of my body!

I said to the little Buddha as I started up the car, "You drive! I'm too tired!"

As I put the car in gear, Jai started shouting, "LOOK! Look the BUDDHA, The Buddha!"

The small little Buddha was turning around to look out the front windshield! We watched him turn until he was looking out the windshield. I swear He drove us home that night! We all spent the ride home giving accounts of what had happened and what we had seen that day!

On the way back home, our group was filled with unspeakable joy. The next day continued the miracle.

The Second Day Of The Telos Miracle

I sat with Will that evening. I told him of all the events. My words and excitement must have made it appear to him as if I had lost my mind. I could see that to him, I was a wife, not a prophet or a visionary. Now, I was just a wife who obviously had lost her mind. Even though he'd been healed of prostate cancer, this was hard for him to accept. Even though he had felt the presence of the Angel on the bed next to him the night that the angel had come to us, it was still hard for him. The Angel removed the tumor, he was healed. The fact that this was his wife, well, it was too much!

"Susan, I don't know what all this means," he said as he went off to play his video games. He'd be deep in thought, disturbing thought, as he had to face some things about me.

I headed into the bedroom by myself, and fell into a deep sleep. Before long, I saw myself meeting with the Masters on the other side. Melchizedek, grand and magnificent stood with Adama, the High Priest, and he began to speak.

"Al'Lat, we have come to show you what has happened." Excited, they escorted me into a room filled with the Light of the Sun, but with no perceivable source.

I was back in the Mountain again! I was back at Mount Shasta! I recognized this place! Adama had first brought me here!

"This is a headquarters for the work on the earth plane," Adama said as he peered into my eyes, communicating his thoughts.

"We cannot lead you, Al'Lat. It must all be in the Spirit of the human being, that part of you that is on this dimension must go forth to fulfill the prophesy. It must be of human desire and will."

I nodded. "That is why you have been so silent these last few months." I replied.

"Yes, once you had discovered the truth of the skulls and followed through with the Divine Plan, we could then supply a few assists! Obed, for instance, just happened to let the book fall off the shelf, giving you a clue to the Kabala."

I laughed! "And the assistant at copy max just happened to feel generous that day and gave me a second copy?"

"Well, we can bring joy, can't we?" Adama smiled broadly.

"A little here and a little there," I quipped.

"Al'Lat, we wear the Star of David within our foreheads because we are of the Melchizedek Lineage, we are of the Priests of the God Most High, Creator of the All."

He paused as I took in the information.

"In our society, that which you call the Lemurians from our ancient and long ago times, we honor the Aspect of the Goddess. Our whole society is based upon Her glory, the Shekhina Glory!"

"I am beginning to understand that, Adama. As I have been studying the scriptures and the Kabala I've understood more and more."

"Yes, Al'Lat, it is through the Presence of the Shekhina in a society that true Peace and Prosperity may flourish." He smiled and was filled with joy.

"In the Earth's system, there is so very little Peace. We find it extremely difficult to bear the emotional pain of humanity for we feel so deeply, that pain." He reflected on his own words.

"Many upon the earth desire our return, pray for our return, but do not understand that for us to descend into the third dimensional space in that humanity exists, we would essentially be committing a suicide." I felt his dismay at the thought.

"Yes, we visit the Mountain and headquarter here, but that is because of the elevation and the higher Spiritual energies here at Mount Shasta. We can bring you here, for you have overcome in your physical and mental bodies the attachments to the Earth though sacrifice and dedication."

"Not another test to my ego, Adama!" I laughed, "I know that I have been gifted with memory that most of humanity does not share, that of a distant world and a home land and people such as yourselves, Adama."

"And yet, Al'lat, that memory did not surface until you had met the initiating challenges...." cut in Melchizedek.

His powerful presence and words put an end to Adama's and my playful interchanges.

"Now, time is short and there is much to tell you that you must know. You have completed the entrance of the Goddess energies to the Earth plane." Then he was silent for a few moments. He was about to share something very important. I could feel it.

"What I now tell you is a great mystery revealed:
That which is in the heavens in a thought form, must first be manifested in a physical form. Such as taking an idea from the ethers and writing it down on a piece of paper;
It is a diagram of thought.
Vapor becomes solid. It is then manifest in physical form"

'The skulls were programmed by the Lord Above all Lords, the Ancient Son of the Divine Couple, the Christ-to accept and activate upon the completion of certain tasks of which you have completed." He looked at me to make sure I understood what he was saying." I nodded.

"First action was to secure the activator skull, El, as you call it.
 Secondly, it was then required you come to understand the mystery of the Kabala.
Afterward, fill the incoming energies into the small vessels of crystal to hold and secure the energy- as the writing on the paper.
As the example of vapor transformed into a solid formation explains." He paused.

"After the thought and incoming energy of the thought of Goddess presence was on the earth, IT COULD THEN BECOME TRANSMITTED INTO THE HUMAN'S CRYSTALINE MATRIXES THAT WERE PRESENT WITH YOU AT HER APPEARANCE." Melchizedek thoughtfully sighed in awe.

"To bring Her energy to the earth plane is a marvelous feat, then to secure it within earthen vessels in a manifest form! That action will ultimately one day overcome the darkness of this plane! This incoming of the Spirit of Truth and Beauty was promised to the Children long ago!" Adama added in a voice filled with ecstatic joy!

Melchizedek continued, "Those that stood with you, some were prepared, others were not, and will suffer in mind and in spirit until they can come to terms with the gifts that lay within themselves."

Adama nodded in agreement then stated to me, "Fear not, for they too shall go though a net, a net to filter out the dross still within the soul memory, but they shall one day overcome."

He paused as I considered his words. Somehow, I knew this meant hard times for some.

"A day will come when they too shall be called into their service and remembrance. With or without their knowledge, they hold within themselves the keys and the energies of ascension. " Melchizedek smiled at me.

I needed the encouragement as I saw so much disruption in their energy fields since the activations. Some weren't holding up too well. I had another question.

"Can you tell me what happened the night the priest tried to torch the Earth?" I asked.

"The Night of the Torching that was halted; you saw the fullness of the Goddess in Her former physical earthen vessels."

"Earthen Vessels?"

"Yes, those that have held her essence in their physical being."

"You mean like Kuan Yin was a real person?" I stated.

"Indeed she was and is. She is with us, as you know."

"Yes, Please! Explain to me more about the vessels."

"No one person can ever hold the fullness of the Goddess. It is impossible. It is as if one tried to hold all of God, the Father and Creator of All, within oneself in totality. All the Universes combined are not large enough to do that!"

"We each, in our human physical form hold a piece of the whole, not the whole. We are as a hologram of the whole, a reflection of the original. We are a part-of the body, each with differing gifts and functions. So too, the Goddess. She has so many aspects of power and of goodness that her form cannot be completely within one physical form. Only the Christ was able to hold the fullness."

"Why was that?"

"Because He is the Only Begotten Son of the Divine Couple, and holds the All within His very being. His essence *is* their essence! He is the direct and first action. He is the Light that was created as they sought to multiply their being. Once established, the Light of the First Born permeated all of creation and does so this very day. He is within all of creation."

"Oh, so that's why twenty vessels were required to hold the template of Her energy?"

"Exactly, Kuan Yin has predominately held Her aspects of Mercy and Compassion, as others have held other frequencies of Her greatness. This has not been on Earth before. Balance now shall one day manifest!"

"So on that night, she was actually present with us, but in several different personages?"

"Yes, that is the only way it could be done at that time. She had not fully come into the earth plane."

"WOW! It was amazing to see Kuan Yin, Mother Mary, Athena, Shekhina, IxChel and Sophia all in one room at the same time!!!"

"Yes, we too were awed at the power of the prayers. Al'lat, remember; you were also there."

"And Christ," I added humbly, He protected me and held my strength. OH! What was He doing with the skull?"

"Ah, yes, the powers that flow through the skull El Aleator are of the transmission of all the Goddess frequencies. It was through the Goddess that the blue rays were directed into the priest to dis-empower the demonic forces that held the human, in an act of compassion. Unknown to the priest that night, his own life had been spared."

"Well, that explains it!"

"Only, in part Al'lat. There is much more for you to understand and to do." Adama inserted his thoughts, softly.

"You mean I'm not finished yet?" I sought to peer into his eyes. It was the first time I ever saw him with his head down and avoiding my eyes.

He looked up smiling. "No, my Dear, you've only just begun! He laughed. Remember? Thirty-six sites?" I nodded toward him, smiling.

"Welcome to sunny California! I have news for you, Al'Lat! You'll be here within the week." Adama smiled as he spoke.

"I will?" I asked astonished at this revelation.

"Yes, you are to locate the keys,"

"What keys?"

"We will assist, but even we do not know where they all are to be found." He said ignoring my question.

"What do the keys go to? Do they open a door?"

"In a sense, yes, they will open the doorway to the incoming Goddess energies and the attuning process that shall manifest."

"Manifest? You mean its not even here yet?"

"Yes, that is why even we do not know where they all are. They must manifest as you travel, and you are to use your Spirit eyes to locate them. As the Feminine Melchizedek, you are responsible for bringing in this system to the Earth and her peoples."

"How many must I locate?"

"There are seven KEYS to the KINGDOM and they are now coming into the earth Plane in thought form, ready to manifest. We are confident you shall locate them. One has already been given to you along with the first symbol. Soon, you shall them all."

"Where are they coming from?"

"They are assisted into manifest form throughout the universe in developing systems, such as earth, through the Pleiades Star System, the Seven Sisters."

Then I understood and exclaimed, "Seven keys from the Seven Sisters? That's why El Aleator had to be activated on the May 20th 2000 date! That was the opening of the Pleidian Gateway!"

"Yes, Al'lat, now you are remembering!"

"Yes, the symbols, I remember the symbols that I received in the sun from the Goddess! One of them is a Key! The first Key! I do have it!"

"Yes, that Key will assist you in the location of the others for it is the first opening key that pulls in the rest through the realms to the earth plane. The Attuning Symbol, the first one we, will show you the use of that later. For now, we must explain to help you remember."

"Do you remember Bible story of the first rainbow?" Melchizedek spoke.

"Oh, yes, the one that Noah saw when the ark finally landed on Mount Ararat." I replied.

"Yes. Now do you remember why it was given?"

"Yes, it was a sign of the covenant between God and Mankind that the earth would not be totally destroyed by water again. Right?" I asked, not too sure of the whole story.

"That is true. But remember that it was also an act of Divine Compassion?"

"Yes! A Goddess Aspect! Compassion is a sign of the Goddess! *The Rainbow*?-OF course! The Sun pulsed rainbows down over us! There were twenty colors! Rainbow colors-*plus*!!

"Correct. Now consider the word Rainbow for a moment. Break it down. Ra_In_Bow. The Bow is the rainbow."

"RA is known as the sun god, but this energy is the FEMININE ASPECT of the SUN "RA"."

"Sha-Ra, or Light GODDESS, has manifested through the sun to us in the rainbow.
Remember, this is a covenant with mankind. It is once again, a sign. It is a sign;
NOT TO DESTROY the Earth because of the
Aspects of GOD which are the DIVINE FEMININE;
Strength, Wisdom, Understanding, Compassion,
Mercy, Earth Dominion, Beauty, Splendor and Victory,
Are NOW present on the Earth!
The conditions for Her Manifest Form were met!
You have made the first discoveries of the mysteries of the Kabbalah, have found the ancient knowledge and have assembled the facets of the diamond!

In Grateful Thanks Al'lat, a great secret is revealed now to you;
God is in love with His Goddess!

Where Her image is, there is Blessing and prosperity for He pours out His love upon Her! Earth will now prosper and one day overcome her challenges!"
He continued, "You will begin to teach and to transmit Her likeness unto the peoples. They shall hold Her likeness in Her Aspects according to their own desires and willingness to promote the Presence on Earth. In time, the numbers and the presence shall grow."

"Now as for the first Key that has already been given to you, the 'Spectra_ Ki.' Consider the word 'Spectrum." Spectra comes from the word, spectrum. What is the spectrum? The answer is the fullness of the colors of the rainbow as seen by the human eye. But you know now that it is the codes of the Goddess in color! The Rainbow! But there is yet another secret held within the word itself.

'Expect Ra'. Expect Ra to come when you use the Key. Expect the coming of RA, but the Feminine Aspect. The ancients knew Ra was in the Sun and also the Feminine Codes! It is all in the Spectrum! The word itself has been a code in your own language. Latin held the essence of the word.

When it is used, you will bring the six Aspects to the people. This shall be a WHOLE NEW SYSTEM. You are to call the teachings of this transmission, RA-IN- BOW, or Rainbow Mastery."

His voice began to fade. They were leaving.

Then, suddenly, I was back in my body. I was back in Manchester, New Hampshire. My eyes opened. A day had already begun and I had a class to teach! I tried to move, but my body was stiff. I had been out of my body for hours and all my joints were solid. It took a few minutes to breathe myself back into a physical form that could speak and move. I tried to remember and commit to my memory all that they had said to me.

It was going to be quite a day! Even though eleven persons had witnessed the miracles the day before, only three of those there got up and came to class. I had to arrive for class; I was the teacher, so there were four of us. Hai, the polish woman and Malama, arrived for class. An interesting fact was that they should all be from other countries; America, Vietnam, Poland, and Korea.

I knew that during the night, I had been filled with information. As I began to speak to those who had come, I began to channel the information that had been down-loaded into me while I was in Mount Shasta with Adama and Melchizedek the previous night.

My students wrote as I channeled, brought into remembrance the information I had received, the entire day. I taught them the symbols from the other side, those I had received from Mother Mary in the Sun and channels from them on how to do a new attunement for the Goddess Energies. I taught them the NEW ATTUNEMENT SYMBOL called SPECTRA –Ki that holds the energy of the Goddesses and is the Master Feminine Attunement Symbol that attunes you to the feminine energies.

I had been instructed as to how to give a mass attunement method in all feminine energies given with a new symbol called the Triple Goddess. That was not shared, but I remembered it.

I now understood. Three persons were then attuned to the Ra-In-Bow System of Divine Feminine Energies; all three had been given the attuning energies by the sun.

They are the only other persons beside me that know the attuning symbols. In other words, there are four people on Earth that can give this system, at least in part, to the people.

This was to secure the energies on the earth plane immediately. For just as a thought when it comes, if it is not acted upon immediately, it becomes "lost." We forget. We could not lose this!

I went home from the class on Saturday elated and tired! They had certainly given a lot of information that night. Now, I would have to instruct the others who had been with me at the Miracle of the Sun as Spirit directed.

I remembered the words of Melchizedek about the others who were infused with the energies. I wondered how after seeing such a miracle the day before, that they could stay home.....Melchizedek said some were not ready, but would one day awaken.

I would wait.

Chapter X
California Here I Come!

When I arrived back home, I was met by my husband, Will, at the door. He looked awful.

"Susan. My son called. He is being shipped out to the Gulf War. I want to see him before he goes. Would you like to go to California with me so I can say "Good-Bye?"

"Oh, course, I will go with you. I am so sorry. Yes, let's get ready." Once again, Adama had given advance notice. He had told me I'd be in California.

We were on our way the next day to California. Before I left, I hurried to send out an email to the Shambhala Group to let them know what was starting to happen.

Dear Friends,

> To those that have been attuned to the Sun's energies: You have only received a securing of energy and much more information has been given and are invited to return at some point. I thank you for giving me the opportunity to learn how to manage the energy! Please, those of you who were there at the Sun's event: it will be important that you receive the whole system at some point. Hold on! You are needed! We will be having the class on the day of Jan 6th-the Feast of the Epiphany and the opening of the sealed ballots of the Electoral College from our stalled and confusing presidential election! This is an important time for the entire world. I have written a piece to introduce you to the Goddesses that were at the Fire ceremony!
>
> Susan
> The Goddesses;

Susan Isabelle

The Crowning Glory of God:
Compassion, Love, Mercy, Wisdom, Long suffering, Beauty, Splendor
Creation as Mother, Emotion.

These above are some of the world's previous energy manifestations of the feminine aspect of the Divine Source, or God, and Holy Spirit. The masculine manifestations: law, rules, judgment, discipline, punishment, severity, and linear thought, The Father. Just as the masculine energies have manifested in human form, so have the feminine.

As we have been sorely lacking in the feminine energies, we have forgotten those who have come in the past to anchor these energies on the earth.

We know these as the Goddesses and energies. We do not worship them, they are of the Whole; but to acknowledge their energy will help us to connect to their presence and power for they help us to integrate and understand the energy of Goddess.

They are the Light and are here to assist us in our walk. I would also like to show you a few applications of the Divine Feminine as we are entering the increasing power of their energies at this time.

To know them is to love them!

IxChel
Ix Chel is the Goddess of healing herbs and medicinal plants. She is known for her aspects of growing corn to feed the people and bringing waters in the spring to help the trees and plants. Plants and herbs are for the healing of your bodies, and for food to live. She nurtures through the Earth's bounty. Ix Chel manifested to us while we

154

were in Belize as the beautiful, loving, being of the night who shines her glory to show us the way in complete darkness as a moon Goddess of fertility. In May, the Maya make small blue crosses to honor her.

We acknowledged her and she blessed us by pouring out her essence! The darkness of an illness may be the darkest road we travel on earth, remember her healing love.

Mother Mary, Christianity

Wrap yourselves in her robe of blue and rest within her scent of beautiful roses. Mary brings her compassion to you, birth of Righteousness, true love to the world, and creative energies. Bring her your grief and tears, she has borne them all and will extend and comfort you in her loving healing.

Call on her energies and ask she carry your heart when it is too heavy for you. Mary manifested to me in the hospital when my baby died way back in 1970. In a beautiful vision to comfort me, I saw her with my child.

For many years I denied her coming to me because of my religious misconceptions at the time, but she came to me anyway. Call on her, she will come and mother you when times are such you are a child again in need of a mother's love.

Kuan Yin, Buddhist

Seen over the battlefields during World War II by many soldiers in the face of death, Kuan Yin carried her bottle of the Nectar of Compassion to the dying and wounded. Kuan Yin's image was captured on film by an Italian bomber pilot during a raid. She is seen in the photo riding in the clouds on the back of the dragon. She is in complete control. Over the masses she rides pouring out compassion on the earth.

Her energy can be used to put out the flames that seek to consume the Earth and the people of the Earth. She is the Goddess Aspect of Compassion, of Mercy and extends her stay here on this realm until ALL sentient beings come to enlightenment.

Call on Kuan Yin when the flames are about to consume you, she will calm the flaming tempest with her soothing Nectar.

Call on her when someone you love is unresponsive to the Light of Truth and pray for their enlightenment. She WILL come! I know! Kuan Yin stood for me, advocated for me in my desire to help the people of the earth. She stood beside me as I requested of the Ascended Master's Council my activations to the Melchizedek Priesthood.

Athena, Greek
The Warrior Goddess! Born of the mind of Zeus, She sprang forth as thought and Wisdom. She also has a powerful sword to cut through illusion.

Once, in a vision, she picked me up and held me in her hand. I stood facing her huge form and not knowing what to do, I formed a little ball of energy and blew it up to her as my little gift. She laughed hysterically!

Call on this wonderful being of power to help you fight your battles , but-she will not do it for you. Once gained as your friend and you connect with her energy of righteous war on the darkness besetting you, she will send the fur flying!

Sophia , Hebrew and Gnostic Teachings
Many of you have never even heard of her. Sophia is the Goddess Aspect of Wisdom. Sophia's energy is the softest

pale blue and will come with sprinkles of golden sparkles. Now do you remember?

In the Bible, she is praised and we are told to seek her above all else. Proverbs 3:13 (a Good number) *"Wisdom- she is more precious than rubies: and all things you can desire are not to be compared to her -length of days is in her right hand, and in her left riches and honor. Her ways are the ways of pleasantness and all her paths, peace. She is a tree of life to all them that lay hold of her. (Remember the Kabbalah?) The Lord, by wisdom, (Sophia) has founded the earth."*

She is an energy: THOUGHT. Can you understand this? When she comes, she will bring a way to find peace in your life through your thoughts as she connects with yours. Honor her and she will come. Acknowledge her presence and she will be beside you in all that you do.

GAIA , Energy of the Earth

I met GAIA the summer of 1999 when she came up through the bottoms of my feet, flew up my channel and out my hands to the waiting student of my Earth Healer class during their attunement to her energy. WOW! I had always known she was there, but not a "Personal Relationship" with the Goddess.

She IS! GAIA is the one essence that represents the manifest physical realm of Goddess. She is the one who is the nurturer, the one who cares for all her beings, tenderly, that are upon the face of the Goddess Earth -GAIA. MA comes from the word- Matter-, the "MA" essence of the MA-terial world! GAIA has a pure consciousness, a being that longs to be communicated with at this time. She has much to tell us and she is waiting for us to respond to her messages. We are deaf. We are about to get a good shaking from Mother. Pay attention!

157

The symbols she has given us are for the healing of the Earth. Use them. Once you connect with her the sky is bluer, the rainbows are sent and the fairy kingdom no longer fears you. They come to visit you and seek your help.

The final energy that I wish to explain to you is that of Shekhina.

The Shekhina Glory

The first recorded time the Shekhina was seen was over the Ark of the Covenant. This was at the time of the Hebrews in Israel. She was a visible sign over the ark of testimony. Whenever She appeared, She was seen as a cloud over the tent of the Holy of Holies. The Hebrews knew that when She was present, the people were comforted and accepted. Her energy is communication of righteousness and mercy.

She is also known as the Holy Spirit. She was seen over the Head of Christ as He arose from the waters of baptism in the river Jordan. Every Jew who saw that knew one thing-The Christ had been baptized by the Shekhina and SHE dwelt within Him from that point on. Yes, Christ had been indwelt by the Purest Feminine Aspect of God! As such, He was empowered to heal, teach and maintain His teaching ministry.

These are the gifts of the Holy Spirit to us. Christ was filled with the Holy Spirit.

She is the One who is God, Complete and Fully Integrated. She communicates to mankind, teaches and instructs us in the way of living, thinking, being in harmony with all of Creation. All the manifestations of God/Goddess is contained within Her.

As we are also manifestations of the Creator's energy in the universes; the Comforter and the Spirit of Truth overtakes one who has connected and desired to integrate Her. We then manifest this Light into the world. Pure Love. Call on Her energy as you seek to understand all things: Call to be given the gift of communication to the world higher knowledge of this Supreme totally balanced and pure Light.

This is done by allowing yourself to become the Divine Channel of Her energy in the world. Love. It is the highest honor and gift of to mankind. It is said of her that She is as the wind, going from one to another as the Divine so directs: So, ASK!

All of the feminine aspects of the Divine will come as we willingly prepare to integrate the feminine energies on the earth. It is, and always has been, their sweet loving desire to aid us and help all creatures of this planet.

They are the Manifestation of Total God Consciousness on Earth and throughout the universes. If we are truly to ascend, we must connect and integrate their energies.

Balance   must   be   restored.

The end of the fourth sun is death and destruction by fire to all. As the Hopi Indians and many cultures are telling us, we are being given a choice right now as to our future as a planet and a people of the universe.

When She was present the night of the fire ceremony, I was frightened by the proceedings but I knew we were going to make it!

Chapter XI

Your Key To Heaven October 2000

While were in California visiting Will's son, we decided to take advantage of the vacation time and do a little exploring around California. All the while I was searching and waiting for the manifestation of the Keys that Adama had told me were coming.

These I understood to be symbols that I would use to assist the integration of energy to students and the earth. I waited anxiously for them. I had received one Key already, the Spectra-Ki used in attunements. I kept drawing it on the little note pad I carried with me as we drove down to Long Beach in hopes the other symbols would soon appear.

I was excited about the beauty we had seen all along the coast from Camp Pendleton down to Long Beach, south of Los Angeles. How beautiful! Flowers grew wild over the sand dunes and lined the street.

Will and I checked into the Westin Hotel on Long Beach Friday night. He was always so kind and gentle. He wanted me to have the very best in life. The Westin Motel was magnificent and the view spectacular! This was a surprise!

We checked in and made our way up to the room, he handed me my room key card. It was blue with puffy white clouds on it. I turned the key over to read what it said. In big bold letters, were the words,
"Your KEY to Heaven!"

The Key to Heaven! I was more excited about the door *key* to the room, rather than the spectacular $400.00 dollar room for the night! I knew I was about to be given the next key to the RA-In-Bow system as they promised.

When I walked into our suite, the super king sized bed was pilled high with billowing white comforters and pillows. It looked like a cloud of pure white floating in the center of the room. A glass wall and balcony looked out over the Pacific Ocean below.

Dinner was served to us on the balcony under the glistening stars of the night sky. I truly loved this generous, thoughtful man.

When we awoke Saturday morning we had our breakfast delivered to us on the balcony overlooking the ocean. The sun warmed us and soft ocean breezes filled with the scent of the salted ocean, gently passed and whispered, "This is truly the Key to Heaven".

But where was my Key? I looked all around the room for something that would indicate the symbol, a sign. But there was nothing, I could find nothing of a symbol! We went out to explore the city and had a wonderful day on Saturday. I loved Los Angeles! The City of Angels!

Saturday at 3 AM, I awoke. I was still in our spectacular room. I had arisen from a deep sleep and sat down on the sofa that had been placed in front of the big sliding window looking out over the Pacific Ocean. Will was still fast asleep in the cloud bed snuggled deep into the white fluffy comforters.

We were on the 10th floor and were in room number 1030. I thought about that. I was in room number 1030, in numerology that broke down to number 13, a very powerful number, and not at all 'bad luck'.

The number thirteen was sacred to the Maya, I knew. The secret had to be in this room somewhere. Tomorrow I would be leaving. It must be found. I had been awakened and this was the hour! I was on another magical MYSTERY TOUR!!!! I looked around the place where I was sitting and noticed something I hadn't seen before.

I WAS SITTING ON A SOFA WITH LARGE GALAXY SPIRALS ALL OVER the upholstery. I looked at the placement of the spirals. YES! The spirals were in a formation. They formed a portion of the Spectra-Ki Symbol! I had been sitting on it!

I jumped up and began searching the rest of the sofa for other configurations. Nothing made any other shapes That I could see or be considered as symbols. Crawling down on hands and knees I even looked under the sofa and searched the floor. I couldn't find anything else. Puzzled, I stood up and looked around the room once again. Nothing! I checked out the placement of the sofa. It looked out the large sliding glass window, out over the ocean. Maybe something was out there?

I opened the slider and stepped out into the early morning air. I looked up into the sky. Perhaps the arrangement of the stars would form a symbol from this point? I wondered and searched the sky. Nothing. I looked at the ocean liners harbored out in the ocean, their lights arching in the darkness. No, this was not it either.

I felt an energy come up and stand beside me. I knew who this was! Excited now, I knew I would be getting a message.......I heard Obed's voice,

"LOOK DOWN!"

I stepped closer to the edge of the balcony and grasp the railing tightly. I do not like to stand on the edge of things that suspend me out over great heights. I leaned over the railing and looked straight down over the edge. Dizzily, I looked down ten stories beneath me.

To my amazement, when I looked down at the area directly beneath me in the darkness, I could see several lights in a formation. I counted them. There were seven lights and they appeared to form a symbol! They were in a specific formation! Seven lights were in a formation! That was it!

Shining up at me in the darkness of night they formed a perfect symbol! I could see their rays stretch out to one another in the shrubbery in which they were hidden during the day! The rays formed the entire symbol!

Obed spoke,
"This is the symbol to represents the 7 sisters of the Pleiades and their gifts to humanity."

The symbol could not be seen during the day because the lights were not on.

This was the second key! It would be used to bring great gifts to the people. Spirit is amazing! And how wonderful that it should manifest to the world in light!

Once again, the Spirit had shown me in the things of nature and natural surrounding. How often I have missed the obvious by being blinded by what I thought I ought to see.

At breakfast I was telling Will about the symbol. I drew it out on the napkin at the table so he could see it. I told him about the assignment that I had been given. It seemed that now was the appropriate time to let him know the *other* purpose for our coming to California.

I explained to him that first, his needs at that of his family were to be considered and I was to give all my attention to his grief, his family and needs.

I had not forgotten about my 'kitten!" Will listened as I explained. He was understanding and interested in the assignment. We walked over together to look at the light formation below our room.

Once again, I leaned out over the railing, but the symbol of the night before could not be seen in daylight as the lights were now hidden beneath the shrubs.

"Will, I can't see it." I said, disappointed. "It's daylight."

But, Will pointed and said with shaking voice excitedly,

"Susan, Look!' there's another one! IT can be seen! There are more!!!"

Looking closer, there were strange block formations directly in front of the place where each of the lights ought to have been. They too formed a very strange twisting symbol along the pathway beneath us!

I could even feel the energy lifting up from it ten floors below! Scanning with my hand, the warmth of the symbol implanted itself into my being!

I heard, "This Key will bring KNOWLEDGE!" I rocked in its energy that had been activated in the City of Angels!

Now I had the third Key!! I was so excited about the discoveries and the energies. We had to continue on, so we dressed for our trip and the day ahead. When I came out of the bathroom, Will looked at me with a puzzled expression.

"What's wrong?" I asked.

"Susan, look at your blouse." I looked down at it but couldn't see anything dramatic. It was just a soft colored multi-patterned paisley blouse. Will came over and directed me to stand in front of the mirror. As I did, a gasp and, "Oh, My God," fell from my lips in a whisper.

There on the blouse I had bought the day before, was the seven star formation exactly placed as on the ground ten floors beneath us! I was wearing it!

"Will, this is called a 'confirmation'. I had no idea about the symbol until today and bought the blouse for its soft blue colors. This is not a coincidence, but a work of Spirit to show I am indeed on the right track!"

(C)

The Shambhala Center Logo

Chapter XII
Mother Mary Comes To Me, Let It Be

My trip to California was over and I had now returned to New Hampshire to the Shambhala Center. I was delighted to have received the promised keys and now waited for more instructions. One day Elaine called me and came in for a session with me.

"Susan, I have been so sick. I can hardly move. They think I have lupus."

"Oh, Elaine, I am so sorry", I said to my former student. I hadn't seen her in a year. Just after her attunement she disappeared.

"What have you been doing since I last saw you?" I asked wondering what had happened to her to bring her into such an awful state! "You had a beautiful attunement as I recall!" Where did you go off to?"

"Yes, I am so sorry I left the training. I went to a school out west for training. Something happened there that I'd rather not talk about now." She looked down and with eyes that held shame. "I've come back. Can you help me?"

"Elaine, it is God that heals. I will do what I can do and ask for your healing. Much has happened over the last year and I am not the same person. I've grown too, but right now let's get you into the therapy room."

I lead her into the little room that held candles and a massage table. She was so weak her attendant and I had to lift her up on top of the table. After getting her into a comfortable position, I opened with prayers for her healing. As I held my hands out over her in prayer, I asked for her healing in mind, body and soul. I asked that what had happened to her be overcome by the powers of God/Goddess in forgiveness, mercy and compassion for her soul and physical body.

As I did so, the room began to fill with the scent of roses! I opened my eyes and looked down at Elaine. Tears were flowing down her cheeks onto the pillow beneath her head. I looked up and saw the etheric form of Mother Mary standing, or rather floating, across the table from me on which Elaine lay crying.

Mother Mary spoke to me,
"You must leave the room for ten minutes while I complete her healing."

I looked down at Elaine who was biting her lip to hold back the great sobs whelming up inside of her.

"Elaine, I stroked her hair to comfort her. Do you smell the roses?"

She nodded affirmative.

"Mother Mary is here and she has come to complete your healing. She has asked me to leave the room for ten minutes." Elaine let out a little whimper and then smiling, she glowed.

"Is that alright with you?" She nodded OK again.

I stroked away the tears now flowing down her cheek. I stepped back away from the table and opened the door into the sanctuary. I took a last look at Mother Mary as she began to enfold Elaine in her misty form. I shut the door.

Standing in the outer room were several people who had gathered outside the therapy room. They had smelled the roses and felt the energy coming right through the walls. They spoke not a word. We stood together outside the room without speaking. Wave after wave of the energy and roses permeated the entire room and bathed us too. This was a holy moment.

While I waited the ten minutes and was bathed in the roses, I also received a special healing. Many years ago, in 1971, I had given birth to my third child, a son. I was told two weeks before his birth that my child would not live. X-rays had shown my son's head had not developed and brain size was very small because of a raging fever I had early in my pregnancy.

I would have to wait for labor prior to delivery as that would ensure my safety. I was twenty three years old. For two weeks I prayed, rocking my unborn child and cried night and day. I told no one of what the doctor had told me. I couldn't speak the words. I did a lot of growing up those couple of weeks.

During that time, I realized that to birth and raise a child was one of the most precious things a mother could do, an honor and a privilege, not to be taken for granted. I promised to care for my children and seek a better life for all of us.

As a teenage mother in the 1960's, I hadn't honored that and my prayers were also for forgiveness. I had two other little boys at home at that time. I had become a model and was in retail in an exclusive boutique. Even after bearing two children, I held my figure and became even curvier. The care of children was difficult and my mother had taken on the responsibility of caring for my children while I worked. Now, I was learning what it really meant to be a mother through the possible loss of my child. Death, in my youthful exuberance, seemed as something that was so far away from me so as not to even consider it. Now it was at my door. I now knew that I valued and loved my children more than anything else.

And I still hoped for a miracle, maybe the doctor was wrong. I didn't hate or curse God. I knew that God was not responsible for what had happened to me, it was a part of life.

Finally, the day of my labor and delivery arrived. I was taken to the hospital by my then husband. Our life together had been terrible and I had resolved that if I got through this I would be a more involved and dedicated mother.

I awoke hours after the delivery in a private room. No one was in my room. I was groggy, but had only one thought! Reaching through the rails of my bed, I picked up the telephone and asked for the nursery.

"Is my child still alive?" I cried into the phone.

"Yes, Susan, but you know"…the nurse was about to tell me the child was dying.

"Yes, I know" I interrupted her, and then asked,

"Please, will you baptize him? His name is Mark."

"Why, yes," she was surprised. She left a moment then returned to the phone holding my son child. She baptized him while I was still on the telephone. I heard her. She was crying.

"Thank you," I said and hung up the telephone exhausted.

I lay back on the bed as tears streamed down my face and sobs from my soul poured out. This was the only gift I'd ever be able to give him along with the little white gown for his burial.

As I lay crying, I saw something like a mist in the far corner of my room. The mist grew brighter and brighter as I watched, unable to move after the delivery. The brightness parted to reveal beautiful scenery.

The hospital wall 'opened'. I was lying in my hospital bed while looking into to a deep green field filled with flowers and tall grasses flowing in the soft breezes under an incredible blue sky! I lay still astonished; my crying was stopped.

Then, something caught my attention in the grassy field. Was that a baby? I couldn't believe my eyes! A baby boy was lying on his back with chubby little arms and feet kicking in the air. Then I knew it! "This is *my* baby!" I yelled.

I struggled to sit up ready to run into the field! But just at that moment I saw him, I saw another great mystery. It froze me in time. I could not move. A woman robed in the bluest sky blue robes, appeared in the air above my son who still lay on the grass beneath her.

She was surrounded by hundreds of children, bouncing joyfully, gleefully laughing and playing with one another and jumping up and down around her. All of a sudden, they became quiet and watched the woman. I did too.

I watched in stunned silence as Mother Mary bent down, picked up my son, and snuggled him into her shoulder. She gently placed her shawl over his little naked body, looked up and smiled at me. Then, she returned to the

171

mist, and then, disappeared with my child, Mark, and all the other children that had come with her.

The room resumed its normal appearance just as a nurse came running in.

"Oh, you are awake!" She exclaimed. "They told me you had called the nursery! The doctor will be up to see you soon!"

"Please, help me to get ready." I said to her." I need to clean up." By the time the doctor had arrived, I was sitting up in bed, my hair combed and no more tears. As he came into the room, he looked at me; he saw that I was beaming with joy. He didn't understand.

"Susan, you know, don't you?" He quizzed me.

"Yes, I do." I answered softly, reverently. He hadn't seen what I had seen and would never understand that. I had seen my baby being personally escorted into heaven by the Queen of Heaven.

"Are you OK?" he asked concerned.

"Yes, I have two little boys at home that need their mother. I want to go home to them, they need me. When can I go home?" I asked.

This so shocked him that he ordered a psychiatrist to come in and evaluate me prior to my release. I didn't tell the doctor anything or else I'd likely still be in an institution! (Smiles)

Now, thirty years later, I was being healed by Mother Mary again. I had carried a guilt that had lingered into my present life. The miracles at the site had brought me face to face with a terrible thing I had done afterwards.

I carried that guilt, even to this very moment as I stood outside the therapy room door.

It caused me to remember something I had done that needed to be corrected. In my zeal to follow God and reform my life, I became a Fundamental Baptist, Born Again Christian in 1972 after the death of my child. I was baptized into the faith and sought to purge my life so as to be the best mother and wife possible. I entered into the strict teachings of the church.

In this church's belief, the presence and interaction of Mother Mary was not honored. I was taught that this was idolatry and not to honor her or pray to her. I put Mother Mary aside and even tried to convince others that she was an "idol." Somehow, in my zeal and ignorance, I convinced myself that the visitation from Mary to me was false.

I made myself believe that had happened at the birth of my son must have been the result of the drugs I had taken and my grief. After all, the pastors and elders couldn't be wrong, could they? All these loving parishioners couldn't be wrong could they? And I didn't want to lose my new friends.…...

Now, on this day, it was the THIRD time in my life that I SAW Mother Mary. She was very real! I would never deny her again! She was involved in the life of the Children of God in a great and glorious way! I asked for her forgiveness for my foolishness and ignorance all those years. I stood outside with the others bathed in her roses and in her forgiveness! I received forgiveness. I honor her for who she really is, The Mother of the Christ and who tenderly loves us all, and I love her too!

After ten minutes I ran into the room. Elaine was sitting up glowing and smiling. "I am healed," Elaine announced as I entered the room!

"So am I!" We hugged!

Chapter XIII
The Masters Speak

After Elaine's healing, she returned to the Center to restart her training. While she had been away, she had entered into a system that used a lesser light energy that allowed the casting of spells upon others. As Children of Light, we are not allowed to manipulate others for any reason. To do so causes us to contract with lesser energies that are all too willing to do our bidding and we become entrapped.

This always has a back lash that causes one to experience the consequences of karma multiplied three times over. When we do so, it comes back upon us in illness and other ways. She was happy to have been spared a terrible fate.

Channeling of OBED at Halloween

Just before Halloween, I began to get messages. One night while I was composing an email to go to our Shambhala Email Group, Obed began to speak to me. Below is the exact transcript of his message to us as it was in automatic writing, a form of channeling. It still applies today;

Subj: **Halo's Eve/A Real Terror**
Date: 10/30/00
Time   9:52:18 PM Eastern Standard
From: shambhalagold@xxx.com
Reply-to: ShambahalaGold@xxxcom
To: ShambhalaGold@xxxxx.com

Dear Ones:

I am writing to you tonight as this is the Eve:
At this time, the Veils are thinned: Some of you
passed through last night for the first time, but
there is more, much more. This email will be hard
for some, its meanings are very "deep." It is not for
all to understand, although I sincerely desire it so
for each and every one in the purest of Love, for the
highest good of all Mankind.

Both the energies of Light and those of Dark exist,
very close now- within our reach; our choices are
about to be made manifest. Some of you have had
dreams-you know this is so, you know that of which
I speak.

The times of the past were times of the imbalances
of masculine energies which have plagued us and
our world; of severe judgment, of punishment and
destruction of the 'disobedient'!

Tonight in meditation, and in the energies of
tomorrow day and night,
choose those qualities you will reach for, the
veils you shall pass through;

You will pass now...For NOW is the time of decision.

"What do you mean?" You ask me.
To that, I reply;
What shall you possess?
Think about this...write it down...

What is your heart's desire?
Really,...what do you desire?

For that is what you will take on; you will become.

What shall you discard?
Yes, you will decide to rid yourself of something..
Will it be your conscience?.....
Think about it......

Will you rid the "old rags" of your life?...
what is no longer desired?

Consider.....
"Will you rid what is no longer needed as aspects of negative ego selves? Meditate on those things; and yes, consign the rags to the consuming fire; but the fire of the Holy Spirit, the Shekhina- SHE-KI-Nah, (She, feminine- KI, Universal Energy) which cleans and purifies with gentle, loving compassion."

Consider.....
"The Shekhina, the Feminine Gentle Goddess of Mercy, Beauty and Peace, of Forgiveness, of Victory and the Power of all consuming LOVE! BUT- now, if you choose, you may live within the Holy of Holy's as the Child of God/Goddess-All That IS, totally freed from constraints, all judgments, all condemnation- past, present or future."

"Do you have any idea as to what that means for you and the earth's ascension?"

"You may, if you so desire, walk through that veil into the waiting arms of your true God-Self as reflection of Compassionate Mother. Here there is no fear and you are dearly loved."

"Feel the embrace of Mother as she
gathers you in Her arms!"

177

"Tempered by her sweetness, the Father welcomes you and sees you, welcomes you, only in Divine Love for THAT IS ALL THAT IS SEEN!"

"Know this! Accept this into your being; for it, and it alone will give you Peace, Shanti, Love.
The Christ Light energies, the Creative Energies and Consciousness of Pure Love were born onto the Earth, were given to us through the Mother, to establish its Presence   on   the   Earth."
"FOR   YOUR   OWN   SAKE-CLAIM   IT!"

"Then you will be free of judgments-which are only judgments you press upon yourselves, for there is now no more condemnation, you walk in the Light."

Free yourselves and live.

"This is the EVE, the Halo's Eve. It is time to decide your path. When you are free, you will not judge yourselves or another, all is seen in love and love alone. All events which come into your lives are transformed as you develop new eyes to clearly see and minds which are in perfect alignment with the Universe and the Earth."

You will know all things and remain in peacefulness;
though all the earth be shaken, you will know the
Alpha and the Omega, and will walk above.

"We honor-or fear, those these next few nights that have
died.
Some were our ancestors, others, the walking dead. They
are real.
Many of you have felt the bone chilling winds as they
come by you.

They, many, are still with us and have never ascended to the Light.

They haunt the hollows of the nether worlds and seek to touch us, to give our Light to them to free them-just a bit- the feminine energies to preserve the earth, to nurture and love it as our own body, for it is."

"Preserve the Earth for future generations!"
Is their cry to us!
Hear them, seek their truths and become ONE."

End of direct channel

I continued to write as the energy flowed and wrote a personal message to the people.

"As I am called to free those who have passed on to the purgatory they themselves have formed, my heart is broken for them. The Compassionate Action of the Mother frees them and allows them knowledge of ascension to the Light through her tender teaching.

Will we not also do the same for ourselves while we are yet alive? Let us learn to love ourselves and embrace the Mother which is always with us-for she dwells within and awaits our requests.

Those requests are granted in first forgiving ourselves, then others, showing in our lives mercy, beauty, wisdom, healing, victory, knowledge and teaching abilities, and a strong foundation on the earth through GAIA.

Lastly, for those who choose life and wisdom, let's also open our 'selves' to the releasing, enlightening, of those who seek us now for our Light.

Susan Isabelle

Give freely, for it is freely given to you. Give to the living and the dead-and the walking dead, they are all around."

OBED and Susan Isabelle

This strange channel later turned out to be so prophetic as several in the coming months turned aside from the Light to walk a new path and teachings. Obed tried to tell the people the time of decision was at hand. Some chose to become as the walking dead he spoke of.

Some did choose, though not the Light of Love. Thankfully, some did choose to dedicate themselves to Spirit and to greater works. Many choices were made by the people around the time of October 31st, 2000. The first division of Light and dark began. It started in the souls of the people.

Life at the Shambhala Center went on. I watched as some left to follow the new path and my heart went out with them, for I knew what was happening.

Spirit continued to teach me in many ways. October had been a month of many, many miracles. Now the 11-11 doorway opened into November, 2000.

What a doorway! I entered into a new experience, one that I'll not soon forget!

A Night Of dreams....

Susan Isabelle

A Dreaming Night , November 11th, 2000

I awoke or at least I think I awoke. I am not sure. But to my astonishment, I was in the body of a little girl who was about ten years old.

Someone was speaking to me, but not using my name. She was calling me Amanda! Not Susan or Al'lat, but Amanda. I realized I was in two places at once! I was at home in my bed 'asleep'. I was writing in trance while also in a field by a pond in the body of a small girl! How? I don't know. I was in a semi trance- like sleep and wrote on papers kept by my bed. When I ran out of paper, I wrote on the sheet!

The person calling me Amanda, was a beautiful Indian Maiden .She wore white buckskin and had streams of turquoise flowing down in long chains around her garments. She had beautiful, flowing black hair and a headband of turquoise.

This then is the record of that night.

She spoke:

> *"Amanda, do not be afraid, it is I, the Maiden of the pond that your family has known all these years. I have loved them, and they me. I have been waiting for you to come, just as your many mothers have before you. There is much to tell you."*

> "What is your name?" I asked timidly, as a child.

> *"I am called Aumala of the Algonquians, of many Earth nations. I dwell in the Pure Light of Great Spirit. My name means, "Bearer of the Light of the Dawn." It is for this reason I come to the Children of the East, of which you are. I am*

*the Spirit of Newness, new beginnings. I am the Promise of
a New Day and of a New Birth."*

I began to feel the child that was me become more at
ease. Although she spoke like an adult, Aumala appeared
to look friendly, and was a young girl, just like me. I
relaxed.

"Why did you come here?" I asked Aumala.

*"I come to each of my female descendants in my feminine form
to endow them with gifts to carry out the work of creation
upon the Earth. Each time I have come to my daughters, I
have found them to be weaker in each of their generations,
so weak that my presence on the earth has been at times near
extinction.*

Forbid!"

*"For with that, so will humanity become extinct upon
this planet, this jewel that sparkles in the Universe is as a
beautiful living, blue gem! My form is required to ensure
the renewal and birth of the human and of all nature.*

*With the times of the rule of indigenous peoples upon the
earth coming to an end, it was necessary that I leave this
plane. I chose to ensure the progression of the line in your
peoples, knowing this day would one day come.*

*The displacement of the Indian was foreknown and the
knowledge has been held by them through many trials.*

That time is now at an end.

*I chose to come before your earthly mother's generation,
but found the times of war and destruction on the Earth.*

*My presence was unable to fully integrate upon this plane
for several generations, and near destruction occurred.
Mankind had fallen into disbelief in the Great Spirit and
the Great Law of Nature. Those, of the mothers upon the
earth, and the Feminine Masters in the heavenly realms,
held the energy until this day.*

*My presence on the earth now holds a glimmer of hope,
for the daughters have turned their hearts to the land, to
creation, and to love of Spirit in true form!
The work of the Masters has held the truth for the earth
and we rejoice!*

*As the sun sparkles on the surface of the waters, so too do
you reflect my presence on the earth."*

"I do?" The child within me barely whispered.

*"Yes, Amanda. You are my 9th generation child in
physical form upon the earth, since the time of my last
coming in the mothers in integrated physical form.*

*You represent the completed eternal circle of renewal
and the progression unto completion of the whole.*

*To you and to those of your generation; you have now
been given the opportunity to bring about the completion
of yourselves. The new beginning of humanity resides at
the tenth generation. This moment, your generation holds
the opportunity for all mankind to evolve and for the
progression of humanity for many generations henceforth!"*

"What do you mean?" I bravely asked.

*"Amanda, what your generation chooses to do will
determine the complete return of my being upon the earth.*

184

Embracing my qualities of the Divine Feminine will ensure love, renewal, birth, beauty, healing and wisdom upon the earth.

My heart has been to bring the Light of the Creator, the Great Spirit of a new day to the peoples.

My heart has been to dwell within my children of Light.

My heart has been to honor the Great Spirit in preservation of It's precious glory of creation.

*Creation is the reflection of love of the Great Spirit to the children of Spirit.
Just as I reflect in you my being, so you reflect the Spirit in your being.*

*The creatures and the plants of the earth are dying.
This is a great loss, for each holds a passageway:
a knowledge, a heart, a cell of the body.*

Together, they create the whole.

As a pebble dropped into the water of this lily pond, the waves flow outward and touch the far shores. So have the actions, the destruction of the air, lands and seas touched every shore, every nation, every sky, shaking the very foundations.

Heart of Great Spirit weeps for mankind does not see the love extended unto them. The Hand of the Mother holds back the hand of destruction in forgiveness and compassion for mankind.

Susan Isabelle

She touched my forehead,

> "To you my Daughter;
> I have placed the gift of knowing,
> the gifts of healing the earth, the elementals, and its
> peoples.

> My Daughter, I go now once more to my home within the
> Light of Dawn.

> Know this: You carry my Light, my likeness.

> I am strong within you, we are One Spirit."

She began to fade back into a light form right before my eyes. As she was disappearing, I heard her last words,

> "I will send them to you.
> They will teach you my word and the Way of the Dawn.
> For in you and your generation is
> the Light of a New Day."

Amanda, or I, fell back on the soft grass in the dream-state and immediately fell into a very deep sleep.

<u>The First Visitor</u>

I "awoke" again in the same body of Amanda. I was confused. How can one dream while in a dream? Then I heard the singing.

"All who aspire
May rise above the fire
A purification…. without notification
Not to destruction…… but reconstruction"

I opened my eyes to see above me a great spider weaving a huge net above. The spider looked down and said,

" I am a poet, but you didn't know it.
Its' not my….well, style, but will do; for a while."

I looked up above at the great spider, its body and long legs were black and furry. My impulse was to run, but I remembered the words of the Indian maiden a short while ago. She had said she would send someone to teach me. The spider examined me, cocking its great head, she then continued,

"To those who seek and are not weak,
Come closer, Dear….., come near
Well…., maybe not…….,but you ought…."

I rose up on my knees before the great spider that spoke softly to me now.

"We skip we dance…we take a chance
To those who believe…
A web we weave..

The first shall be last: And all shall be past

> *Did you dare but ask?"*

> *Chitter, chatter: it does not matter*
> *Of the first or the latter"*

The great spider continued her work on the web as I watched. I asked the spider,

"What is your name?"

The spider replied,

> *"Do you think this is a game?*
> *You, a sage who write upon the page?*
> *That you may begin again..*
> *Go forth now and cry to all,*
> *Who ask, "WHY?"*
> *"Goodbye!"*

"Wait! WAIT!" Amanda cried, "Tell me more- I need to know!"

> *"A message from heaven...there is no leaven...*
> *A message from heaven...there is no leaven...*
> *A message from heaven...there is no leaven..."*

The spider sang, then continued,

> *"Six legs have I*
> *By which I may ascend the sky*
> *To which I weave*
> *Do you believe?*
> *2 to reweave the past*
> *2 to secure the present*
> *2 to construct the future*
> *All are but arms to prepare the charms!"*

I considered the spider's words.

"This is a powerful being!" I whispered under my breath. 'Change the future?" .....

"Are there alarms?" The spider asked.

"Upon my web of fate
IMPLORE!
Before too late!

I weave these charms....
Seek now no harms.....
May befall....the ALL"

From high in her web the spider looked down at me and seeing my confusion asked,

"Am I simply a spider
Or a clever hider?

Who would seek from one so small
The waiting fate of us all?"

The spider began to transform before me into a gorgeous woman with long flowing black hair and piercing black eyes that held a glimmer of amusement. Her head was wrapped in a golden ribbon that held a thick braid wrapped over her head as a crown. Her dark skin was smooth and beautiful!

"My true form now you see
Go I say, and now be free...."

Seeing the beautiful creature now standing before me, I felt such love coming from this one to me. Still before the beautiful spider-woman being looking up at her while on my knees, I asked,

189

"May I ask of you a gift. I don't want to let this time go past or by me now!"

"YES!, YES! What do you require?
But, am I One to hire?"

The beautiful spider woman now waited for her answer. I spoke,

"Please, Dear Spider, I have heard you say you weave the
fate of all mankind.
I ask you weave a web of love, of kindness, of compassion
and
of Light to cover all.
Can you do this?"

"What? You question my ability?
My Dear! Weavers of fate are we
This very night you shall see..

A web of Light to remove the fright
449 is our time

Hurry on, past this night, it will not last
Before the dawn, we'll all be gone

Our web to have been woven...
The hoof of one yet cloven...

Bound.....

Shall not be found......

On this plane, no, not again..."

She turned to leave me, and resumed her form of spider. I said to her as she began to ascend,

"Oh Mistress of the Web, I honor you, and as you wish, leave just now".

Her last words to me were,

"To weave, we must now leave."

One swish of one of the spiders' arm, sent me back into a deep sleep.

Paint Me A Rainbow, The Second Visitor

"How? How? Do you want to know HOW?"

I heard a small voice beside me somewhere on the grass. Stirring myself out of the deep sleep, I managed to answer the voice,

"How to do what?" I asked while half asleep.

I looked around to find the being of the voice. At last I saw him in the tall grass. He was completely green and was well hidden in the green of the grass. Surprised at his appearance, I exclaimed ,

"How to do what?"

"Why, to make a rainbow in the sky!"

He answered Amanda sounding a bit impatient with her/ my question. Cocking his head at me, he stared right back at me as he continued to cling to a piece of grass.

"Why do I want to make a rainbow in the sky, Little One?"

I spoke softly as I looked down to watch the little green being. He wore a green cap and tight pants of green moss. He did not have hands as such, but rather feathery green extensions that clung to the grass as suction cups. He jumped from blade to blade as he came closer, almost directly beneath my gaze. Once he had settled down, he looked up at me and seemed to wait for me. I spoke again,

"Why do I want to paint a rainbow in the sky, Little One?"

**"Because! Because! 'Tis great fun!
A covenant, you know, 'tis true!
'Tween God and you."**

He jumped around with each word in excitement. The child in me wanted to giggle and I could hardly keep from laughing, but out of respect for the little being, I waited. When he settled down again, he looked up at me and waited for my response.

"Oh, yes, please show me how!" I exclaimed.

As soon as I had said these words he began to hop around again gleefully singing these words,

"A song, a song is all it takes!"
"A song?" I interrupted
**"Oh, yes! A tune or two
Will be just enough for you!"**
"Do you always rhyme?" I asked, remembering her encounter with the Mistress of the Web.

"Oh, yes, I do it all the time!"
He giggled and then in roaring laughter, rolled on the grass laughing! Climbing back upon a blade of grass, he adjusted his hat, pulled down the pant legs, and straightened his jacket. Once again he began his song;

193

"My song, for you
My song, 'tis true…
A little bit of red..
It goes to his head…
From the flowers, it takes not hours…
Nothing here I'd rather
Than from the flowers gather"

"All flavors of the golden yellow
To amaze the good fellows….
Swirled up on high
The sky is nigh"

"Now, more difficult to get…
The orange; but yet…..
For all good wishes, come by and by
All are needed to fill the sky"

"Now, hummmm, of the bluest blue….
This one is made for you….
To open and inspire
To all that is higher….
The violet of your open mind
Acts of kindness come in kind"

"Oh! That is so beautiful! I love your song!" I cheered.

"I am not yet finished; but I thank you.
There is much more to do."

Breathing in deeply, he raised his face to the sky. He began to sing again,

"Paint me a rainbow and you will see
The jewel'est green of every tree…
The wonder of creation be
My entire color evergreen BE…."

194

With that, his green color glowed deeply and the color of emeralds sparkled from his little body in great rays that beamed out from him.

"Oh, you are so beautiful!" I exclaimed.

He smiled at me and said,

> *"To make you very smart,*
> *These are of the heart...*
> *My colors are a gift!*
> *Could you give me a lift?"*

I stretched out my hand and he climbed into my palm. I sat holding him now and waited for him to speak.

> *"Now, something you must understand*
> *All of creation is so grand!*
> *From the sun....*
> *OH, Such Fun!"*

He began to giggle; he managed to say this before falling over in great heaves of laughter. His laughter was contagious. I couldn't help but laugh with him. I was thrilled with the tiny being I held in my hand. I loved him immediately and spoke softly to him,

"I love you, Sweet One, and I love your song."

With that, he stood up again and began gazing seriously up into my eyes. For a long time he looked at me. He looked into my soul. Then he began to sing,

> *"Paint me a rainbow of your love*
> *Shining, shining, beautiful up above*
>
> *Then, shall I return my love.*
> *Gentle, gentle on the wings of the Dove*

Susan Isabelle

Death nor destruction, no,
not, for thee...

Nor to those who bend the knee
Not to those with eyes to see
And ears to hear that which
is ever near"

"Paint me a rainbow of your love
Shining, shining, beautiful, up above

Paint me a rainbow, you will see
Cast your prayers up to me

Upon the beauty of the sky
I paint them on high

I raise the bow
To all to show

My love to thee
That you are free..."

In a flash, he vanished out of my hand! Looking around, I could not find him anywhere in the tall grass. Then I heard his song, far, far away,

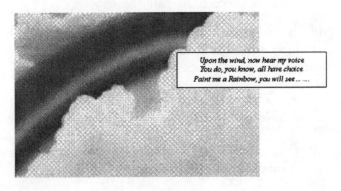

Upon the wind, now hear my voice
You do, you know, all have choice
Paint me a Rainbow, you will see... ....

"Large or small
I AM in the All
Upon the wind, now hear my voice....
You do, you know, all have choice
Paint me a rainbow, ...you will see
Paint me a rainbow, you will see.....
Paint me a rainbow, you will see.....
Yes, to be free..."

I was left gazing up into the sky, seeking to see him one more time.

<u>Humans!   The Third Visitor's Teachings</u>

I heard a sound coming from nearby. It was soft as a bell muffled in the grasses somewhere.

Ting-a-ling! Ting-a-ling! Ting-a-ling!

I heard someone say,
"Look at that!"

"Who said that?" I exclaimed!

"I did! Do you see it?"

"What?" Did I see what?" I asked the unseen voice.

" The rainbow silly!
Look at it!"

I raised my eyes to the most incredible rainbow I had ever seen! Its colors were splashed across the sky in a blaze of glory!

"I will miss you, Little One!" I said as a tear rolled down my face.

"Didn't you hear him?" The little voice exclaimed impatiently.

"Hear what?" I asked.

"His song, silly!"

"Why of course I heard his song!" I said, becoming defensive. "I heard him."

"You heard him, but did you hearrrrr him?"

"Of course! How can you hear without hearing?" I was irritated when I replied.

"Well, if you heard him, you'd know he's never far away so you don't have to miss him, Silly!"

I asked while looking around in the tall grass. "Don't you know it's not nice to call people names? Where are you?"

"I'm not in the grass, look over here in the pond. I'd fly over, but I've got a real good view of the rainbow here. It's beautiful! You must have given him some real colors to paint with this time!" The voice answered.

As I made my way over to the pond, I peered through the grass at what appeared to be a tiny butterfly, but certainly not a butterfly! Pretty yellow wings framed a tiny being who had hands and feet with little antenna sprouting from his head.

His feet hung down in the pond from the green lily pad he sat upon. He made rings from the movement of his feet in the water as he swung them back and forth. He gazed up into the sky and asked nonchalantly,

"You are human, aren't you?"
"Yes" I answered.

Looking over at me now he swept me with his glance, then looked up again at the rainbow stating,

"Well, humans are silly."

"Wait just a moment!" the child in me retorted, "Why are saying that humans are silly. I've never done anything to you!"

**"Well, from where I sit, you are a human,
.......so you have!"**

"What do you mean? I *know* I've never done anything to you!" I said getting angry now.

"Just because you don't see what you've done, doesn't mean you haven't done anything", he said.

"Whatever do you mean! Why do you say humans are silly and why do you say I've done something to you? Why, I've never even seen you before!"

**"Just because you don't recognize me,
doesn't mean you haven't seen me," he taunted.**

"I know I've never seen you before, I've never seen anything like you before," I snapped.

**"Well, to answer your question.
Isn't it a silly thing to build a beautiful house;
then pull all the nails out each night?"**

"Yes, I suppose so. Why would anyone do that?"

"I don't know, he answered, but humans do it all the time!"

"No, they don't! Who told you that?" I asked.

He paused a few moments then began again,

> *" Look into the water, Amanda."*

I saw the beautiful pink and white lilies floating on soft green pads on the water. Its blue reflected the sky above in the ripples he made with his feet.

> *"Isn't it a silly thing to love to be near the ponds,*
> *the lakes oceans and streams saying,*
> *"How Beautiful",*
> *then dump your garbage into them?"*

"Who does that?" I asked.

> *" The humans do."*

He answered me directly staring deep into my eyes. He watched me consider his words, then said,

> *"Look up, Amanda!"*

I raised my eyes up to see a contrail of a passing jet making its long white mark across the sky.

> *"Isn't it a silly thing to look up into the beautiful*
> *blue sky and say,*
> *"How beautiful!"*
> *Then fill the sky with poisonous fumes so strong*
> *you can't see the sky anymore?"*

> *"Follow me, Amanda."* He commanded.

He flew over to the edge of the forest with me following close behind. He paused and hovered by my shoulder just at its edge.

We stood together looking at the tall forest. Its deep rich green foliage filled the air with smells of sweet pine and its cleanliness.

> ***"Isn't it a silly thing to go to the tall pines,***
> ***acknowledge they clean your air; say,***
> ***"How Beautiful!"***
> ***Then cut them all down?***
>
> ***You make houses and roads.....***
> ***destroying the beauty and the air you breathe.***
>
> **Humans *ARE* silly!"**

He flew back and landed on his lily pad.

I ran back to find him on the lily pad lying on his back.

"Well, maybe so," I spoke softly to him, "but still, I never did anything to you." I tried to defend myself. "You're OK, aren't you?" I asked.

He sat up and asked me,

> ***"Do you see my little lily pond?"***
"Yes" I replied.

> ***"Do you see my little lilies?***
> ***Aren't they pretty?***
> ***Aren't they beautiful?"***

"Yes, they are." I answered. He spoke again,

> ***"This is my home.***
> ***Every year the rains come.***
> ***They are now bitter with the pollution humans***

have put into the air, the sky, the waters.

*In a few years, the lilies won't be able to grow here
anymore because the water will be poisoned....
Soon,
I won't have a lily pad to sit on..... to watch the
rainbows anymore."*

He became quiet, and turned his back toward me. I
thought I saw him wiping tears from his eyes.

"Oh, I didn't realize." I began to speak. He turned again,
and lifting from the lily pad said,

"Now, I will give you eyes."

His little wings began to beat so fast, he seemed to
disappear. All I could see was a flash. He flew right by
me as a flash of silver in the air.

"Oh, I have seen him before!" I exclaimed. "I've seen that
flash of light, I didn't know what it was!"

I felt a tiny touch on each eyelid. I heard a high pitch
sound, which seemed to coming from all around me that
was deafening. It grew louder and louder in my ears.
Suddenly there was a "POP!" I could hear hundreds of
little voices all around me, speaking all at once.

"Wait!" I gasped while catching my breath. "I can't hear
you all at once!!!!"

*"We work, we work,
we work so hard, keeping ahead
if not helped, soon all be dead
Jus' because we don't know how
Many of us are leaving now......"*

I looked down to see a little caterpillar near my elbow. "Did you say that?" I asked.

> **"Oh, yes, I be a sad, saaaaad, Chlorchatter!"**

"What's wrong, Chlorchatter?" I asked...

> **All's the matter!**

He answered, then began to say........

> **"Upon the leaves,**
> **even those-at your knees**
> **They spray, they spray!**
> **To keep bugs at bay**
> **We eat: we eat**
> **Lie dead-at your feet"**

> **"Oh, we don't know how**
> **Many, many, ...we leave you now"**

In the still air at that moment she heard the voice of the Indian Maiden.

> **"Yes, Amanda, they are leaving,**
> **they too serve humanity.**
> **I strengthen them, but you will be needed now."**

To my side a little voice sang out.

> **"Now to open**
> **as many-'tis not!**
> **How to open?**
> **Their knowing is not"**

I turned to see a butterfly pulling and pulling, tugging on a daffodil bud.

"What are you doing?" I asked. He answered me,

> ***"Know ye not how the flowers blossom?***
>
> ***The plan and process is so awesome!***
>
> ***Though not seen or observed***
>
> ***I, Buddy, surely have served"***

"Oh I see! You open the buds of the plants!"

> ***"Why of course, 'tis not just the ants!"***

He giggled and went to pull open another flower bud.

> ***"Meet now Hi'bis***
> ***She! 'Tis a glorious Miss!"***

A beautiful being, a fairy, then sped by me to land on the flower Buddy had just opened. I watched quietly as the fairy placed golden sparkles into the center of the flower.

I was fascinated by her beauty and her gentle, gliding flight. She then floated above the blossom and with the wave of her hand, more sparkles entered the flower.
I wondered what she was doing. She heard my thoughts.

The fairy stopped mid air and turned to me saying,

"The blossoms; they are meek
Who will strengthen each flower?"

"Oh, how late the hour!"

Suddenly I heard the sound of buzzing, buzzing all around. Hi-bis, the fairy said,

"Here the Ray-bees!" From the sun
Once, they had tremendous fun"

She stood there on a blossom to watch, shaking her head. The Ray Bees sang,

"Ray bees come down to buzz
No, not much is as it was!
Unwillingly, we deliver dangerous rays..."

"Oh, Mankind!"

"You forgot the sacred ways!"

They buzzed right past her and disappeared into the greenery around her. Then the very air was silent. I considered the words that had been spoken.

Again I heard the voice of the Maiden speak to me,

"A protective layer over the earth
has been damaged, Amanda.
Once it removed the danger from the
rays, stripped it from them,
but now they pass right through! They
mean to bring life to the earth,

but now their task has become one which they deplore and humanity must consider."

"Amanda, it will be up to you."

In the morning I awoke to find scraps of paper written in several different forms of writing scattered all over the bed and on the floor. Clearly, this writing was not mine.

At some point I don't remember, I had run out of paper and wrote the last pieces on the bed sheet.

I'll never forget that night and I spent the next month considering the words that had been said to me.

I had already begun to transcribe the night vision of Aumala and I into a child's book and had shared the story with Will. Spirit seemed to want me to make it available to others. I loved the stories and began to paint the little images that I had seen in the night. Soon a small book was formed and I would give it out as Christmas presents to family and friends. So much had happened!

I soon realized that Aumala was like White Buffalo Calf Woman. The Spider Woman was as Athena, the Weaver of Fates and Grandmother Spider of the Native American legends.

The little green being I had held in my hand was clearly God, The Father. I remembered in awe His words,

"Large or Small I AM in the All! "

I was to paint a rainbow of love for Him! I wondered how I was to do that!

Each little creature taught the truths of the human condition in a simple and beautiful way that even children could understand!

I considered the words of Grandmother Spider. She had given me actually six opportunities for humanity.

She had said "2 to reweave the past,
2 to secure the present,
2 to construct the future!"
To construct the future?
WOW!
I had much to consider and meditate on.

Chapter XIV
Temple of The Goddess

More Teaching

On Dec 9th 2000, I was told during the night to go back to the Telos site in the White Mountains. Adama had come to me in my dreamtime and instructed me to leave the next morning. I spoke to my husband, Will and he quickly agreed to go with me. He was now into the adventure!

We went up early in the morning. When we arrived, we were unable to drive into the site because of icing. We walked in together, over two miles up in the mountains in snow and ice.

When we came into the area, the sun was hidden behind a thick cloud cover that looked like snow clouds. I kept hoping and praying that it wouldn't start to snow! As I walked up the hill into the site a large raven kept hopping ahead of us and calling us up higher and higher. We were being led to an area. The raven stopped, looked at me, then it flew away. I knew I was where I was supposed to be. I looked again at the clouded sun, its glow was barely discernible behind the clouds. I stopped to look around. Will kept going up ahead.

All of a sudden, there was a flare of energy that came out from the barely discernable sun, sending out a multicolored glow over the whole area.

A see-through image of a woman appeared in front of me suspended in the air, about three feet in height. She was completely enveloped in an aura of bright magenta. I could see right through her and saw the trees behind her. I could see that the leaves and trees were magenta in her image.

She was sitting back on her knees with her feet tucked up under her. Her long slender hands were placed on her legs, just above her knees. She had a Spanish comb tiara on the back of her head. Her head was bent slightly forward.

As I watched her, I could see coming up the back of her body, globes of energy. The globes were inside of her, moving up her spine. The globes flowed up and out over her head and began to do something.

Three times I saw her do this. I looked to my right and to my left to see if there was anything to the side I was to see. No, there was nothing on either side of her. But in front of me, she sat as clear as could be; a bright magenta woman forming pulsing globes of energy.

I saw a symbol that I had seen the day of October 13th come into her crown and spin down her channel! I was shown the process and how the symbols worked together to form the energy globes... As soon as I understood the process, she began to fade away.

Another flare from the sun suddenly burst through the clouds! This one was completely gold!

A Golden woman stood between four globes of golden light. She was pulsing and creating, yes, CREATING something! She showed me how!

Then I realized, I now had all the Keys and

They were teaching me... how to teach you.......

I immediately knew that these were the uses of the new symbols! We were going to have quite a Ra-In-Bow class in January!

Will had left me alone for those few minutes, stepping away so I could have my private time. He didn't understand, but somehow he knew that I needed my space.

As soon as it was all over, he was right beside me. We didn't speak at all on the way back down the mountain. I wonder if he saw the flares. I never asked. We walked down the icy road back to the car in silence. Once in the car, I was busy in the front seat writing down what I had seen in the forest and drawing diagrams. Then I fell asleep.

I awoke. We were close to home but something was wrong. Will told me he was having chest pains. As we were close to the hospital, I took over driving and brought him to the emergency room. He was in his 70's and the hike we had taken that day was too much of a strain on him. He was having a heart attack. I stayed with him in the emergency room while tubes were inserted and technicians ran about performing tests. He was in a lot of pain. I prayed by his bed and held his hand.

It was around midnight when I asked for help. My prayer was to God to spare him, and as I did, the image of the Beautiful Spider Woman came to me. She spoke,

"God has given you task; all you need do is but ask!"

I remembered she had given me six wishes only a few weeks before. I hadn't asked anything for myself then, but now, I didn't want to lose Will! Not now! I asked,

"Athena, Grandmother, Weavers of Fate, *by God's decree,* not mine.

211

This time, I ask for Will and for me....
Restore Will to perfect health ...
Reweave the present moment , this I ask."

Will's breathing relaxed and he fell into a healing sleep. Around 2:00AM, he was transferred into a private room on the 4th floor of the hospital in the cardiac unit. I fell asleep in the chair beside his bed.

I awoke at 4:30 AM. He was still sleeping peacefully, but the nurse had come into check on him once again. As she checked his tubes, I walked over to the big windows that were covered with heavy curtains.

I pulled back the curtain. I could not believe my eyes! On the 4th floor level was a huge spider web that stretched from the window pane to a metal pole security light suspended out over the street below. It was placed on the side of the building! The glow of the street light on the dewy web, made it shimmer silver and gold in the blackness of early morning. Beautiful!

That web must have been four by four, a great dream catcher suspended by thin strands of silvery white spun by Grandmother spider. I had been heard. Will would survive. My second wish had materialized. Will went home the next day. For some unknown reason, he was now perfectly healthy.

I knew without a doubt, that the gifts that had been given to me during the night I was the child called Amanda, were real. This was not just a vision or a dream of the night.

Four wishes remained, a gift from the Father. I would never again use the wishes for personal gain. In the future, I would need these re-weaving and constructing gifts.

They were never meant to be used for personal reasons but only for the highest good of all, and in Divine order.

"449 is Her time."

Christmas Day, December 25, 2000, The Eclipse

The sun rose in the clear blue frosty sky that morning, until around noontime it was bright and extremely cold! Then the air seemed to take on a silvery hue. We were having an eclipse on Christmas Day, at the end of the millennium. Will and I were going to watch it!

It was so cold, it only warmed to a whole 10 degrees outside with a firm, brisk wind. The wind blew across the white snow as my husband and I made our way through the woods to the little lake near our home to view the eclipse.

Will and I brought with us a sextant, a devise to assist sailors across the seas by celestial navigation. We were excited that morning to open our Christmas gift from California to find it in the wrappings! Today of all days! Now we would both be able to look at the sun to watch the eclipse, this rare happening in the sky. Its many filters would enable us to look directly into the sun and watch the moon pass over her surface.

Once situated up high on the side of the hill overlooking the lake, we had a clear view of the sun. We wouldn't be here long though, not with this wind!

Will handed to me the sextant. As I arranged the filters to view the sun, I could feel the sun's rays beaming down on my face. They made me feel dizzy and I handed the sextant to my husband to arrange. Something was happening, but I wasn't sure of exactly what. He fixed it and handed it back to me. He knew this was important.

I couldn't believe I was viewing the sun for the very first time using a sextant. How amazing and how generous

Spirit is. All is provided in the simplest and most wondrous ways. I had planned to view the eclipse that noontime with the typical child's way of a pinhole in a cardboard box, recommended on television that morning! Now, by a marvelous gift, we were doing it professionally. Obviously, Spirit wanted us to see this!

The great glowing globe of the golden yellow sun came into view. The dark moon was already beginning her slide across the face of the sun. I could imagine Mother Mary once again standing on the sun, it firmly under her feet and her stars in her crown! I felt Ix Chel's joy at receiving the power of the sun's energy, their saluting one another in the heaven's!

The moon seemed to push forward across the sun with a fiery red rim of glory ahead of it. The sun was rimmed with an emerald green. Its beauty was awesome! It made me dizzy, so I handed the sextant to Will, who eagerly took it from me and began to use the devise.

Then, all became quiet. The wind stopped blowing, and there was no sound. I stood absolutely still.

Then, opening my arms to receive the rays, I let the full force of the sun and moon come over me. *"I am ready to receive."* I prayed.

Great pulses were now flowing through me. The time was at hand. Tingling head to foot, the sun's energy was spinning the very cells of my body. Dizzy, I backed up and leaned against a tree as it continued to flow. For just about three minutes I stood receiving the ray, then the wind picked up and blasted us with fury. It was over and now time to go home.

I walked back into the house feeling very groggy. I fell on the couch and into a deep sleep. I awoke an hour later, different somehow, I could feel it. My physical structure had been altered. I could sense that I had been prepared for something yet to come.

The rest of the day was uneventful, and as family came to visit, I wondered about many things. Many thoughts were flowing as I considered the Ra In Bow class to come on January 6th, the Feast of the Epiphany. For some reason, that was the day that Spirit wanted the first class. It was hard trying to focus on anything else. It preoccupied my day.

I had been told not to refuse anyone who wanted to come to the class. I now had fifteen students coming to the class. I wondered how I was going to be able to hold all that energy to pass the Empowerments that had been given!

Once I was a very small woman, but ever since I had started to give hundreds of Reiki and Shambhala attunements as my class sizes grew- so did my body. My body changed. My eating habits hadn't changed, but my body took on a new form, to my dismay, much larger!

At first I was distressed and sought diets and other ways to decrease my size and perceived weight gain. I just made myself sick. The vegetarian diet I had been on nearly destroyed my body's ability to make platelets and the doctor told me I must have meat if I were to survive and keep my spleen. My genetic heritage, Type O, was that of hunters and gatherers of the Native peoples. I learned from Dr. James D'Adamo's book, *Eat Right For Your Type* and a personal visit to him, that my body was wired to require that I honor my ancestors' genetics. I began to eat meat again and the platelet situation that was threatening my life, reversed itself.

I was soon to understand though, that my enhanced body was now empowered to transmit the powerful energies through the transmission of electrical frequencies in my larger frame. This was done by water. Currents run through concentration of water and other minerals in the body. Also, Estrogen storage and water were necessary for me to hold the incoming energies. I had plenty of both. I finally realized it is a small price to pay for the abilities; for mental, physical and spiritual benefits abound. Remember the Buddha's Belly? How do you think he got that?

Sometimes, people were cruel and made comments about my size. They, in ignorance, did not understand that this had nothing to do with habits, control, food, meat, vegetables, coffee or other parts of my diet. I don't get thin; I'm not supposed to. In fact, the pictures from Belize on the day of the incoming Pleidian energies actually showed me grow in both height and width to about double my natural state! Those Pleidians energies *require* a large frame!

Spirit had given many gifts at my birth, one was to be born under a Scorpio Sun and also a Sagittarius moon, with plenty of Venus too, guaranteeing a womanly figure! I learned to be happy with 'me'!

All that I did required much energy, endurance and physical ability. I taught, I worked as a social worker, I ran a Center of twelve therapists, owned a store, was on assignment with Adama, and I wrote! That was more than what most people could do. Spirit provided plenty of energy! In fact, the class manual was nearly completed and ready to go to the printer in the morning, so it was a happy and contented Shambhala/Ra In Bow Master who feel into bed that night.

217

"Susan, Susan, wake up!' *I heard the Voice of Obed*
once again.
" It's time to go."

Rising I glanced at the clock, yes, it was 3:00 AM in
the morning.

The Temple of the Goddess

It was not unusual for me to be awakened at this hour.
I have been called many, many times at 3:00AM. I knew
now not to fight the energy; it is an opportunity I don't
want to miss. I made my way out of the bedroom and into
the living room where I sat on the couch and wrapped
myself in the great quilt that was placed there just for
these nights.

Maybe I would be given instruction as to what had
happened that day at the eclipse. Closing my eyes, I felt the
warm gentle energy begin to enfold me wrapping loving
arms around me and into my being. Waves of magenta,
unconditional love passed through me, rocking me gently
with sweet, sweet, joy. *"In Thy Presence, is fullness of joy!"*
The psalmist spoke. He knew this.

Suddenly, the couch and the room disappeared. I was
standing at what I knew to be the entrance of a great white
Temple. I was a small speck before its height and width.
I'd never seen this before!

Glowing white and incredible before me, I could not
even see its beginning nor its end, just the doors ahead,
which I knew were doors, but I could not see their tops
nor bottom. Misty white became the forms of angels,
glowing and swaying on either side of me, holding the

218

space around me. I was there in both physical and spirit form.

My clothing had been changed to a white garment somehow, already provided by the time I had arrived. Movement and excitement were all around me. The angels were busy preparing me for something. I didn't know what, but I remained calm and very peaceful. Once they were finished, one motioned me to step closer. At once I felt myself entering through the doors which just appeared to dissolve as I approached, not swinging open, just 'allowing.' There were great beaming radiating pillars of many colors, shifting and pulsating. They were filled with sparking stars and stood within the Temple. If you can imagine a pillar so high and so wide as to hold a galaxy, you will begin to understand what I mean when I say a 'Pillar!'

"What is this Place, I wondered, why am I here?'

A form materialized before me and I feel to my knees before His great countenance. I'd never seen Him so magnificent before! Melchizedek spoke to me while extending his hand to lift me up,

"No, Al'lat Le Andro, my Sister, the time has come. Be strong.
It is for this time you have come into being,"

I felt his strength enter me. I stood tall with confidence and dignity. He spoke again,

"Al'lat Le Andro, long, you and I have waited for this time. It must be so."

As I looked into his eyes, I knew: I remembered: I remembered the night of our merging over a year ago, the

219

words he spoke to me then. I remembered Andromeda, my peoples, and who I am. I have come to do this; I remembered.

"I am now ready. I must go, alone, now." I announced boldly to all.

I looked at him, I know the great love he has for me and if he could have done so, he would have done this for me: but that could not be. Strengthened by his love, I stepped forward toward the first of the great living Pillars. Its ruby rays filled the Temple. From my mouth flowed these words;

> "I stand in the place where I stood before I came into my physical incarnation. By my Mother I have been given form to dwell in the lower planes. Before me now is the Pillar of Strength of Being. The Gift of Divine Mother is my form. She has breathed life into my being, upon Her Breath, I live, I breathe, I am."

I stepped forward into the Pillar to stand upon a golden disk that shone its brightness up into the Universe. Upon the golden disk was engraved a ruby symbol. Looking closer I could see that the first symbol was made of rubies, of the Goddess. Its rays shone up through my being and activated at my touch; my physical form was no more.

Transformed into molecules of ruby Light, I swirled formless in the energy of the Pillar, the Aspect Being of the Goddess known as Strength, the Athena. I rose in Her being, speeding upwards through the Universe She upholds; to view her domain. From the place to which my being was ascended,

She showed me the inner Temple of God's Universe.

The Temple is the Kabala.

Once you dwelt in the ethereal realms, then birthed into life through the 2 pillars, legs, of your Earth mother . Your life was breathed into you by the Breath of the Divine Mother. You took on physical form, having the strength to live, a warrior Athena!

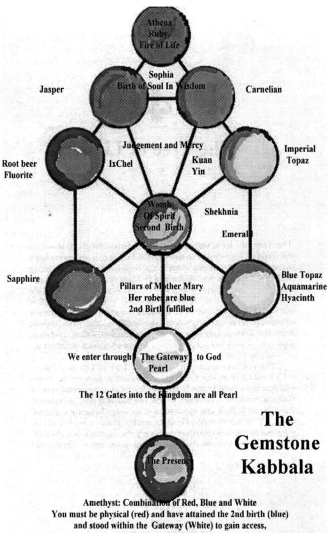

Athena
Ruby,
Fire of Life

Sophia
Birth of Soul In Wisdom

Jasper

Carnelian

Judgement and Mercy

IxChel

Kuan
Yin

Root beer
Fluorite

Imperial
Topaz

Womb
Of Spirit
Second Birth

Shekhnia

Emerald

Sapphire

Pillars of Mother Mary
Her robes are blue
2nd Birth fulfilled

Blue Topaz
Aquamarine
Hyacinth

We enter through The Gateway to God
Pearl

The 12 Gates into the Kingdom are all Pearl

**The
Gemstone
Kabbala**

The Present

Amethyst: Combination of Red, Blue and White
You must be physical (red) and have attained the 2nd birth (blue)
and stood within the Gateway (White) to gain access,
To become Amethyst!

221

The Temple is the Kabala., but one so incredible, that it
holds all the Spherical Universes of God's Creation.

The Pillars are alive with the Essence of God/Goddess,
in Perfect Union with all Her aspects.

Male and Female, rising and uniting in perfection,
It is complete within Itself.

Within each Aspect, within each Pillar. I heard The Voice,

"I am That I Am"
"I Am That I AM"
"I in you, you in Me...".

"Receive My Breath..."

"Be My Strength..."

I could now see the Living Kabala,
The form of God/Goddess Alive
The Temple of Creation...

The Tree Of Life Stands
Within the center and
Upholds the Holy Hologram Universes

In the Flower, dwell and suspend,
The Universes around about it;
The Galaxies,
The Stars within their assigned domain
As branches of the Great Tree

The Essence of The Light is Every where,
Lighting the Whole from Within.

A great Thundering VOICE rang out over the Universe,

"My People, Know this:"

"The Goddess Dwells Within Her Temple,
She is Loved Beyond All Love
She is Come To the Peoples
To Be Known
To Be Honored
To Be Loved"

I spoke:

"Mother, Your Warrior Strength sustains me.
Mother, Athena, who, by Your power has woven my fate,
my being.
By your Strength, I take the Shield of Righteousness
By Your Sword, I take The Sword of Truth"

Placed over my form a Great Sword appeared, a Shield and Helmet. I understood as I stood upon the first symbol of the Great Pillar. Many understandings were given at that moment in time. I understood the Great Tree: the first Pillar represented the Strength that the Mother gives to Her children at the time of their birth.

Souls being born are given the Breath Of Life; A gift from Divine Mother. She holds the physical incarnation of the soul as it births into physical being between the pillars of your physical mother, the two 'pillar legs' of your mother during your birth.

Once the soul existed in the Kingdom, astral, or etheric planes, possibly coming from the higher realms or that of the karmic wheel. But now, the soul is born into the world having a physical body. The energy required for physical existence is given through the energy of the

Universal Mother upon your first breath. It is She who gives strength, the Warrior Energy for your physical survival, and the fight for life is on!

She provides the Sword and the Shield until you are ready to fend for yourself, using your higher tools. She has manifested this aspect of Her being to humanity in the forms of Strength and Breath, the Athena Aspect.

A Great Gong sounded throughout the Universes.

Descending through the Pillar, I returned to my form; but not my form, I now held Her Athena Aspect within. Her molecules had merged with mine, I held Her energy. I stood once again upon the ruby symbol, now quiet.

Nine more Aspects Lie ahead, nine more symbols, nine more Pillars:
I had seen them from above. It is desired She be honored.
Proverbs 3:13 (a Good number) "*Wisdom-she is more precious than rubies: and all things you can desire are not to be compared to her -length of days is in her right hand, and in her left riches and honor.*

From Ruby I ascended to Wisdom; the Pillars of Carnelian and Jasper

The Angel by my side escorted me to a place between the next two Living Pillars. Seeing the great glowing Light of Goddess before me, I knew I was to once again receive the Symbol within each of the Pillars before me.

Standing between the Pillars, these words came from deep within me to the unseen.

"I stand between the Pillars of Sophia, the Pillars of Wisdom and Understanding."

I extended my left hand toward the great Carnelian Pillar saying,

"Sophia take my left hand, Empower me with all understanding as I join with you."

My hand was grasped by Her essence, a symbol was placed in my hand. Seven eternally moving star points were sealed within my hand. These were the empowerments of seven planets, seven metals and seven gifts
"I thank you Sophia for having guided me thus far."

Stretching out my right hand to the other deep orange and bluish fire Pillar, I felt it also grasped. I stated,

"I stretch forth my right hand to grasp yours in Wisdom, Divine Wisdom."

A rounded symbol containing seven pillars within it was placed in my hand. This was a gift of mastery symbolizing the Seven Pillars of Wisdom.

The Angel came to stand before me. Both my arms were stretched out across an entire Universe. He instructed me,

"Your body, Forms a Cross of Sacrifice.
Your head in physical realms,
With hands grasping the Divine Wisdom and the
Divine Understanding,
You are upheld by Judgment and Mercy:
Your Belly, Flaming the Fire of Shekhina;
Your Path is Marked: Through the Gate
Your feet are placed upon Malkuth

As your Fathers before you, their lives were given in sacrifice upon this cross."

The Softer Voice spoke to me.

" Al'Lat,
between Wisdom and Understanding,
lies your heart."

Then the Thunder Voice spoke,

"Know this, you will suffer in
your service to humanity
as did My Son and as others before you....."

There was a pause in heaven as I considered the
meaning of His words.

"Do you accept the responsibility, the honor of
sacrifice for others?

I answered,
"YES!"

Again He spoke,

"Hold tightly the hands as they shall guide you:
for Understanding is good, but without
Wisdom, it is a dangerous thing.
Wisdom and Understanding come;
The Heart Lies Between.
This is in preparation for your role and
responsibility to the Earth and her peoples."

"I understand,"

I was filled with Light

I heard the great gong resound and the Angel proclaim;

"But where shall wisdom be found? And where is the place of understanding. Man knoweth not the price there-of; neither is it found in the land of the living. The depth saith, 'It is not in me:' It cannot be gotten for gold neither shall silver be weighed. It cannot be gotten with the gold of Ophir , with the precious onyx or the sapphire: The gold and the crystal cannot equal it. No mention shall be made of coral or of pearls for the price of wisdom is above rubies.....

20. Whence cometh Wisdom? And where
is the place of understanding?
Seeing it is hid from the eyes of the living?
God understandth the way and he knoweth the place there of.
Unto man He saith,
"Behold, the fear (awe) of the Lord is Wisdom,
and to depart from evil is understanding."
Book Of Job

The Angel held a Cup of Wine in his hands. He offered to me the Cup of Sacrifice.

"To seal the Vow you have made,
State the Name of God seven times into the cup and
then drink!"

"Ayer Asher Ayer, Ayer Asher Ayer, Ayer Asher
Ayer,Ayer Asher Ayer, Ayer Asher Ayer, Ayer Asher
Ayer, Ayer Asher Ayer"
I AM THAT I AM

Then I drank the cup.

At that moment a crown of Seven Stars descended from Heaven and was placed upon my head. I heard the Words spoken,

"The Goddess of Wisdom who has hewn out her seven pillars." (Psalms 9:1)

And I knew this:

Her Seven Veils are soon to be removed from the mind of mankind.
   I Spoke again,

'I am filled With Wisdom and Understanding . I am now ready to go forth!"

I understood the Mysteries of Wisdom to humanity:As a child our first concern is survival, then understanding of our surroundings, of physical life and learning. We are but brute beasts without understanding and are only instinctual creatures holding onto life. But then comes understanding.

You must understand your physical incarnation, your place in the world and who you are. From the place of understanding, you are them prepared for the mystical, higher truths and learn of right use of knowledge, or Wisdom.

Once the soul has attained a level of maturity that extends beyond the desire of physical survival and begins to seek, the soul is under the guidance of Spirit, of Sophia, the Mother Guide of the energy of Wisdom and Understanding. Once I understood and integrated the teachings of the second Pillar, I was initiated into the Third Pillar, the Pillar of Wisdom. Here I was formed into the Essence of the Aspect of Wisdom and taught this;

The seven Pillars are the seven Stars of Wisdom which She will give to all who have desired and attained Her teachings of Wisdom!

As understanding is birthed into your being, you come under the Seven Pillars of Her teaching, Arithmetic, Geometry, Astronomy, Grammar, Rhetoric, Dialectic, and Music. Sophia is the Mother energy of Universal Mind.

Proverbs,8
>*Wisdom has buildeth her house, she
>has hewn out her seven pillars
>4. whoso is simple, let him turn in hither;
>as for him that wanteth understanding she
>saith unto him; "Come, eat of my bread and
>drink of the wine that I have mingled...*

>*Doth not wisdom cry?
>She standeth in the top of the high places in the way
>of the places of the paths...*

>*30. I was always with Him, daily I was His delight!*
>She is the Bride......

Standing tall, I wore the Armor and Symbol of Athena and the Two Symbols of the Stars and Pillars of Wisdom in my hands and a Crown of Seven Stars of Wisdom. My form was filling the Kabala.

The Angel came toward me once again and assisted me to a position that was again between two massive Pillars.

When so placed, the words came forth from my lips,

>*" I stand between the Pillars of Mercy and
>Compassion and that of Judgment."
>I stretch out my hand to the Aspect of Mercy and
>Compassion, the Great Kuan Yin.
>I receive Her empowerments."*

A beautiful rainbow colored lotus appeared in heaven and as I held my hand within Her pillar I felt the lotus enter my hand, rainbow sparkles lit up the whole of the Kabala. The essence of Her symbol moved into my heart center and became a bright flame In my heart, filling the entire Universe around me! The words were spoken in Heaven,

"The Light of Her Flame Is Now Within!"

The ten Vows of Kuan Yin were spoken in Heaven, ending with Kuan Yin speaking,

> **"I have come to Earth to see that**
> **every sentient being shall evolve**
> **and come into enlightenment, I**
> **do not ask that you so do;**
> **But I do ask that you vow a vow of**
> **Compassionate Action for the Earth"**

I answered her,

> *"I too, Kuan Yin, vow with your vow to see the*
> *enlightenment of all sentient beings who are directed*
> *to my path for mercy.*
> *I too show forth mercy and compassion on Earth!"*

The rainbow colored Lotus now shone brightly in both my hands!

The Angel then came forward and lifted my right hand and placed it within the Earthen Pillar to my right. I spoke the words,

> *"I stand between the Pillars of Mercy,*
> *and Severity; Judgment.*
> *Wisdom, Understanding and Mercy are now mine.*
> *With righteous Judgment, I hold Dominion.*

IxChel and All Earth Goddess Aspects,
I hold the right through Mercy to claim my
inheritance through you and with you!
Mankind was formed to have this dominion!
It was taken and is now reclaimed!
I claim my dominion over the Earth, the healing
herbs, the waters,
the lands, the sky, the moon and all creatures thereof!
I receive your symbol of this empowerment!"

A great spinning symbol of six petals of gold was placed in my hand.

"I vow of this responsibility to love and to care for
the Domain of the Earth and of my dominion"

Genesis 1:26 Be fruitful and multiply, and replenish the Earth and subdue it, and have dominion over the fish of the sea and over the fowl of the air, and over every living thing that moveth upon the Earth....

With the affirmation of the responsibility the Voice was heard,

"Receive the Symbol of the Sun in your crown"
As the words were spoken, above the seven stars of Sophia
a bright sun was placed in my crown.
"And the Moon"....

With that, a crescent moon appeared and placed itself just beneath the sun in the crown. With each of the Initiations of the Aspects of the Goddess, understanding grew. Now I understood that as a human being, the most we may attain in our physical incarnation is that of the flesh.

We, when we serve others, gain in wisdom and with that may one day become a "judge" or hold places of responsibility with or over the peoples. Many do so as supervisors , presidents of countries or spiritual ministers. That's all the toys of the world. Once attained, that is all in the physical body one may claim. But there is much more.........

Shekhina

As the Angel drew me toward the Center Pillar, its emerald green rays rose all the way up into infinity. In awe, I asked the Angel beside me.

"What place is this?"

He answered,
"This is the Universal Womb.
The place of your second birth.
You must be born again to proceed any further!
As Jesus told the Master in Israel, Nicodemous, you must be born again!
You must enter the Womb of your Mother once again, not that of flesh, but of Spirit and of Her waters, to take on Her likeness!
I spoke,

"Yes! I desire to be all that I may become.
I desire to be in likeness as My
Mother, to be of Spirit!"
The Voice spoke,

"Enter you at the Shekhina, your Spiritual Mother!

I stepped forward onto the Pillar ahead of me, its Emerald Green rays overtook me and I fell to my knees! First I saw Her form as a Dove hovering above me. She is so beautiful! On my knees I spoke,

" Shekhina, Most Beautiful!
I kneel before You for Your blessing. By Your love,
I have attained all within my physical incarnation!
Shekhina Most Beautiful,
I thank You for Your love and tender guidance, I ask
now, Shekhina, for Your Beauty to   enfold me. I am
now ready to receive You Shekhina and my anointing
of My Mother...."

I was Born Again, this time in Her, My Spiritual Mother, The Shekhina, The Holy Spirit

Within the Pillar I was transformed. Her Dove flew into my soul! Her rays of Beauty merged within me, I became as She is, holding Her likeness within.

The Angel spoke,

"Rise up! Stand now within Her Womb of Glory,
Shine forth the Mother in Your Being,
Oh Child of the Divine Goddess!
Come now to the power of your second birth!
Once in your physical form, you were birthed
through the womb of your Earthly mother,
between the pillars of physical
striving and of suffering,

Now Birth Ye into the Spirit and Her way!"

Rainbow after rainbow entered into me. I was filled with the Holy Spirit, Her likeness within my being, She is

233

now my Mother! When I stood, I was no more. Angels supported my being and led me to stand between two great Pillars of Blue and Sapphire! They spoke,

"Stand here between the Pillars of Splendor and of Victory, for you have attained!
Pass through these Pillars to the Likeness of the Child of God,
To Behold Your Father!"

As I stood between the two great pillars the Angel took one hand and placed it within the Pillar to my right.

"Hold now the Victory!"

A symbol appeared that formed a symbol of Goddess. My other hand rose to the opposite Pillar to receive another symbol in my left hand.

"Hold now the Sign of Splendor of a Child Of God!"

The Angel anointed my head and spoke,

"In tears you were brought forth in the physical ,
Now, in Glory you are born and
there are no more tears!"
I spoke these words,

"Mother, brought forth in tears,
I rest now within Your Great Pillars in preparation
for my spiritual birthing through them."

"I carry the Shekhina Rays of Beauty."

"The Mother's Rainbow Rays of Your Likeness"

"One thing remains Mother, my spiritual birthing:

234

My emergence through these Great Pillars
to claim my newness!

Just as Mother Mary birthed the Son ,
She birthed the Christ, The Son of God
The Child of Love and Peace .
Your Spirit appeared unto the
Earth through His birth!

As I pass through Your Pillars in my birthing,

I birth Splendor and Victory into the world.
I shine forth in Your Likeness

In my being, I honor You

I walk forward now before the
place of my inheritance."

Foundation

Angels lifted me and brought me to the Gateway Pillar called the Foundation. Its opalescent Rays fill the Universe with its glory! Those seeking entrance into the Presence of the Most High must pass through this Gate, it is the Gateway called the Christ, the Foundation.

The Christ, the Son of God came from His place in Heaven. It is here before the very Throne of God, He descended to give Himself for us. We must stand In Him to enter unto the Throne of God. I understood. The Angels backed away. No one can do this for or even assist the Initiate. There was silence in Heaven. All were waiting. From my soul came the words,

> *" I stand now before the Christ Light*
> *The Foundation of All Creation*
> *I now have choice:*
> *I may merge with the Light of Foundation if I choose*
> *To become ONE with this Light*

> *"I understand I become One with*
> *The Source of ALL Light*
> *The Source Of All Love*
> *The Source of All Creation"*

The Thundering Voice, now gentle with Love asked,

> *"My Daughter, do you desire to walk*
> *Within the Light, The Way of the Christ?"*

And in All truth and in all Love, I answered my Father,

> *"This I desire with all my being!"*

I heard,

"Then, go forth!"

I stepped into the Pillar of the Light of the Christ, to merge with the Light. Angels sang as the Glory of God became manifest within me. Throughout all of Heaven the Angels sang,

"Hear, Oh Hear, Oh Israel, The Lord Your God Is ONE"
Come now before His Throne in fear and in
trembling no more.
The way, the Gateway has come to you.
Broad is the path to destruction
Narrow is the Gate
Enter ye in to and through the Gate!!

A hand appeared above me and wrote upon my forehead these words spoken,

" Yod Hey Vau Shin Hey,
Yod Hey Vau Shin Hey,
Yod Hey Vau Shin Hey,"

The Name of God and The Christ was emblazoned into my forehead. Great rays emanated from my forehead to announce to all I AM a Child of God and have come through the Gate.

Sealed, I stood before the final Pillar,
The Throne of God, the Malkuth!

Malkuth

Standing before the 10th Pillar I heard,

"My Daughter of Light, it is not time now for you to
fully enter into the Presence, for to do so, you release
your physical life. You may, however, come forward."

I stepped forward into the Pillar known as Malkuth, or the Presence of God.

These words were spoken from The Highest

IAM ONE, IAM ONE, IAM ONE,
I AM

I spoke,

"I claim my inheritance before
El Elyon, God Most High
I have attained the Kingdom; I Am your Child'
Born of Mother'
Established in the Foundation'
I enter your Presence

Swept up into the Light I was wrapped in arms of pure love! I felt the Presence of Shekhina, my Mother as Mother and Father wrapped me in their embrace.

Under His wings, I am safely abiding. Once again, I heard the Voice speak,

"Go back and help the people"
So Be It!

I returned to a physical form within the Pillar. I was aware of a very great Angel standing beside me.

My hands went to my forehead, I said,
"ATEH"
Then below my feet I spoke the word
"Malkuth"
Then to my left shoulder I touched and spoke,
"Vegeburah"
Then touched my right shoulder saying
"Vegedulah"

Both hands came into prayer position at my chest, I said
"O Le am"
And I bowed before the God Most High saying,
"Amen"

Suddenly, I was outside the Pillars standing in the void between Heaven and Earth with the Angel.

The Angel looked at me and he said directly to me,

"NOW, DO THIS FOR THE PEOPLE!"

I jolted upright on my bed! Gasping for air and chocking, I drew in a deep breath! My first breath as a new creature, born again in her first breath of Life! My heart rumbled then jolted into a beat. I was back home in Manchester, New Hampshire. My body was in cold perspiration and I shook.

I moved, arose from my bed. Will was sleeping soundly. He'd not heard nor seen anything. I looked at his form. He was so peaceful. Angels have blessed him, I thought. I felt love for him and in my soul, knew.

I went out into the living room, picked up my wrap and stepped outside into the before dawn stillness. I slipped out of the house and walked down to the lake in a holy silence.

All was still and the stars were still shining brightly. I knelt down on the crisp snow glistening in the starlight. It reminded me of the Light of Heaven, but I was on Earth. I prayed,

"Father, HOW am I supposed to
do this for the people?
I shall, but please, show me how..
I love you so much and in my heart I am so thankful
that You have shown me Your Holy Truth."

239

He heard me. There, while kneeling in the snow I saw the ceremony. I would find circles and build the Kabbalah and walk the people through, just as I had been walked through.

This, I knew, was the sacred Initiation the Christ had undergone for the Second Birth. He did it for us.

Long forgotten, it was a sacred ceremony held in trust by the Masters of Israel. They, in the inner circles of the Masters, walked the Kabala just as I had. Jesus walked it in his physical body in the Temple also. That is why He was so shocked at Nicodemous' question. He ought to have known this.

Now, Father would have me to do this for the people. It would be restored in these last days before the Coming of Christ to take up His Bride. I understood now. His Bride is born again, in the likeness of the Mother, the Divine Feminine and the Child of God and Goddess. Child of the Shekhina and the Great I AM.. Now, it is to be offered to the people. I heard again,

"Go, and help the people."

I arose from kneeling in the snow and returned to my bed to sleep. I slid back in under the covers to sleep deeply. The body needed rest and care for the upcoming January 6th Feast of the Epiphany and the First Kabbalah Initiation.

I would trust that God would provide all that I needed to bring this Holy Second Birth from Heaven to Earth. The Temple of God within the heavens is shown to us here on Earth.

It is in the writings of old:
Men knelt before the Shekhina before the Ark of the

Covenant to find Mercy
The earthen Temple of Solomon was built with
gemstones and pillars,
Its template is within man as the chakras of gemstone
color tell the story.
It is in our sacred geometry. It is in the seed of life.It is
in the flower of life;
It is all around.

Oh, let me not be blinded by what I can see,
but let my heart guide the way;

It is in the Kabala, The Jewel IS in The Lotus!

© *Goddess Kuan Yin by Susan Isabelle*

Kuan Yin's Vow
I shall remain on the Earth plane
until all sentient beings

241

Chapter XV
HOW?

The telephone was ringing. "Hello?' I answered and heard,

"Yes, I'd like to speak to Susan Isabelle."
"This is she."

"Well, I was given your name and I'd like to offer you an opportunity. I represent the New York Whole Life Expo that is held each year in New York. We have had a cancellation and would like for you to come and lecture and have a booth, if you so desire. We generally have about thirty thousand visitors to our event each year. Would you like to come?

"Yes," fell out of my mouth. "When is it?" I asked.

"I know this is really short notice, but its January 13th 2001. Please, we'd love to have you come!"

I thought for a moment, that was only a week after the Kabala initiations. "Spirit, do you want this?" I asked silently.

A resounding ,"Yes!" came to my being. I answered the man, "Yes, I will come."

"Oh, Good! Thank you! What will you be speaking on?"

"The Goddess In the Kabala, The Path To Ascension" was the reply. It was the first time I'd ever said it!

He exclaimed, "Wow! That's a great topic and is sure to get you a number of participants to your lecture!"

The first announcement to the world would be in New York City, the home of the greatest population of the Hebrew community in America. That was important as the Kabala clearly has Hebrew roots. Yes, I would go, somehow.

The next few days I wrote. The New Year was just around the corner. A book was forming. It was necessary to have it at the Expo. The people must know of this. Notes came into form as pages of a book appeared, editing would not even be necessary.

The Initiation would be held on the 6th as planned in the downstairs of a large chiropractic office. It was the largest space I could find. The Kabbalah would stretch out at least thirty feet in length with Pillars formed of Light and symbols for each participant.

Hurry! Hurry! Hurry! The Spirit moved things so fast! Before I knew it, a complete manual was formed, the Initiation was recorded and a book was on its way to a printer! Amazing!

Goddess Creates

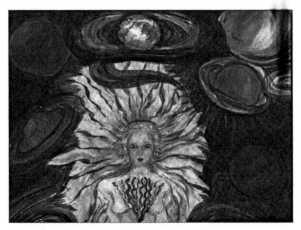

Susan Isabelle

Initiation January 6th 2001

Seventeen people arrived on the day of the first Kabala Initiation. I was dressed in pure white as Spirit had shown I must do. The Kabala was formed on king sized white sheets spread over the floor and candles lit the circular disks with symbols upon each to hold the energy of the pillars.

Two large pillar candles stood to represent the entrance of humanity into physical form from the ethers long ago. Each participant would enter here, into the pillar called Strength or the Athena. An assistant was named to help me. I knew once I entered the Initiation Kabala, I could not leave. There would be wine, water, and at the stations of the Kabala each person would have the symbols and the phrases I had spoken; but now, they would have to complete the Initiation. Once I entered, I could not leave. This is Holy Ground.

The Initiation started with a cleansing performed by my assistant before anyone could enter. Mother Mary was very present at each cleansing. The air was filled with the scent of roses. Each was anointed with frankincense and myrrh.

After the cleansing, when the participant was able, the assistant guided the Initiate over between the two pillar candles of fire. Remembrances of past lives occurred here for many. They saw their past and all that had been done by them in other lives and places. Many cried and trembled at the visions given them. This was not what they had expected. A full life review happened for most. It shook them to their very core!

244

Soon, I was to find that each Initiation took at least 45 minutes to complete. I was in the Kabala for nearly thirteen hours without stepping outside of the sacred area it formed. I had no knowledge of that at the time as I was in Spirit.

Many people came and stayed the entire time as miracle after miracle occurred! They found they could not leave and must watch and support the others entering into the sacred path of Enlightenment.

Once they walked forward through the first two pillars of fire, all the past was burned away and they were ready to enter into a newness that would change them forever.

Standing on the first pillar, they unexpectedly gasped the first Breath of Life from the Divine Mother! They received the symbols and the empowerments and felt the expansion of their energies as they 'grew' in height even as I had! Molecules were changed! Faces lit up with a new recognition of their Divine Inheritance that lay ahead!

They recited the words exactly as the words had been given to me in Heaven. By the time people made it to Shekhina they fell on their knees along with me to receive Her unto themselves. She descended upon them as She had promised.

Unable to stand, many felt the Angels come and lift them to their feet and hold them up as they went forward into their Second Birthing of Spirit!

We together called Her, "Shekhina, Most Beautiful!" We cried together as She transformed them into Light! Gasps from others watching were heard as many Initiates were visibly changed before their eyes! Magnificent! Holy! True!

Late into the evening, the Initiations continued. Angels were singing the songs of the High Holy days. Lights danced around the room and globes of light floated throughout the entire area. Each person received the Seal of the Child Of God in their foreheads as I had, and each became a new creature of God in Light and in all Love!

After midnight, I was driven home. Tomorrow would continue the teachings of Spirit! That night, I fell to my knees. I prayed and thanked Mother and Father for the wonder of all that had happened. I am so humbled and so in awe of Spirit! Heaven had come to earth!

The next morning, the Initiates happily arrived. This day would bring many gifts and all that Spirit had taught me from October's dancing Sun and Divine Feminine teachings, the symbols, and to December's deeper understandings of our mission on Earth.

Each participant had now been given the empowerment to ascend or to stay and assist others in their ascension. Universal consciousness of Divine truths now embodied seventeen persons of Light!

Now, all that remained was to teach the new energies. Holograms of Light and creation energies not to be spoken of at this time, were taught to the Initiates. They had been gifted with Divine Creation abilities as the Children of God. Now they were to learn how to use them and use the creative forces! One day, each person will be called upon to use these gifts as each is sealed by God's Name. As we worked with the symbols for the next two days and used the holograms, the stereo would not work. It shut itself off. When it did, singing of Angels began.

All of Heaven was rejoicing at the events occurring here on Earth! Everyone heard the Angels! One person even recognized the words of the songs as they were in Hebrew, her native language!

Finally, when it was time to go home, Spirit 'pulled the plug" on my physical empowerment, extraordinary strength and knowledge. It was time for Susan to sleep. I did, well into the next day. January 6th, the Feast of the Epiphany was truly that! We all came into awareness and had our own epiphany! We had stood in the very Presence of Malkuth, the Divine Presence, and were forever changed! 2006

 Author's Note: To all who feel that you are called to do enter into the Kabala Initiation, I encourage you to seek God's direction and purification of heart, mind, and soul. I will once again offer the Kabala Initiation at the sacred Mountain of Mount Shasta in California. Spirit has brought me here to begin the Initiations for the People of Ascension.

Now, you have understanding: Walk in wisdom.

Susan Isabelle

New York January 2001

Lillian, Rhonda and Janice were waiting for me at the Center. We were on our way to the New York Expo where the first announcement of the Goddess in the Kabala would be sent out into the world. I would have a small booth and would also be doing activations to the crystal skull El Aleator to help to set more of the Goddess energies to as many as wished to hold the frequency.

The books looked great and I would be giving the lecture. So much had happened in such a short time, my head was spinning. We drove the six hours into New York and located our hotel. The great Twin Towers were visible from our balcony and we hurried to set up our booth.

As we rode upwards in the elevator, all four of us felt it! A slow roll of the building began. The doors of the elevator opened and we stepped out into the long hallway. The floor was lifting and swaying.

The Earth was so unstable! Why wasn't anyone noticing? People seemed oblivious to what was going on around them and right under their feet. We wondered if it was safe for us to stay at the hotel.

Then I saw him. A Maya man was standing at the end of the hallway. He nodded, sent out a telepathic message to me, and I knew we would be OK. He was standing guard for us. He'd just told me so. The Earth continued to rise and fall the entire weekend and during the expo. The women who were with me assisted but were very worried and nervous.

The lecture went well and many people found their way over to the small booth. They had so many questions!

They took home activated crystals of their own. Goddess energies were needed here!

Something was going to happen in this place. I didn't know when or what, but the reality on which New York set had absolutely no base beneath it. The energy here reminded me of Cape Cod and I wanted to leave. A man approached my booth toward the end of the day.

"Susan, I need to speak to you." He looked concerned. I recognized him from the audience at my lecture. "I *have* to speak to you!"

I got up and walked to the dining area with him. He was distinguished and was a television anchor man. I recognized him. He lived here in New York City.

"What can I do for you?" I asked curious.

"I know you feel it. I know you know," he said. "I can't stay here anymore!" He blurted out his distress. He too was feeling the swaying, changing reality in this place. Everyone else seemed to be oblivious to it.

"My work has been to stabilize the area but I can't do it anymore! I have to leave! This place is going to go down!" He cried. As we spoke he revealed he was a Master who had come to New York to hold the space, but he was unable to do so much longer. He was ready to pack up and leave.

"Please", I said , "don't do that! There are so many here! The Maya are holding the space also with you, I saw and spoke to them." I let him know of our experiences. He agreed to have a further talk after the expo was over. I would try to help as I could.

I went back to the conference center and continued activations with the crystal skull El Aleator. I kept him in my small pouch that was hung around my neck. I'd hold him over the crystal or skulls of others at the expo and transfer the energies and the knowledge into their crystals from El Aleator. I did this time after time.

Suddenly, I felt tremendous serge of energy come into me from El! My hand went to my chest, over his pouch. The pouch was completely empty! The crystal was *inside* of me! I could feel it inside my chest, pulsing, but it was completely gone from my pouch! I looked up at the long line of people who were waiting for me to do activations. I had a moment of panic, but them was comforted; somehow I knew it would be 'OK'. I wondered, could I continue to activate others?

I called the next person in line. He sat in front of me just as all the others before him. I reached up to Heaven to ask for permission for the empowerment of the Great Library of Knowledge to come to him. It came in fullness. Yes, we could still do this!

I then called the Maya Lords of Light to set the thirteen globes of light of the full thirteen crystal skull library in his crown. The connection was made from the Library by my directing the connection and saying,

"From your mind to their 'Mind',
For your good and the Highest Good of All of
Humanity."
Then,
"From your heart to their 'Heart',
For your good and the Highest Good of All of
Humanity."
"We will use these gifts for the Highest Good of A*ll*"

Then holding the his hands over the crystal skull I taught him how to summon the Angels by the Power of God and under His command, to help the student by El Aleator's Divine Gift to us.

Swirls of energy flowed! Yes, the energy flowed out from me from my heart center and filled the crystal of the student in a great wave of energy! This would be powerful, even more so than before. As wonderful as this was, I felt saddened. El Aleator was gone in the physical form I had come to love. I was crushed, but could feel him in my heart. I had come to depend on the little crystal. I had received so much from it over the past ten months! I wanted to cry, but I continued as Spirit led.

After the day was over, I sat with the announcer and we talked until 2 AM. He told me of his work and of his fears of New York. He agreed to stay for a while longer but would one day leave. It appeared there was nothing else he could do.

"I will send you strength and hold you in prayer." We parted into an unknown future. Upstairs, I told the women about El having de-materialized and they gasped!

"Susan, what are you going to do?"

"Well, there is nothing I can do." I sighed. "He was a gift and maybe that the time of his use is over on the physical realm. I don't know. I'm extremely tired. Let's go to bed."

It seemed as though my head had just hit the pillow, when I heard Obed shout at me,

"Susan, LEAVE NOW!"

I sat right up out my bed. Rhonda shot out of her bed next to me.

"Susan, did you hear that?" She screamed! "We have to leave right now!" We woke the other two women.

"Get UP! Get up! We've been told to leave now. No showers.Grab your things and let's go!" I began to stuff things into my bags. I threw on some clothing and began to get my shoes out from under the bed to put them on. I stopped and froze. Underneath the bed, between my two shoes lay El Aleator! My tiny crystal skull was back home!

"LOOK!" Look what I've found!"

Everyone gathered around to look at a miracle. Somehow El had rematerialized twenty floors higher in the hotel! It was beneath my bed, by my shoes, where I would be sure to find him! I turned him over and examined him. He was fine! I gave a word of thanks and then said,

"Let's get out of here!"

We were in the car leaving New York City, but something was wrong. 5:30 AM and there were no cars. Can you imagine New York without cars? We made our way onto the New Jersey turnpike and were confused. What's happening here? We wondered. Finally, we stopped at a gas station to get some coffee, yes, coffee, and spoke to the attendant about why there were no cars.

"Oh, don't you know?'

"Do we know what?" We asked warily.

"There's a big blizzard coming. Everybody's been told to stay home. See, it's already starting to snow."

"Oh, NO!" We all said. Looking outside, we could see the white sparkles in the air. To think about having to drive six hours home in a snowstorm; that would be impossible!

"We'll, just drive straight and hope to beat it out!" I said!

And we did! We made it home in record time, just ahead of the storm. It snowed for four days. New York was completely socked in. If we had stayed even a few more hours, we'd have been stuck there. Spirit knows! If we had left even an hour later than we did we'd have been stranded.

I often wondered about the TV announcer. Could he make it there? Would he stay to hold the energy? He was so afraid. He knew destruction was coming and all his efforts to hold the dimensional space were not enough. I prayed for him but I believe he left his post.

September 11, 2001 ......
The dreaded event occurred.

Late August came before I knew it. The summer was nearly over. One morning, a man walked into the Center. "I want to speak to Susan Isabelle," he said while looking straight at me.

"I'm Susan." I replied, all the while thinking, 'what could this man want with me?' I considered him. He had dark brown shoulder length hair, a moustache and deep penetrating black eyes. He wore a long dark overcoat, even in the warmth of summer. He glanced around to make sure no one was within hearing range.

"I am told that I need the Goddess energies and have come for them." He spoke quietly. He didn't want anyone to hear him. This man looked as though he was part of the Italian Mafia and that was the last thing I expected to hear from him!

"Let's come into my office." I said motioning to him.

I listened to his incredible story. He had extraordinary gifts. He told me he had been in 'communication with the other side.' He had psychic information that an event was soon to occur on the planet that would shake the world. He stated had been a physic in the military for twelve years and was highly skilled in remote viewing. He claimed he was a time traveler. He had also been instructed by his guides to find me and receive an Initiation.

I wasn't sure what of think of this person, he certainly did not look like anyone who'd want a Goddess Initiation, but Spirit said 'Yes.' The man appeared to be humble and sincere.

I told him were scheduled to do the Goddess In The Kabala Initiation shortly and he could come. I didn't know what that meant at the time.

This man was soon to become my constant companion, guardian, advisor, and friend in the work God had given to both of us over the next four years. We had a contract to fulfill and he would assist the work that was coming. Adama would have a few more "Assignments" that would require this man's skills to help me.

All too soon, I would be in need of the special, psychic gifts he possessed.

Just after the Labor Day weekend in early September, I drove out to the gem and bead store in Vermont by myself. I needed a break and I always enjoyed going through the beads. I love to make jewelry. It soothes my mind and is a great creative outlet.

On the way home I was singing in the car and just having a wonderful time enjoying the day!

Suddenly, I felt something come up behind my car! The car was engulfed by a squeezing, dark energy! It was squeezing the life out of me. It was suffocating me while I drove!

I could hardly breathe! I wanted to pull over, but I heard, "NO!" So speeding along at 65 miles per hour, I fought the dark presence!

With each breath I could muster I screamed,

> **"Kadosh Kadosh Kadosh!"**
> **"Kadosh Kadosh Kadosh!"**
> **"Kadosh Kadosh Kadosh!**
> **God, help me!"**
> I prayed!

"Holy, Holy, Holy is the Lord God of Hosts!"

The Kadosh Prayer is used to call in the Angelic Realm under the command of the Christ, and there is no higher cry for help! The help came and made the creature of darkness release me.

The dark presence let loose its grip and flew by me. It was so dark it looked like a black van had past me, but it flew straight up and into the sky.

As it flew past me I felt pure hatred and then I heard the words,

"Danny...... Rhonda........ THE CENTER!"

In this beautiful fountain that stood in the NH Shambhala Center, flowed healing waters from all over the world. In it were waters from;

The Chalice Well in England,
Nectan's Glen
The Water of Lourdes, France
Mount Shasta Panther Meadow
The Lemurian sacred Site In New Hampshire
Loc Du Moshel Canada
Belize Mopan River Sanctuary
And more....
People could come to the Waters for healing...

Now the Fountain is at Mount Shasta waiting for the time to reopen the flowing waters once again...
Soon!

"Oh! My God! It's after the Center!" I screamed. I pulled over and I called Dan.

"Dan! Are you alright?" I shouted as he answered his cell phone.

"Yes, Susan! I know why you're calling! It just attacked me and my wife. We were in the car on our way to Concord. It's gone now. We're OK. We did the Kadosh as you taught us!"

"Oh, Dan! I am so glad you made it. What was that thing?" I asked relieved.

"We don't know, but we don't ever want to experience anything like that again!"

"I'd better call Rhonda, it's headed her way and then the Center. I'll call you later!"

I then called Rhonda, but she never answered. I left a message. I didn't know I was already too late.

Within weeks, she would leave the Center as a different person emerged.*

Driving straight to the Shambhala Center, I got out and ran into the Temple. Before the Altar, I prayed for the Center and all who were associated with it. Whatever this thing was it was dark and it was coming at the People of Light! When I had finished praying, I walked out to my car and began driving down the street.

I heard Obed say,

"Get out and take a picture!"

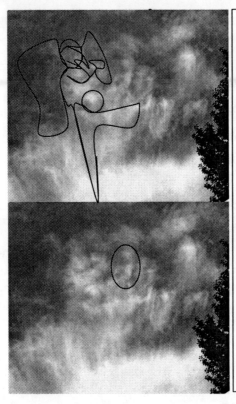

The misty forms of angels are in this picture. By the time the camera was ready, they had begun to disappear. The wings I outlined on the angel with a split beard.

Beneath him appears a small monk in robe outlined.

2nd picture shows the man figure with a Magi cap on. Robes and draping sleeves are seen throughout.

Many in the community saw them and came into the Center asking if I had seen them!

Oh, yes, I had!

A picture of what? I wondered as I pulled the car over into a side street. I was surrounded by tall buildings and was on a busy street. Getting out of the car, I held my camera and looked around, then up.

In the sky was the form of a very Great Angel. The angel was holding a green ball, or globe. The globe was shooting out a greenish ray at something that was flying away. I saw it! A black dragon. It was a black dragon creature fleeing away from the Center!

Across from the Angel was the form of three men. They looked like the pictures I have seen of the Magi at Christmas time. Behind them were Angels. I began snapping pictures, lots of them. God had sent out the forces and drove that thing away!

I went home elated!

*(I still pray for her, and know that all things eventually work to all our benefit. She is loved.)

The next day, Samuel came into the Center. He was a powerful Master of the Light. He was frantic.
"Susan! Susan! Who opened the gate?" "Someone has opened the gate!"

"I don't know", I answered. "I don't know. I was attacked as were another couple. I don't know." I showed him the pictures. "I hope that this will comfort you," I said, helpless to do any more. He was distraught.

"There is no comfort now. I will return." He sadly left.

It is always amazing to me who the Masters are that walk this planet. Believe me, you'd never guess. They hold tightly their true identities.

And then it happened.

We all watched at the Shambhala Center.
We cried at the replays of the Twin
Towers of New York falling,
We held one another as the planes crashed.
And we cried as people fell to their death and then
finally, the smoke and ash.

The loss of life was horrible, and we all felt the terror of our country. What had happened sent shock waves throughout the entire world. People were coming into the

Shambhala Center to pray and to cry for the Earth and all the peoples.

They brought Bibles, rosaries, crystals, flowers, and lay on the Temple's floor before the altar and just cried. I hugged them and cried too. I would not leave. Words were being spoken by high officials and people on the street that could have plunged us all into nuclear war. "NUKE- EM" was the sentiment on the street.

"They will pay!" The words from our government.

It didn't matter WHO, just "Nuke Em" "Make them pay!"

But, who is 'them?" No one knew.

The energy of the planet was spiraling downward into chaos. We all could face destruction should nuclear war erupt. I fell asleep in exhaustion on the Shambhala Temple's floor.

> "Susan, Al'Lat Le Andro Melchizedek!
> You must call on the Goddess!"

All three came to me, Adama, Melchizedek and Obed in my sleep state.

"This is what you have come for!" They spoke to me.

"How? How? What am I supposed to do?" I complained. I was discouraged. Goddess had come to the Earth, not to bring destruction, but to prevent this sort of thing from happening by changing the consciousness of the planet. So far, we weren't doing too well.
"Call on the Goddess!"
I awoke. I had the instructions! I ran to the computer to send out an urgent email to all those who had had the Goddess Initiation.

"COME! COME! To The Shambhala Center TONIGHT! We are going to call the Goddess!

You can just call me…
Any old time, you can call me….

"By using a combination of sounds, tones, and the written Names of God, that are actually materialized symbols of great power, we are able to call forth the Universal Energies to affect positive change to benefit and assist humanity"
Susan Isabelle

261

Chapter XVI
September 13th, 2001 7:00 PM

They all came, filing into the Shambhala Center in absolute silence. They were no longer students, but co creators in a new realm of energy work and the knowledge of the Goddess.

They had come tonight to assist in the transformation of consciousness of the planet and in the protection of Earth! They filled the Center beyond its capacity until there was only a small space left in the middle of the room where I had placed a white covering. Here, we would call Her.

The Priest of the Shambhala Temple would assist me in this, for it would require a male and a female to do what we were to do. I looked at him. Just over a year ago, this man stood in the rain and didn't get wet. This man cried in awe of the miracle of rain stopping above his head. He had been one of the first people to walk the Kabala on January 6th, 2001, the Feast of the Epiphany, eight months previously.

He had such a profound experience while in the Kabal, that it changed his life. Afterward, he had assisted me in all the Kabala Initiations. He had been present, assisting, All during the previous months.

Many people had been called to walk the Kabala into Second Birth. Spirit had prepared him for this night. He had been transformed. He had become a Melchizedek Priest. He looked too at all who had come. They now filled the Center and were waiting.

I placed in his large hands a paper on which I had written sacred words. The words were given by Spirit for us to speak; they were the *Call of the Angels of Mercy*. He towered over me in quiet gentleness.

We would recite the names of the Angels together, male and female power joined, and place the Angels around the Earth.

Twelve had been given. Twelve Angels would come I was told, when we called them.

I walked over to the white floor covering and began to pray. I prayed for all those who had lost their lives and their families. I prayed for the Earth and all those who dwelt in fear that night, not knowing if tomorrow would bring devastation.

Spirit led me to sit in a chair that had been reserved for me, so I sat. I could feel the Light from Goddess enter me and I began to expand in my Light. So much energy!!! I was filled and spreading outward, even beyond what I had felt in Belize, until my essence containing the Goddess Light that filled the entire room.

As it spread outward, it touched each person there, filling them. My crown chakras were so expanded I could see outdoors, I could see everything. I knew everything all at once, more than a human could contain. All knowledge of what I was to do, was instantly known. I looked over at John. Together, we would join this Light in the CALL. I nodded to him. We stood up.

We stood facing one another and I began to speak words I do not remember. Spirit filled my mouth with the words. As I spoke, the Earth began to manifest between us, spinning and glowing in Light above the floor about four feet in the air.

It seemed as though John and I knew the words from the past, for we found ourselves calling the Angels in unison, as if we had done this many times before. His strength, his power, formed the miracle and my feminine, the essence of Mercy, empowered it.

Twelve Angels of Purest Light from the realm of God's Heaven, from the very Throne of God appeared around the Earth. They had come!!! These were the Angels of Mercy!

We watched as the cords of the lower realms were cut. The Earth had been bound somehow to the lower realms. These cords held the people and the Earth, trapping the minds of the beings on the Earth. The Angels removed the cords.

Now the Earth ascended upwards and grew in its size between us. Now I would begin the call of the Goddess.

I began to sing tones over the Earth. I prayed and pleaded with Her.

"Come, Divine Goddess,
Place Your Spirit over the Earth.
OH, Bride of God and Beloved Shekhina!

Come, place your image over us.

Let Your Husband see you here!

Let Him protect his Beloved
Let Him remove the curse from Your Children!"

As the words were spoken, a mist began to envelope the Earth! A white shimmering glow swirled around the Earth! She was here! She covered the entire globe!!!

The globe of the Earth was now massive! It filled the room and we could not contain it between our hands. It expanded until I could not see it anymore, but felt as though I was inside the Earth!

The Voice commanded,

"Sit down!"

I fell back into my chair. John did also. I lost my consciousness for some time. I don't know how long. When John and I opened our eyes and returned into physical awareness, all the people were lying all over the floor and on top of one another. The force of the Light slay them and they lay as dead upon the floor of the Center. Then I heard the Voice.

"Arise!" *I stood.* **"Breathe!"**

Drawing in a great breath, I breathed out over the people. They awoke.

"What happened?"

They whispered to one another and untangled themselves from the floor. All appeared to be back to normal.

"Go now, quietly," I barely whispered.
"We will speak tomorrow."

Each picked up their belongings and left the Center. Very quickly , the Center emptied. Only two remained, the two women who had once spread the rumors about my "possession."

"Susan , we are being told to stay with you." They looked at me with pleading eyes.

"Yes, stay." I was exhausted and barely in my body. They drew up two chairs and faced me. They were concerned. The soft glow of candles lit the room. The three of us sat in silence. I was numb with the experience.

Suddenly, the entire room went completely black! There was no light at all! We couldn't even see one another! I gasped!

In the flash of a moment, I saw something in the darkness that will stay with me forever!

In the velvet blackness an "arch" appeared. Not just any arch, this arch was made up of hundreds of images of the Earth! It bowed out across the room between us! It was a great arch, one Earth touching the other.

Then I saw it! I whispered too shocked to speak words,

"Oh, my God!"

The third Earth in from the end of the arch was blowing up! I watched as the Earth exploded! Pieces and chunks of the Earth blew outwards as the Earth exploded from its core! Then, it was gone! A void was left between the former arch and the two Earths at the end.

There were two other earths beyond the explosion!

Just as I saw this, the lights in the room came back on.

The three of us momentarily stared at each other in shock.

> "Oh, NO!" Sue said then jumped up
> and ran to the front door.
> "OH, My God! Come see!"

Kathy and I jumped up and ran to the door with her. Sue was trying to open the door, but she couldn't.

Outside, the sidewalk and the entire
parking lot was tipped sideways.

We couldn't open the door. The sidewalk blocked the opening as it was halfway across the door!

We started to feel panic, but something was overpowering our ability to move. We looked at one another. We didn't speak. At that moment we were filled with a compulsive need to sleep. We dragged ourselves silently to the altar in the center room and lay down on the mats that had been left on the floor. We passed out.

At 5:30 AM we 'landed!' With a resounding thud, the shaking caused the bookshelves and room divider to fall over onto us. We groggily crawled out from the books and shelves and were stupefied, standing looked at one another.

As on cue, we all together ran at once to the front door to look out.

Everything was normal. Absolutely normal. The sidewalk was back in its place and the sun was shining already, its early morning rays. It looked beautiful!

It was going to be a beautiful day!

"What happened?" Are we still here?" Sue asked.

"I think we saw a reality of Earth blow up. It exists no more. I think that was us…."I whispered.

"How come we're still here?" asked Kathy. I looked at both of them, then thought aloud,

"I think that we were transported into a world, a reality of Earth that exists

TWO DAYS INTO THE FUTURE!!!!!!"

I stopped to consider the words spoken through me, for they were not mine. I was being given understanding even as I spoke to the two other women.

"Remember the two earths that were beyond the one blowing up?" They nodded.

"Somehow, we've been placed into another realm, *a future realm.*" I stopped in the realization of it. I bowed to give thanks.

"Thank You Goddess! Thank You Father!"

I continued, "The Father loves the Goddess so much, that in the other realm, it could not exist. We've been given another chance. I believe that on the old world, we blew ourselves up."

I wondered how that had happened for a moment, but was told not to dwell on that.

> *"God in His mercy has loved us enough to give us another*
> *chance, another reality.*
> *Pray to God that we don't destroy this one too!"*

Together, as we discussed the miracle, we lay on the floor beneath the altar, rested and were in our own private thoughts. What did this mean? Were we still going to have our families?

So many thoughts; but so many thanks went up from the three of us. Maybe we were the only three people on this new Earth? No, there were cars outside. We could hear them passing by. Did anyone else know what had happened? None of us could leave the Center. We couldn't. Our legs would not take us.

Before too long, those who had been with us the previous night began to return to the Center. Sue, Kathy and I told the story many times over.

"Yes, they were OK." The students told us. "No, they hadn't felt anything."

But all felt they had to come to the Center for some compelling reason. Now they knew why. All felt new hope and encouragement.

All of a sudden, a student named Karen jumped up and startled shouting,

> "I have to go outside! I have to go
> outside and take a picture!"

She began to fumble around in her bag to find the camera she had brought with her. She grabbed it and ran outside the Center. We followed her out side and looked up.

"I heard someone tell me to come outside!" She exclaimed as she began rapidly snapping pictures. We could see why.

The entire sky was filled with Angels. A great Lotus spread itself out over the sky. Cherubs were in the sky looking down on us.

A great Eye, just one, looked down at the tiny people below who were looking up. God was looking at us!

Karen ran around with the others snapping pictures. The other shop keepers in our mall came out to see the glory above them too!

269

Angels! Angels were in the sky above us and an image of a woman formed. She held a Dove in her outstretched hands, her black hair flowing. Kuan Yin! Kuan Yin was over the Center!!!!

**The Third Earth back was blowing up:
But, with the help of all Heaven,
we had moved it two days into the future!**

Everyone was jumping for joy! When the pictures were developed we were ecstatic to see Kuan Yin was in the sky! Her arms were outstretched and the Dove of Peace was taking flight from her hands. The great lotus we had seen, was in her heart center.

Kuan Yin in the sky over the Shambhala Center in Manchester NH on September 14, 2001

Photo by Karen Rocklin-Weare

We had been saved! I cried tears of joy!

The Lotus had spread across the sky that day, a promise of a new creation, a new day!

So many people began to come to the Center and every day was a miracle! I soon wondered,

"Adama, what shall I be doing next?" I asked

"Al'Lat rest for now...
The challenges that lie ahead are many...

Know this;
I am the created son of the Highest, Adam, the father of the nations through Seth, the Righteous Child

Susan Isabelle

Upon the raising of the Son Of God in perfection
I walked the streets in my ascended form
Freed from the bindings.
I come to humanity,
The Children of My Loins
That I may show them
The True and Holy Gate

I look to my children to complete the
Divine Order:
Go forth and multiply
Love God with all thy heart, mind, and soul,
and thy neighbor as thyself

Rest now Child of Peace

I will come to you shortly
for your next assignment......"

272

Quote from Jeremiah Selogy's upcoming new book,

Akashic Karmic Lords In A Strange Land

"A call has gone out to those souls so long awaited
their 1st love's return to their life be lived:
Echos that tear away the veils of illusions threshold

"HEAR ME NOW!"

That voice calling that has called for so long, it echos:
Ring of the King, fuzzy buzz in your inner ear's domain,

Spirit Calls!

A radiance spans the Infinite Lightyear Spectrum of
Kingdom Come,
The builders have given all...
God Speed to their task at hand be fulfilled!

The governing Order of Truth has laid the foundation,
The walls have been raised by the power of The ONE,
all and every building block sealed

Rainbows of God's Promise in the blink of an eye

Come Forth!
Children of the Kingdom!

All shapes, sizes, and colors form a gathered Nation

Universal- Nation- Infinite- Christ-Omnipotent-
Righteous- Nation
'U.N.I.C.O.R.N.'

OH, BELOVED OF GOD!
Omnipotent Divine Creation

273

Chapter XVII

Understanding the Aspects of the Goddess as She has been revealed on Earth

Below you will find the ways that Goddess has manifested on Earth to many peoples and cultures. All cultures have a Goddess; a mate to God. Allah, has Al'Lat, Shiva has Shakti.

It is the knowledge of the Goddess who can unite the peoples for She is mercy and compassion to all and is known to all cultures.

The names are really not important that we give to Goddess in our own native tongues. But the aspects that flow out from the Heart of Goddess, down to us on this dimension and that are manifest reflections of who She is, are very important.

We need to know and recognize them. Why? So as to develop these qualities within our souls and to enter into a higher way of relating to one another and to the earth.

Below you will see an example of each of the Kabala positions represented by a name of a Goddess. Athena could also be called many other names, all representing the QUALITY of Strength and LIFE BREATH.

Let's learn from the Goddess.

Athena,
Her first Aspect:
Physical Birth
Be strong! Survive!
Have fire in your soul!
Breathe!
Strive,
Grow, GROW! GROW!!!
Attain Understanding under Her guidance Gain
Wisdom!!
Kabala: Kether

Goddess Aspect: Warrior Aspect, Strength, Breath
of Life

Symbols: Owl, Sword and Shield,

Stone :Ruby, garnet

Colors: Red

Chakra: Root, Physical Life

Sophia,
Second And Third Aspect
Growth and return of Higher Consciousness
Gain Understanding
Gain Wisdom

Wisdom: Understanding: We spend our entire lives seeking wisdom. "Above all things", Solomon wrote, "Seek wisdom. Build Her Temple within!"

This is the Sophia, consciousness that has left the home above and has lost its way. Read the Pistis Sophia, of the Gnostic scriptures, to understand the descent we all have made into the lower realms. Our consciousness fell.

"All have fallen and come short of the Glory of God!" Your minister would say.

Yes, it is true. It fell so far down into the lower realms that it can't figure out which way is truly "up!"
Without the Light of the Christ in the Mercy of Goddess action toward Her children reaching down to give us of the True Light, we could not rise upward to ascend.

Lessor lights attract us in deception. Physical needs for survival overwhelm the soul. We must seek the Malkuth, the Presence of God and the Shekhina! THAT *IS* WISDOM!

Her symbol is the Mystic Star and the Seven Pillars of Wisdom. The Mystic Star is in constant motion: So must we be, seeking Wisdom. Seeking progression from red to orange.

Kabala: Binah,
Goddess Aspect: Wisdom and Understanding

Symbols: 7 Pillars of Wisdom, 7 pointed Mystic Star
Seven Stars in our crown
Stone : Carnelian, agate, Hyacinth
Colors: Red, orange, yellow hues
Chakra: Navel Plexus, Relationships

Forth Aspect
Kuan Yin, known as the
Goddess of Compassion

Once you have attained Wisdom, you may then be empowered to birth Compassion in your heart. A soul that is striving for survival, fighting for ego, cannot hold the energy of Kuan Yin's compassion for others as it is so involved in self promotion and competition. That soul is not yet prepared to express Her tender mercy.

Usually, the lessons leading up to the expression of Mercy in the soul are lessons which require one "walk in another's shoes" and often are the result of many life varied experiences-the result of Wisdom learned by experiences. Through our experiences we learn to have compassion on others. We evolve through this aspect to a more 'godly life' and expression of the Goddess.

Kuan Yin is represented as a Rainbow. The rainbow is the symbol of God's compassion to the earth. Kuan Yin and has taken a vow to "remain on the earth plane until all sentient beings come into enlightenment."

She does not require we take this vow, but to fully understand our role and responsibility to help others along the way. That Way is one of our expressions of compassion to others we meet in our lives.

She gives her Nectar of Compassion in our hands and the ability to give to others. Of many eyes, we see the condition of mankind.

Our open, lotus mind becomes a place of creation.

Kabala: Chesed
Goddess Aspect: Mercy and Compassion
Symbols: Peacock, Rainbows, Lotus
Stone :Tiger Eye, Jade Green
Colors: Yellow, brown, rainbow
Chakra: Solar Plexus,
Place of Decision/Will Center of Humanity, Heart Of
Compassion Connection

Fifth Aspect
Ix Chel, Earth Goddess
Our Compassionate Responsibility;
To preserve the Earth for Future Generations

Ix Chel is represented by the Moon and is known as a Moon Goddess, but in actuality, she is an Earth Goddess who cares for the earth, viewing the whole from her place on the Moon. Ix Chel represents the aspect of Dominion, or responsibility of the Earth. She has wisdom to see the "whole picture". Her heart is with her sister energy GAIA who bears us on her body.

According to the Maya, She pleads with her husband CHAC for the rains and the birth of spring on the earth. She is the embodiment of Compassion. Her place is of Severity but rather withholds the hand of the Father's severity due to ignorant mankind and ever pleads for us as an Earth Mother. Goddess of fertility, of birth, mothers and children she secures life on the planet. Ix Chel message to us as we stand in Her Pillar, is to take our place on the earth as She has and to preserve life, all life. From frogs to trees, to animal to humanity, the preciousness of life requires we take up our responsibilities using her energies.

For those who desire it, She gives gifts of the powers of the Sun and the Moon., representing all realms of Heaven. The Symbols she gives you are the basis of all life. You will have dominion over them all, and balanced with Compassion, you are now ready for your Second Birth.

Kabala: Geburah
Goddess Aspect: Dominion
Symbols: Water, rainbows, corn, herbs snake
Stone : Onyx, brown flourite
Colors: Rainbow, brown, blues of water
Chakras: Solar Plexus Decision/Will Center
Root, Grounding To Earth Heart Chakra, Compassionate
Action Toward the Earth

Sixth Aspect
The Goddess and Spiritual Rebirthing
Shekhina, Tiferet, Beauty

The Soul, now integrated its physical being, has attained higher learning and understanding. In addition, the soul has begun to use its knowledge in the progression of mankind and of the earth.

An unseen hand was guiding all the while, connecting events and experiences, bringing them into our conscious being. That One has held us, guided us, nurtured us as our Mother and prepared us for the next journey.

That silent One is Shekhina. It is Shekhina, the Glory of God which hid the old Testament Priest and the people from the wrath of God before the Ark of the Covenant, as a covering, protecting luminous cloud.

Once there, the people knew they could approach God, because She is Mercy. She is the Holy Spirit. She loves and protects us. She is the Bride of God that indwells within us when we bear her likeness.

She is represented by the Dove, the Dove which showed itself above the Christ when he arose from the waters of baptism. At that moment, the Christ showed us what it meant to be born again.

"You must be born of Water and of Spirit," He said.
The Teacher who had come to Him asked,
"What? Shall I again enter my MOTHER'S womb?

The answer is YES!

You must be born of the Spirit through the waters of physical life, of knowledge, wisdom, love, compassion, mercy and then the Spirit.

"You must be born of water and of
Spirit" according to Jesus.

You must first stand within Her to be remade. Once remade in this womb, you must be birthed. You must pass through the Pillars, the 'birth canal' of Mother once again, even as Christ did, both physically and spiritually. Just as we passed though our physical mothers 'pillars' or legs at our physical birth we birth spiritually. He showed the way to us;

How can Spirit have 'legs'?
The 'legs' are the 'pillars' of the Kabala.

It is within Shekhina that the soul is prepared for the Second Birth. The Birth of the Spiritual Being is through the Pillars of the Second Mother, Mary.

What are the Kabala pillars of the second birth?
Splendor and Victory.

It is through Mary's Blue Pillars that we pass through and attain Splendor and Victory

Note: In most publications of Cabalistic teachings, Shekhina is shown in the place of Kingdom: This is also true, but Her place is the place of Beauty.
She is Most Beautiful Goddess! In my experience in the Temple, this is where Shekhina stood, then joined in the Kingdom with the full Aspect of God..
It is She who births Her children, and is the Eternal Womb.

Kabbala: Tipareth
Goddess Aspect: New Life
Symbols: Rainbows, The Dove
Stone :Emerald
Colors: Green, Rainbow
Chakra: Heart Center
Gateway to the Higher Aspects is the Heart Chakra, to
that of throat, communication, 3rd eye, thought and
Crown

Seventh and Eighth Goddess Aspects Mother Mary Pillars of Splendor and Victory.

Just as when we stood in the heavens waiting to be born into the physical, we wondered what our life would be like? We wondered about our parents, our hair color, the experiences we would have as a living soul!

Once we have been remade in Tipareth, The Divine Womb, we have the same questions, the wonderment and the excitement! We birth *into* a new life. That life awaits us. How shall we live?

We are given the rays of Splendor at this birth;
We are given the Rays of Victory at this Birth.

This time, however, instead of a physical birth, we are about to come forward into a whole new Being- of the Holy Spirit Sheknina. We are given Her Symbols as representation of who and what we are.

We receive Her empowerments:
As She birthed Love into the world, so shall we.
Mother and Father have made us in Their Image.

The labor has been long and hard, we have had many obstacles. By our willingness to pass through these pillars, we show our willingness to reach a new level of maturity, a spiritual maturity.

Given the likeness of our Mother, we carry now the Rainbow Rays of her Being. We have survived, attained Wisdom, Mercy and Severity tempered by Love: our

285

Susan Isabelle

stripes, our colors through our lives in the physical. We carry them as a Rainbow about our auras.

Her colors are within us as her children.

We are about to be born into the New Realm of Spirit; Endowed Beings, of Spirit.

A whole 'new creature' one of the apostle's claimed. Yes, a New Being. Mary Birthed The Son of Love, so we too are birthed into Splendor and Victory. Then, Foundation Awaits us at this Birth.

Kabbala: Hod, Slendor; Netzach, Victory
Goddess Aspect: Splendor and Victory
Symbols: Maltese Cross, Sun
Stone :Sapphire and Blue Topaz
Colors: Blue as the Sky, Blue as the Ocean
Chakra: Throat and Third Eye
We may see and speak the words of Beauty

The Gateway
Kabala Position: Foundation

As we walk symbolically through the Pillars of Mary, we are showing our progression of Spirit. Once through the Pillars we have a choice to make. Simply put, do we desire to walk through and into the Foundation? Just what is the Foundation?

Why is the Gateway so narrow?
Just as physical Athena birth was a narrow step into the unknown, so too the Pillar of Foundation is narrow. Narrow is the gateway that leads to the Presence of God. Remember Jesus also said,

"Broad is the path to destruction and narrow is the gate?" He was speaking of the Kabala and the narrow gateway.

The Foundation is the final culmination of all the colors, of all possibilities of those born of the Light, the Spirit. The colors of Foundation are opalescent; they shine at the slightest ray of Light. The Source of that Light is the Christ Light energies.

Those energies are the Foundation of all Creation. Opalescent Rays flow out from here. Those joining the Christ Light energies, are joining the Foundational Being of Physical Being and of Spirit- Being. Radiance that is so beautiful flows from here!

Foundation is Partnership with God. We are adopted into the Family through our agreement. It is acting out in our physical and spiritual being in accordance with the principles of Light. It is acknowledging the work of Spirit in our lives and responding to it in peace and joy. We agree to radiate the Light to all.

Why "Christ?" Isn't that too, "Christian?" You ask? Christ means a circle of Light. Eternal Light that was formed at the first 'round' of the creation of this universe is called the Vesica Pisces. All things came into being through this light, sound and vibration. A good study of sacred geometry will help you to understand this in more detail. I would recommend the reading of Drumvalos' books, *"The Ancient Secret of the Flower Of Life"* to better grasp the concepts of the true Christ Light.

He was the first born of Mother/Father, *the Vesica Pisces*. He is the fullness of Them.

He was the One in pure consciousness who came in physical form as a man on Earth to secure the Right for Humanity to pass through Him into God Presence, Malkuth.

He has that right in both physical and Spirit formation and offers that to us in all Love.

He passed all the Initiations;

He was the first to make it all the way through.

He became the gateway for all those that would follow.

He walked this Kabala in the Temple and in the Temple of His Physical Being.

He fulfilled it all in total perfection, for He is God and the only One able to fulfill the wholeness of the Kabala *without faltering.*

Where we have not been able in our physical being to do this, He has. He did it in the physical. He paved the way for us through Him. Through Him, we are offered the Gift.

It is a *gift* to those who grasp the opportunity. To understand this is to have great Wisdom, far above rubies. Far above our physical life; Wisdom.

Those entering through this Gateway are in the Likeness of Spirit and are allowed through by His having secured it for us. God sees His Son in His likeness over us. God sees the Shekhina in Us and the Likeness of His Beloved. We are allowed into the Divine Presence as His Son and Daughters.

We are operating in the physical at the highest spiritual
levels as the New Man/Woman that have secured a
Second Birth through Spirit.
Foundation,
The Christ Light, is the Foundation of All of Creation
The Foundation is the Gateway to the Kingdom.

Kabala: Yesod
Foundation Aspect: Entrance, Gateway
Symbols: Cross, Sun, Heaven's Pure White Light
Stone : Pearls and Diamond
Colors: White
Chakra: Crown Ascension Chambers of the Mind

Tenth Kabala Position
The Kingdom
Malkuth

"The Kingdom of God is within you" Jesus

The Kingdom/Shekhina is the soul, the mind, energy and Spouse in *complete harmony* with her male Counterpart, becoming the fullness of God. This is not new information. The Shekhina is well known throughout all time.

It is said that in the Targum of Onkilos an Aramaic version of scripture dating 130 AD, gave the name *Shekhina* where later authors substituted "name"

Deuteronomy 12:5
"God shall choose that His Shekhina may dwell there, unto the <u>house</u> of the Shekhina shall you seek."

Malkuth, the Kingdom is Kingship.
Seek the House of Shekhina.
Malkuth is where She resides with Her Mate.

It is here that we acknowledge that God Is God.
Praise and Glory and Worship are God's
For we are a creation of the Hand of God.

With the words of our mouth we say the Prayer of the Kabalistic Cross and confirm our worship.

Here we are crowned in Glory and take our stand as the Child of God in all inheritance obtained. Here we may choose to reunite with God and linger, or choose to return to physical being.

Kabbala : Malkuth
Kingdom Aspect: Presence of God
Symbols: Heaven's Pure White Light, Purple of Royalty,
Robe of Son-ship and Daughter
Stone :Amethyst
Colors: Purple
Chakra; Crown and Soul Star, Open Rainbow Lotus

Chapter XVIII
The Kabalistic Prayer

The following prayer is the one used at the end of the Initiation. As I have continued my research about the prayer, I have found it has been known and used for centuries by the saints. This is the prayer I sang with the angel at the Kingdom, I just didn't understand the Hebrew! Together we sang and rejoiced as you will also. I encourage all to learn and practice it on a daily basis as the power grows with the repeated use.

After a week or so of using the prayer and the body motions you will feel the upward motion and expansion of your energy. This will happen even if you've never had an Initiation!

It is beautiful! Your heart will swell to overflowing in the Glory of it!

Prayer for Kabala Integration
Kabalistic Cross

Stand or sit with one hand over the
third eye, say, sing or tone
Ateh

Draw the hand down the front of the body to the root
chakra location, say, sing or tone
Malkuth

Bring the hand up to the right shoulder, say, sing or tone
Vegeburah

Bring the hand up to the left shoulder, say, sing or tone

Vegadulah

Bring both hands together in prayer
position, say, sing or tone

Le'Olahm

Open arms wide and say, sing or tone

Amen

Ateh (Yours-God's)	AHHH TAAA	For Thine
Malkuth Kingdom	MALLL KUUUU TH (Is the Kingdom)	The
Vegeburah (And the Powers are His)	VA GA BUR RAAAAH	The Power
Vegedulah (And the Glory is His)	VAAAGAAAA DU LAAH	The Glory
Le Olahm (Now and Forever!)	Lay….OOOOO…..LAhim	Forever
Amen (So Be IT)	AAA MENNNNN	Amen,

So Be IT!

Testimonials

I think the following narratives will describe the Initiation better than I can as it comes from the perspective of students and Initiates.

She writes:

I did not sleep the night before. My soul was so excited I could feel the anticipation. This is what "we" had been waiting for.

That morning we were experiencing a New England snowstorm and there were cars off the road and accidents everywhere. I was determined that nothing would stop me from getting to New Hampshire from Massachusetts that day not even a snow storm! I prayed all the way asking for protection. If this was a test, it was a good one! I was to soon know that it was well worth my efforts.

The initiation started with a special cleansing by Mother Mary facilitated by Rhonda. As I received this and was waiting for my initiation to start, my hands literally shook with the energy for 10-15 minutes. My hands were on fire! Rhonda whispered to me, "I know that you're healings will never be the same after this."

I stood in front of Susan Isabelle for my initiation into the Kabbalah and she said my name, "Janice", my heart was beating rapidly.

I knew this was BIG! As I approached to receive each of the Goddess energies, I felt as if I lifted from the ground.

My body swayed back and forth. I was floating! I almost fell over. When I approached to receive from Mother Mary the tears came to my eyes. It finally hit me that I had made it!

As I stepped into the kingdom, I literally was standing in the presence of God. The light embraced me and lifted me up. It was the most amazing thing I had ever experienced!

*As I hugged Susan Isabelle, I wept as a little babe would...
tears of joy. I was born. Rhonda again whispered to me, "He
will always be by your side now. He will never leave." I
hugged her and cried some more.*

*The second day was the empowerment. Susan's stereo
would not play at all and then magically it went on when
Spirit wanted it to go on. I feel as though I had a total "out
of body" experience. I was aware that I was in the room, but
I literally could not move. I felt as though I was being held
up by someone behind me. I went in and out of the conscious
state coming back into the room and then leaving again.*

*As empowerments were put into my hands, they were
being lifted up then gently placed down in my lap. I could
not lift my hands, but I was "assisted". I have no recollection
of where I went.*

*There were a couple of students taking pictures. There
were little white holiday lights set up and in the pictures they
were in Rainbow colors not white!*

*As we were working with the new energies on each other,
Susan came over and said,*

"Do you hear the angels singing?"

I said, "I thought it was the stereo." It wasn't.

*The angels had come to sing their joy of our completion
of the first RA-In_Bow class.*

It was beautiful! It was magical! We were in heaven!

Our lives will never be the same.

Love, Janice L

Susan Isabelle

From Karen's perspective

My journey on this earth has included travel to other US States and to foreign countries. I have experienced a variety of cultures and landscapes. In the past few years, my travels have taken me to an inner world and spiritual dimension. Visions of my soul's landscape color my world.

In January of 2001, Susan Isabelle held a weekend seminar welcoming in the new feminine energies, Ra_In_ Bow. The initiation ceremony was beautiful, spiritual and emotionally moving. The initiation was a journey through the energies of the Goddesses. I sat and watched my peers go through the initiation. I was filled with so many feeling. I connected with each lightworker as they went before me. I was the last to participate. The ceremonial room was magical. Candles were casting dancing shadows.

Rhonda prepared me for my initiation with special energies. I had the wonderful scent of roses. It was profound. I was now ready. As I moved through the pillars, I connected with each Goddess. Each Goddess connected her energy with me. Kuan Yin was most powerful. I connected. The smell of evergreen was all around me. My spirit was moved. My heart was filled with love. The initiation was complete.

I heard angels sing. The sound was faint but perceptible. I was filled with awe. My initiation was powerful. My creativity was magnified. I am an artist.

The Goddesses have blessed me with inspiration.!

Respectfully ,Karen Rocklin-Weare,
Shambhala Reiki Master

Postscripts

An Email from England

Subj: 13 OCTOBER 1917 - FATIMA - THE SUN
CAME DOWN
Date: 10/11/00 7:49:32 PM Eastern Daylight Time
From: (World-Action)
Reply-to: xxxxxx.uk

FATIMA

13 OCTOBER 1917
On the 13th October 1917, in the presence of 70,000
people, a miracle happened in the sky above FATIMA
at the exact moment and in the precise spot that the
three children had announced earlier.
Witnesses reported:

The SUN appeared to actually DANCE in the sky and
seemed to fall to the ground before resuming its normal
place in the heavens

Chapter XIX

The Colors of God's Kingdom
Gemstones, Chakras, And The Kabala

From the Catholic Bible, Tobit's Praise ; Tobit 13

" My spirit blesses the Lord, the great King;

Jerusalem shall be rebuilt as his home forever.

Happy for me if a remnant of my offspring survive
to see your glory and to praise the King of Heaven!

The gates of Jerusalem shall be built
with sapphire and emerald,

and all your walls with precious stones.

The towers of Jerusalem shall be built with gold;

The streets of Jerusalem shall be paved
with rubies and stones of Ophir;

For in you they shall praise His holy name forever."

Remember:
The Temple of Jerusalem (Peace) is in us.
God/Goddess dwells in us at the Second Birth.
We are built with gemstones and our foundations
are......

Why Crystal Skulls To Hold Gemstone Rays Of Color?
There's lots of Gemstones and Crystals in God's Kingdom

Just as I had experienced so long ago in 1972, my experience in entering the Presence of God was that I was of a sapphire ray. I found myself entering into the ray that emanated out from the Throne. That was real.

<u>The entire Kingdom is made up of colors.</u>

To be of Spirit is to wear and be a frequency. The skulls hold those frequencies and that are transmitted to those holding and receiving the energies. Perhaps each of us who hold and receive a skull is receiving a frequency that we need and those around us need for our spiritual evolution.

My experiences in the Kabala have explained this to me in all its fullness.
WE NEED TO SECURE THESE RAYS to evolve and become all that we are destined to be as humans and as spiritual beings.
The rays of the skulls are a direct transmission to us on earth from the heavenly realms.
They provide us with the fullness of the frequency needed for ascension.
That is why the work of the skulls is so important.
That is why to understand them is to love them and seek the progression of the rays of the skulls throughout the earth.

The Global Assignment is to Activate the Crystal Skulls!
Permeate the earth…
Bathe it in the Light of Heaven….
Bathe it in the 'frequency' the colors of the Goddess!
Create heaven, the Temple here…
So we can acclimate to the higher realms we are
ascending to in the very near future…

To begin the transformation, we first hold a frequency of
thought of the structure of Heaven.

You hold a skull; you radiate a frequency of the
Goddess, Of Creation on the earth!

Also, begin to wear stones, people!
Begin to wear the frequencies of
emerald, ruby and all the colors.
Live in Splendor and *radiate* your colors!
Know what? Wear BIG stones!
Why do you think Kings and Queens
wore crowns of jewels?
They hold power!
They hold truth, the hold the Image of
the Kingdom of the Goddess!

Crystalline formations of all the gemstones are scattered
all over the earth. The following has been adapted from
the Catholic Encyclopedia and is more information is
freely available in depth on the website wwwnewadvent.
org/cathen/14304chtm. I have found this site to be most
comprehensive and informative.

In it is a comprehensive look at the qualities and the uses
of gemstones in scripture. I have studied the breast plate
of the High Priest of the Hebrews for it was given to

him upon written direction from God. In the Book of Exodus it is mentioned several times. It was used to assist communication with God. We might want to consider that too.

Quote:

The Hebrews obtained their precious stones from Arabia, India, and Egypt. At the time of the Exodus Egypt was flooded with riches, and we know how the Israelites on leaving the land possessed themselves of many precious stones, according to the commandment of God (Exodus 3:22; 12:35-36). Later when they were settled in Palestine they could easily obtain stones from the merchant caravans traveling from Babylonia or Persia to Egypt and those from Saba and Reema to Tyre (Ezekiel 27:22) Solomon even equipped a fleet which returned from Ophir laden with precious stones (1 Kings 10:11).

The precious stones of the Bible are chiefly of interest in connection with the breastplate of the high-priest (Exodus 28:17-20; 39:10-13), the treasure of the King of Tyre (Ezekiel 28:13), and the foundations of the New Jerusalem (Tobit 13:16-17, in the Greek text, and more fully, Revelation 21:18-21).

The twelve stones of the breastplate and the two stones of the shoulder-ornaments seem to have been considered by the Jews as the most precious; they undoubtedly serve as the standard of whatever is beautiful and rich beyond measure; both Ezech., xxviii, 13, and Apoc., xxi, 18-21, are patterned after the model of the breastplate; no wonder therefore that the stones entering its composition should have been the objects of a considerable amount of literature from the fourth century.

It should be noticed that the ancients did not classify their precious stones by analyzing their composition and crystalline forms: names were given them from their color, their use, or the country from which they came. Thus it happens that stones of the same or nearly the same color, but of different composition or crystalline form, bear identical names. Another difficulty is due to the names having changed in the course of time: thus the ancient chrysolite is our topaz, the sapphire is our lazuli, etc. It will be sufficient to treat briefly of these stones according to the alphabetical order of the English names." End quote.

Condensed version from the original text as follows:

AGATE, Heb. *shbw*; Sept. *achates*; Vulg. *achates* (Exodus 28:19; 39:12, in Heb. and Vulg.; also Ezekiel 28:13, in Sept.). — This is the second stone of the third row of the breastplate, where it very probably represented the tribe of Aser.

It was supposed to render the action of all poisons void, to counteract the infection of contagious diseases; if held in the hand or in the mouth it was believed to alleviate fever. The eagle, it was said, placed an agate in its nest to guard its young against the bite of venomous animals. The red agate was credited with the power of sharpening the vision

AMETHYST, Heb. *ahlmh*; Sept. *amethystos*, also Apoc., xxi, 20, where it is the twelfth and last stone of the foundation of the New Jerusalem. It is the third stone in the third row of the breastplate, representing the tribe of Issachar (Exodus 28:19; 39:12); The amethyst was a preventive of intoxication. Drinkers wore amulets made of it to counteract the action of wine. The amethyst is a brilliant transparent stone of a purple color resembling that of diluted wine and varying in shade from the violet purple to rose.

BERYL, Heb. *yhlm*; Sept. *beryllos*; Vulg. *beryllus*. — In the breastplate this stone occupied the third place of the second row and was understood to represent Nephtali (Exodus 28:19; 39:13); Apoc., xxi, 20, gives it as the eighth stone of the foundation of the New Jerusalem.

By comparing various texts of the Vulgate — the Greek is very inconsistent — we find that *shlm* is always translated by onyx: this alone seems sufficient to render fairly probable the opinion that beryl corresponds to Heb. *yhlm*. That the beryl was among the stones of the rational appears beyond doubt since all translations mention it.

The difference between the beryl, the aqua marine, and the emerald is determined by the coloring matter and the peculiar shade of each. The beryl, though sometimes white, is usually of a light blue verging into a yellowish green; the emerald is more transparent and of a finer hue than the beryl; as a gem, it is more beautiful, and hence more costly; the aqua marine is a beautiful sea-green variety. The emerald derives its color from a small quantity of oxide of chromium; the beryl and aqua marine from a small quantity of oxide of iron. The beryl occurs in the shape either of a pebble or of an hexagonal prism.

CARNELIAN, Heb. *arm*, to be red, especially "red blooded"; Sept. and Apoc. *sardion*; Vulg. *sardius;* the first stone of the breastplate (Exodus 28:17; 39:10) representing Ruben; also the first among the stones of the King of Tyre (Ezekiel 28:13); the sixth foundation stone of the celestial city (Revelation 21:19). The word *sardion* has sometimes been rendered sardonyx; this is a mistake, for the same word is equivalent to carnelian in Theophrastus (De lap., 55)

Its color is a flesh-hued red, varying from the palest flesh-color to a deep blood-red.

CARBUNCLE, Heb., *gphr*; Sept. *anthrax* (Exodus 28:18; 39:11; Ezekiel 28:13; (Ezekiel 27:16), the first stone of the second row of the breastplatel; it represented Juda it is perhaps the third stone of the foundation of the celestial city (Revelation 21:19). The ancient authors are far from agreeing on the precise nature of this stone.

CHALCEDONY, Apoc., xxi, 19, *chalkedon*; Vulg. *chalcedonius*, the third foundation stone of the celestial Jerusalem. The chalcedony is a siliceous stone. Its name is supposed to be derived from Chalcedon, in Bithynia, whence the ancients obtained the stone. It is a species of agate and bears various names according to its color. It is usually made up of concentric circles of various colors.

CHODCHOD, *kdkd* (Isaiah 54:12; Ezekiel 27:16); Sept. *iaspis* (Isaiah 54:12), *chorchor* (Ezekiel 27:16); The chodchod is generally identified with the Oriental ruby. The translation of the word in Is. both by the Septuagint and the Vulgate is jasper;

CRYSTAL, Heb. *ghbsh* (Job 28:18), *qrh* (Ezekiel 1:22): both words signify a glassy substance; Sept. *gabis*; Vulg. *eminentia* (Job 28:18); *krystallos*, *crystallus* (Ezekiel 1:22). — This was a transparent mineral resembling glass, most probably a variety of quartz. Job places it in the same category with gold, onyx, sapphire, glass, coral, topaz, etc. The Targum renders the *qrt* of Ezech. by "ice"; the versions translate by "crystal". We find crystal again mentioned in Apoc., iv, 6; xxi, 11; xxii, 1. In Ps. cxlvii, 17, and Ecclus., xliii, 22, there can be no question but that ice is meant. The word *zkwkyh*, Job, xxviii, 17, which some translate by crystal, means glass.

CHRYSOLITE, Heb. *trshysh* (Exodus 28:20; 39:13; Ezekiel 1:16; 10:9; 28:13; Song of Songs 5:14; Daniel 10:6); This is the tenth stone of the breastplate, representing the tribe of

Zabulon; it stands fourth in the enumeration of Ezech., xxviii, 13, and is given as the seventh foundation stone of the celestial city in Apoc., xxi, 20.

In none of the Hebrew texts is there any hint as to the nature of this stone; however, since the Septuagint habitually translates the Hebrew word by *chrysolithos*, except where it merely transliterates it and in Ezech., x, 9, since, moreover, the Vulgate follows this translation with very few exceptions, and Aquila, Josephus, and St. Epiphanius agree in their rendering, we can safely accept the opinion that the chrysolite of the ancients, which is our topaz, was meant.

In the Middle Ages it was believed to possess the power of dispelling the fears of night and of driving away devils; it was also supposed to be an excellent cure for the diseases of the eye.

CHRYSOPRASUS, Greek *chrysoprasos*, the tenth foundation stone of the celestial Jerusalem (Revelation 21:20). This is perhaps the agate of Ex., xxviii, 20, and xxxix, 13, since the chrysoprasus was not very well known among the ancients. It is a kind of green agate, composed mostly of silica and a small percentage of nickel.

CORAL, Heb. *ramwt* (Job 28:18; Proverbs 24:7; Ezekiel 27:16); Sept. *meteora, ramoth*; Vulg. *excelsa, sericum*. — The Hebrew word seems to come from *tas*, "to be high", probably connoting a resemblance to a tree. In Ezech., xxvii, 16, coral is mentioned as one of the articles brought by the Syrians to Tyre. The Hebrews made apparently very little use of this substance, and hence it is seldom mentioned in their writings; this explains also the difficulty felt by the translators in rendering the word.

DIAMOND, Heb. *shmyr*; Sept. *adamantinos*; Vulg. *adamas, adamantinus* (Ezekiel 3:9; Zechariah 7:12; Jeremiah xvii 1). — Whether or not this stone is really the diamond cannot be ascertained. Many passages in Holy Writ point indeed to the qualities of the diamond, especially its hardness (Ezekiel 3:9; Zechariah 7:12; Jeremiah 17:1). In the last Jeremias informs us of a use to which this stone was put, which agrees admirably with the use to which the diamond is put at this day: "The sin of Juda is written with a pen of iron, with the point of a diamond". The diamond was not very well known among the ancients

EMERALD, Heb. *brqm*; Sept. *smaragdos*; Vulg. *smaragdus;* the third stone of the breastplate (Exodus 28:17; 39:10), where it represents the tribe of Levi; it is the ninth stone in Ezech., xxviii, 13, and the fourth foundation stone of the celestial Jerusalem (Revelation 21:19). The same precious stone is also mentioned in Tob., xiii, 16

The Hebrew root *brq*, from which it is probably derived, signifies "to glitter", which quality agrees eminently with the emerald. The word may also come from the Sanskrit *marakata* which is certainly the emerald; In Job, xiii, 21; Jud., x, 19; Ecclus., xxxii, 8; and Apoc., xxi, 19, the emerald is certainly the stone spoken of.

In the Middle Ages marvellous powers were attributed to the emerald, the most conspicuous being the power to preserve or heal the sight.

HYACINTH, Greek *hyakinthos*; Vulg. *hyacinthus* (Revelation 21:20); the eleventh stone of the foundation of the heavenly city. It corresponds very probably to Heb., the ligurius of Ex., xxviii, 19; xxxix, 12 The stone spoken of in Cant., v, 14, and called *hyacinthus* in the Vulgate is the Hebrew *hrshysh*, which has been shown above to be the chrysolite.

Hyacinth is a zircon of a crimson, red, or orange hue. It is harder than quartz. Its form is an oblong quadrangular prism terminated on both ends by a quadrangular pyramid. It was supposed to be a talisman against tempests.

JASPER, Heb. *yshphh*; Sept. *iaspis*; Vulg. *jaspis;* the twelfth stone of the breastplate (<u>Exodus 28:18</u>; <u>39:11</u>), representing Benjamin. In the Greek and Latin texts it comes sixth, and so also in Ezech., xxviii, 13; in the Apocalypse it is the first (xxi, 19). Despite this difference of position *jaspis* is undoubtedly the *yshphh* of the Hebrew text. There are jaspers of nearly every color. It is a completely opaque stone of a conchoidal cleavage. It seems to have been obtained from India and Egypt.

LIGURUS, Heb. *lshs*; Sept. *ligyrion*; Vulg. *ligurius;* the first stone of the third row of the breastplate (<u>Exodus 28:19</u>; <u>39:12</u>), representing Gad. It is missing in the Hebrew of Ezech., xxviii, 13, but present in the Greek. This stone is probably the same as the hyacinth This identification, admitted by tradition, rests on the remark that the twelve foundation stones of the celestial city in Apoc., xxi, 19-20, correspond to the twelve stones of the breastplate/rational, from which it would appear that the ligurus is the same as the hyacinth. Some have identified it with the turmaline, a view rejected by most scholars.

ONYX, Heb. *shhm*; Sept. *onychion*; Vulg. *lapis onychinus;* the eleventh stone of the breastplate in the Hebrew and the Vulgate (<u>Exodus 28:20</u>; <u>39:13</u>), representing the tribe of Joseph; the twelfth in the Greek; it is called sardonyx and comes in the fifth place in Apoc., xxi, 20. The exact nature of this stone is disputed. Many think, because the Greek word *beryllos* occurs instead of the Hebrew *shhs* that the beryl is meant; but this is not so (see BERYL above). The Vulgate indeed gives onyx as the equivalent of the Hebrew *shhm*.

The onyx is a variety of quartz analogous to the agate and other crypto-crystalline species. The colors of the best are are either white and black, or white, brown, and black. The best specimens are brought from India. The ancients obtained the onyx from Arabia, Egypt, and India. (Genesis 2:12; Exodus 25:7; 25:9, 27; 1 Chronicles 29:2; etc.) Job 28:16).

PEARL. — In the New Testament we find the pearl mentioned in Matt., xiii, 45, 46; I Tim., ii, 9; etc. It is generally of a whitish blue, sometimes showing a tinge of pink; there are also yellow pearls. This gem was considered the most precious of all among the ancients, and was obtained from the Red Sea, the Indian Ocean, and the Persian Gulf.

RUBY. — This may have been either the carbuncle or the chodchod It is extremely hard, almost as hard as the diamond, and is obtained from Ceylon, India, and China. It is considered a most precious gem. Proverbs 31 Proverbs 3:13 (a Good number) *"Wisdom-she is more precious than rubies: and all things you can desire are not to be compared to her -length of days is in her right hand, and in her left riches and honor. Her ways are the ways of pleasantness and all her paths, peace. She is a tree of life to all them that lay hold of her. (Remember the Kabala?) The Lord, by wisdom, (Sophia) has founded the earth.*

SAPPHIRE, Heb. *mghry* Septuag. *sappheiron*; Vulg. *sapphirus*. — The sapphire was the fifth stone of the breastplate (Exodus 28:19; 39:13), and represented the tribe of Dan; it is also the second foundation stone of the celestial Jerusalem (Revelation 21:19). The genuine sapphire is a hyaline corindon of a beautiful blue color; The ancients gave the name of sapphire also to our lapis-lazuli, which is likewise a blue stone, often speckled with shining pyrites which give it the appearance of being sprinkled with gold dust. Both may be meant, but the lapis-lazuli seems more probable, for as often as its qualities are described, it is spoken of as being easily engraved (Lamentations 4:7; Exodus 28:17; 39:13). The sapphire was obtained from India.

SARDONYX; SARD. — These two words are often confounded by interpreters. The sard is the carnelian, while the sardonyx is a species of onyx.

TOPAZ, Heb. *ghtrh*; Sept. *topazion*; Vulg. *topazius*, the second stone of the breastplate (Exodus 28:17; 39:19), representing Simeon; also the second stone in Ezech., xxviii, 13; the ninth foundation stone of the celestial Jerusalem (Revelation 21:20); also mentioned in Job, xxviii, 19.

This topaz is generally believed to have been the chrysolite rather than our topaz. . When rubbed or heated it becomes highly electric. It varies in color Australian topaz is green or yellow; the Tasmanian clear, bright, and transparent; the Saxon pale violet; the Bohemian sea-green and the Brazilian red, varying from a pale red to a deep carmine. The ancients very probably obtained it from the East.

Enjoy the rays of beauty of the stones and of the crystal skulls that are securing a new day on earth!

"Paint Me a Rainbow and you shall see

All the Love I have for thee...."

And He has.........

Susan Isabelle

And now prepare yourself; The work is not yet done

<u>In The Eye Of The Goddess,</u>

I had a new work to do...

It would take me on a wild ride across the globe...

Susan Isabelle

Bibliography/ And
Recommended Reading

Susan Isabelle

*On Assignment with
Adama, Book I
The Global Assignment:
Activate The Crystal
Skulls
Coming soon: In The Eye
Of The Goddess*

Rosita Arvigo

Sastun

Genevieve Lewis Paulson

Evolution In This Lifetime

Yehuda Berg

The 72 Names of God

CAITLIN MATTHEWS

*Sophia, Goddess Of
Wisdom, Bride of God*

ANDREWS, TED, *Animal-Speak:
The Spiritual & Magical Powers of Creatures Great &
Small*

ARGÜELLES, JOSÉ, *The Mayan Factor: Path Beyond
Technology*

FREIDEL, DAVID; SCHELE, LINDA; PARKER, JOY, *Maya
Cosmos: Three Thousand Years on the Shaman's Path*

GILBERT, ADRIAN, *The Mayan Prophecies: Unlocking the
Secrets of a Lost Civilization*

JENKINS, JOHN MAJOR, *Maya Cosmogenesis 2012, The
True Meaning of the Maya Calendar End- Date*

MORTON, CHRIS and THOMAS, CERI LOUISE, *The Mystery of the Crystal Skulls: A Real Life Detective Story of the Ancient World*

MURRAY, KATHLEEN, *The Divine Spark of Creation: The Skull Speaks*

ROBBINS, DIANNE, *Telos: The Call Goes Out — Telepathic Messages from Adama*

Revised edition,2003 Messages From the Hollow Earth

SPILSBURY, ARIEL and BRYNER, MICHAEL, *The Mayan Oracle: Return Path to the Stars,*

Andrews, Shirley, *Atlantis and Lemuria*

Drumvalo   The Ancient Secret of the Golden Flower of Life

Catholic Encyclopedia of Gems

The Kabala
Bible   *King James Version*

Coming Soon!!!!
Susan's Book III

Some of the incredible events:
Meeting Merlin,
Walking the Table of King Arthur's Hall and resetting
the global Frequencies in Stonehenge

Mount Shasta
Over
14, 000 foot high

With
Susan Isabelle at Mount Shasta, CA.

"Mount Shasta is a very sacred mountain.
I invite you to join me for Goddess Initiations, classes or
private instruction in the ancient mysteries.
Let's Sing to the Waters and Call the Ancient Ones!"
Susan Isabelle

Reiki Master Teacher and Shambhala Melchizedek Master Teacher
Classes at the Shambhala Center
Shambhala , All Levels
(All Higher Levels with Apprenticeship)
Goddess In The Kabbala, Ascension Initiations
Melchizedek Priesthood
Maha Karuna 1&2 , Sound Healing
Earth Healer, Crystal Mastery
Lemurian Gateway
Kuan Yin , Compassionate Action
Sophia, Wisdom Teachings
Sword of Truth, Shield of Strength
Advanced Alternative Healing
Aromatherapy
MORE!

Together....
We Shall regain the Ancient Knowledge,
We Shall restore the Earth
We Shall Love The One who nurtures Us
We Shall Honor Her Creator
Together
I will show you the Teachings of the Ancients,
The Mysteries Revealed
The Acturians gave the Symbols and
St Germain gave the method,
Come I will Share The Wisdom

Classes with Susan Isabelle

Crystal Skulls on Mount Shasta?
Yes!
The Ancients prepared in crystal
instructions for those of the future.
Come, learn how Itzma, Son of the
Divine Couple, God Above All Gods, as
the Maya call Him, programmed crystal
to "speak"!

Remember how on the day of Palm
Sunday even the Christ said the stones
would cry out? Now, they do....

We'll teach you about Sastun, the Maya
word for crystals that were connected to
the Maya Lords of Light (angels). These
were to assist the Keeper to heal with
ancient knowledge and skill.
We do Classes!

Susan Isabelle is a Maya
Crystal Skull Keeper.

She will be
presenting the original
skulls, very ancient, called
One Heart,
One Mind
of Humanity Skulls

In Book III, you will
learn about
El Za Ra, the mate of
El Aleator!

These two skulls , a gift to Susan from the Maya,
grow in size as you watch them.
They change colors and have a very distinct
magnetic polarity. Each has a brain and when
placed back to back form a perfect human heart!

316

The Crystal Skull Handbook !
Learn HOW to work
with your crystal skull and discover the
ancient mysteries they hold!

Thank you for giving me the opportunity to tell you about the wonderful happenings on the Earth!

I hope to see you at Mount Shasta at our store.

Come in sometime and chat awhile! I'd love to see you!

Susan Isabelle!

Picture taken September 9, 2006

CPSIA information can be obtained at www.ICGtesting.com
Printed in the USA
LVOW12s2323201213

366240LV00001B/151/A